NEW BOY

NEW BOY

JULIAN HOUSTON

G RAPHIA

AN IMPRINT OF THE HOUGHTON MIFFLIN COMPANY

BOSTON

ACKNOWLEDGMENTS

Several people have contributed to the development of this book. Leslie Epstein and James Carroll, both wonderful writers, have, at timely moments, fanned the embers of my desire to write fiction when they were about to turn cold. Katherine Butler Jones, who grew up in Harlem during the forties and fifties, read the entire manuscript and offered many helpful suggestions. I am particularly indebted to Susan Monsky, writer, teacher, and coach, who has shown me ropes I did not know were there and has helped me to become a better writer. My agent, Wendy Strothman, suggested the idea for the novel after reading one of my short stories, and sold it to Andrea Davis Pinkney, vice president and publisher of the Children's Division of Houghton Mifflin. Both have believed in the book and in me as a writer from the beginning, for which I shall always be grateful. Emily Linsay, my first editor at Houghton Mifflin, and Eleni Beja, her successor, provided invaluable assistance in helping me to understand and respond to the expectations of a publisher in bringing a book to life.

Fiction writing, it is often said, is a lonely undertaking. For this writer, it would not be possible without the understanding and support of a loving family. My son, Daniel, my daughter, Elisabeth, and my beloved wife, Susan, who reads every word I write and whose comments are always offered with wisdom and affectionate candor, are the bedrock of my work.

Copyright © 2005 by Julian Houston

All rights reserved. Published in the United States by Graphia, an imprint of Houghton Mifflin Company, Boston, Massachusetts. Originally published in hardcover in the United States by Houghton Mifflin Company, Boston, in 2005.

For information about permission to reproduce selections from this book, write to Permissions, Houghton Mifflin Company, 215 Park Avenue South, New York, New York 10003.

Graphia and the Graphia logo are registered trademarks of Houghton Mifflin Company.

www.houghtonmifflinbooks.com

The text of this book is set in 12-point Bulmer.

Library of Congress Cataloging-in-Publication Data
Houston, Julian.
New boy / by Julian Houston.
p. cm.
Summary: As a new sophomore at an exclusive boarding school, a young black man is witness to the persecution of another student with bad acne.
ISBN 0-618-43253-1 (hardcover)
ISBN 0-618-88405-x (paperback)
[1. Prejudices—Fiction. 2. African Americans—Fiction. 3. Jews—United States—Fiction.
4. Boarding schools—Fiction. 5. Schools—Fiction.] I. Title.
PZ7.H8225Ho 2005   [Fic]—dc22   2004027207

HC ISBN-13: 978-0-618-43253-0
PB ISBN-13: 978-0-618-88405-6

Manufactured in the United States of America
MV 10 9 8 7 6 5 4 3 2

To the memory of my mother,
Alice Jackson Stuart

chapter one

"It won't be easy, you know," said Cousin Gwen. "They won't take any foolishness up there. Especially from a colored boy." She was standing on the sidewalk in front of her apartment building in a wrinkled pink housecoat and worn bedroom slippers, giving me some last-minute advice. Her face was the texture and color of a raisin. Her eyes were penetrating.

My parents and I had driven up the night before on our way to Draper, the boarding school in Connecticut to which I had been admitted. We had spent the night at Cousin Gwen's apartment in Harlem, and now my parents were sitting in the big Buick Roadmaster, waiting for me to climb in. "This is quite an opportunity you have," said Cousin Gwen. "It's so rare that any of our boys have a chance to go to these schools."

"I'm looking forward to it," I said, doing my best to sound confident. Until she retired, Cousin Gwen had been a schoolteacher in Harlem for forty years, and as I listened to her, I felt like one of her pupils. It occurred to me that forty years of teaching members of the race had left her with an unerring ability to detect imposters.

"You'd do well to keep to yourself at first," she said, "until you know who you're dealing with." Looking back, I'd say it was the best advice I'd ever been given by any adult, including my parents, although I didn't pay much attention to it at the time. I was eager to get going and she must have recognized it. "Well," she said with a resigned sigh. "Just remember when you're up there, they'll need you back home when you're finished. Don't end up like Joe Louis."

In those days, the life of Joe Louis was a cautionary tale for every colored boy from a comfortable home. *A big, yaller nigger,* as my father would say, Louis was the son of an Alabama sharecropper who became the heavyweight boxing champion of the world. He would make the white folks jittery just by climbing into the ring. In the photographs I saw of him as a child, he was always pokerfaced, the kinks in his hair greased to perfection. He was the most famous Negro of his day, and he made millions of dollars. And lost every cent. He could knock you out with a six-inch punch, but he didn't know what to do with his money; so he trusted the wrong people. They would come to him like courtiers, with a promise of something for nothing. "Just sign here, champ," they would say, and he would sign, lending his name to a candy bar, a milk company, a restaurant, a toy doll, a saloon, assuming all of the liability for a fraction of the assets. By the end of his career, he was penniless, reduced to greeting guests at the doors of nightclubs and working as a referee at wrestling matches to pay off a tax debt too huge to comprehend. Through ignorance and carelessness, he had allowed his chance at independence to slip through his fingers, and had been returned to slavery by the government.

We reached the school just before lunch. I reported to the headmaster's office with my parents, and the secretary, a tall, dignified woman with short, iron gray hair, directed us to the dining room. "We've been expecting you," she said with a soft smile. "Mr. Spencer would like you to join him for lunch at the headmaster's table."

The dining room was bustling when we entered. Four hundred pink-faced boys in jackets and ties, more white people than I had ever seen in one place in my life, were seated at long wooden tables noisily comparing notes about summer vacations, summer romances, course assignments, and teachers. And just as the school's catalogue had described, at the head of each table sat a member of the faculty "to insure civility and to promote appropriate discourse." At the opposite end of the table sat a student in a white cotton jacket who was assigned to wait on the table for two weeks.

Tall, pale, and slender, in a brown tweed jacket and a bright red bow tie, the headmaster, Oliver Spencer, stood when he saw us entering the room and walked over to greet us.

"Well, this must be the Garrett family," he said. "I'm Ollie Spencer." His wide smile exposed a mouthful of crooked, tobacco-stained teeth. I could imagine my father, who was a dentist, cringing at the sight. Mr. Spencer extended his hand, which my mother accepted without removing her glove. She was still conducting a final inspection, before deciding, once and for all, whether to leave her only child in this place.

"Did you have a good trip?" said Mr. Spencer, making what I came to recognize as headmaster small talk. He pumped my father's hand and then mine with an excess of enthusiasm, not waiting for a reply. "Come and join us for lunch. We've saved three places for you." We began a brief but conspicuous journey to the headmaster's table, observed by everyone else in the dining room. For several seconds, amid the din of voices and the clatter of tableware, a hush fell over the room and conversation stopped while everyone took a good look. I was the first, you see, the first colored student in the eighty-seven-year history of the place, and I suppose they could be forgiven, at that point, for gawking.

My parents and I were seated next to each other, at the head of the table, and introductions were made all around. Across from us sat Mrs. Spencer, plump and hearty, with rosy cheeks and long blond hair piled loosely on top of her head. She was wearing a white cotton blouse and a pale blue seersucker jacket. For some reason, she reminded me of a teller in a bank. Seated next to her was Mr. Wilcox, a mathematics teacher and a dour man, with a bald head, a bristling mustache, and heavy, tortoiseshell glasses that he preferred to look over rather than through. And next to Mr. Wilcox was Peter Dillard, president of the sophomore class, the class I was entering, who was wearing a navy blue blazer and who looked as though he had recently stepped out of the shower. Of the three, Mrs. Spencer seemed most curious.

"Well, how are things in Virginia?" she asked. Her eyes were gleaming. I was uncertain if she was asking about the weather or if she wanted to know the truth, but my father intervened.

"Hot," he said. "It's always hot this time of year."

"Well, it's been pretty warm up here, too," she said. "We've had very little rain. My garden is just parched."

My mother had been silent up to that point, and I was wondering what she was thinking. I had been looking at dried-up gardens in our neighborhood all my life, and I had never heard one described as "parched." I wondered if mother had, and what she made of the headmaster's wife.

"Very fine school you have down there in Charlottesville," said Mr. Wilcox, biting off his words like pieces of raw carrot. We let the comment twist slowly in the wind, hoping no one would catch its scent. Of course, Mrs. Spencer did.

"Oh my, yes!" she squealed. "The university! Tell me, how is Charlottesville? I haven't been there in ages. Such a lovely town, don't you think?"

"We sent three seniors there this year," chimed in an aroused Dillard, the class president, as lunch arrived, lugged on a large metal tray by a student waiter.

All three seemed oblivious to the fact that until very recently I could not attend the University of Virginia, under any circumstances. I wondered how widespread was this ignorance among the rest of the school population. I was certain my parents were uncomfortable with the implications of this discussion. They had tried to shield me from the indignity of segregation whenever possible—arranging to take me wherever I needed to go so that I didn't have to sit in the back of a segregated bus or streetcar, refusing to patronize any shop or restaurant or theater that maintained a COLORED ONLY section—but they never pretended that it didn't exist. I could imagine my mother giving the three across the table a withering look, dabbing the corners of her mouth with the end of her napkin, and rising from the table to say to Mr. Spencer, "We have obviously made a mistake. We have no intention of leaving our son in a school like this. Thank you for your time." Instead, Mr. Spencer put a baked chicken breast on each plate and passed the plates around, together with stainless steel serving bowls of peas and mashed potatoes, and the subject was not pursued, to my great relief.

It had become clear, before the end of the first hour of my first day, that the world I had just entered was utterly different from anything I had previously encountered. I was on my own. I would have to fend for myself, and I was thrilled by the prospect.

"There will be a meeting of all new boys in the auditorium this afternoon at four o'clock," said Mr. Spencer, toward the end of the meal. "Between now and then, you can get your class assignments and your books and find your dormitory room. Dillard will give you a hand." I had finished lunch and was eager to get started, but first, I had to say goodbye to my parents. They

6

were still eating, however, and the headmaster's table in the dining room seemed hardly the place for such a parting.

"Do you play any sports?" asked Dillard from across the table. In truth, I hadn't played any organized sports in Virginia because there were none, other than in high school, which I had attended only for one year. We were not allowed to play on the Little League baseball or football teams, and the only way we could walk onto a golf course was as a caddy, which my parents refused to allow me to do. I played a respectable game of playground basketball and could hold my own in football and baseball, but I had never been coached in anything.

"A little basketball, a little football," I said, hoping my vagueness would cause him to drop the subject. Instead, he seemed to take it for false modesty, and his eyes widened.

"Really?" he exclaimed. "Boy, can we ever use you. Football practice starts this afternoon. Why don't you come over to the field?"

Everyone at the table was looking at me, waiting for my answer. Although I didn't realize it at the time, I was about to define myself.

"Not this afternoon," I said. "I need to unpack and get my books. Maybe some other time." Dillard gave me a long look of disappointment. My parents, on the other hand, seemed to heave a joint sigh of relief.

The lunch dishes were cleared away, and my parents stood up and shook hands with everyone. I told Dillard I would meet him at the dormitory in a few minutes, and I got up to leave.

"Would you like to be excused?" said the headmaster. I gave him a puzzled look, and he gave me a good-natured smile in return. "At Draper, boys are expected to excuse themselves from the table before leaving," he said, smiling again, with a kind of low-wattage, paternal grin.

"Excuse me, sir. May I be excused, sir?" I said. Everyone at the table beamed, including my parents.

"Catches on fast," said my father with a smile. "That's a good sign." I had passed my first rite of initiation into life at the Draper School, but it was certain not to be my last.

"We're very glad to have you with us, and I hope you'll feel free to come and see me whenever you have a problem," said Mr. Spencer, still flashing his benign, all-purpose smile. "And, yes, you may be excused."

I walked out to the car with my parents, observing that we were still the object of curiosity on the part of everyone around us. Not only the students, but the adults, from the teachers to the groundskeepers, gave us long looks, though it was not easy to tell what they were thinking. A few seemed friendly and some seemed cool, but most of the expressions were blank as a piece of paper that had not been written on.

The drive over to the dormitory with my parents gave us our first and last opportunity that day to exchange in private our impressions of the school. I was about to be left alone, truly alone, for the first time in my life. The two great pillars that had supported me up to that point were about to be removed.

"Well, you're on your way, son," said my father. "They certainly keep the place looking nice," he mused, steering the Buick past manicured lawns and the graceful, towering elms that covered the campus. He was fond of bromides, and maintained a barrel of them for use in every situation. Later, after much thought, I realized that they were one of the tools of his trade. Patients came to him expecting the worst, and his first task was to put them at ease by talking, but only about little of consequence.

Mother, on the other hand, was a schoolteacher like Cousin Gwen. She was used to having only fifty minutes to work with, so she got right to the point. "You're going to be under a microscope while you're here and don't you ever forget it. Not for one minute. Just when you think you've been accepted and they're treating you like everyone else, that's when something will happen that will cause you to remember that you're a Negro. The only contact these people have had with our people has been with maids and shoeshine boys, and you can imagine what that's been like. I didn't see another colored face in that dining room, not even back in the kitchen. So you're it. You're going to represent the race, and from what I've seen and heard, they've got a lot to learn." She leaned over the back of the front seat toward me so that I could kiss her cheek, and as I did, I realized that it was wet with tears. "Make us proud of you, son," she said.

As we were unpacking the car, Dillard arrived to help me take my things to my room in the sophomore dormitory. It was a long, three-story brick building, with an entrance set off by four tall white columns. My room was on the third floor, with a dormer window that looked out on the campus, the surrounding hills, and a part of the golf course. There was a bed, a desk and chair, and a built-in dressing cabinet. It was not as large as my room at home, but it was comfortable enough. My parents, who had accompanied us up to the room to take a look, approved.

"Is there an adult in charge of the dormitory?" my mother asked Dillard as we were all walking back down to the car. Dillard pointed to the far end of the long corridor and a door with a brass knocker facing us. The door was shut.

"There's a master living on every floor," he said. "You don't see them that often, but they'll have you in for punch and cookies once in a while. They're mainly here to make sure things don't get out of hand." The three of us chuckled at Dillard's remark, and strolled out to the car. Everything about the school seemed to be in such perfect order, the graceful elms, the manicured lawns, the handsome buildings, all constructed with red brick that had aged beautifully, and the pristine white columns. The footpaths had been paved with the finest gray slate and did not contain a scrap of litter. Even the birds seemed to have been trained to fly away to deposit their leavings elsewhere. It was hard for me to imagine things getting out of hand in such a place.

All of the schools I had attended before had been hand-me-downs, used by the whites until they were falling apart, when they were ready to be abandoned to the Negro hordes. At least, I thought, I wouldn't have to worry about a leaky roof in my algebra class at Draper.

We were downstairs at the car, and my parents were preparing to leave. Dillard handed me a sheet of paper.

"I picked up your course assignments for you," he said. "You still need to get your books from the bookstore, which is behind the main building. I've gotta head over to the field for football practice. You sure you don't want to come?"

"I'm sure," I said. I knew I was fortunate to have a choice. Draper had awarded me a small academic scholarship, but most of my tuition was being paid by my parents, which meant that there was no expectation, when I arrived, that I would have to earn my keep by wearing the green and gold of the Draper Dragons.

Dillard said goodbye to my parents, shook their hands, and headed off to the football field.

"Seems like a nice young fellow," said my father in his blue serge suit, his hands clasped behind his back, surveying the campus again.

"Are you sure you packed that extra pair of pajamas I left out for you?" said my mother. I assured her I had. "What about underwear? Are you sure you've got enough underwear? What about your gloves? Remember, it gets cold up here." She was having trouble leaving, and it should not have surprised me, for I was the embodiment of her dreams, the life she had nurtured from her womb and then tended in the hoary, weed-choked garden of the South, until the decision was made to send me away to firmer, richer soil. Nevertheless, I was absolutely desperate for them to go. This was supposed to be *my* experience, and I wanted to have it on my own. I was too young to understand that it was also their experience, indeed, their adventure, in a world they had dreamed about and read about but never inhabited. Now they were going to live in that world through me, but the price of the ticket was steep. When they returned home, my bedroom would be empty. At dinnertime, the table would only be set for two. And they would no longer have to transport me from place to place so that I wouldn't have to ride in the back of the bus.

We exchanged brief hugs and kisses, and both of them seemed to be fighting back tears as they climbed into the Roadmaster. I felt, at that moment, looking at them seated behind the windshield of the huge black sedan, that in the brief trip north, they had somehow aged; that without their realizing it, time had caught up with them and was passing them by, and now, having brought me as far as they could, they were about to return to the past. Dad turned over the big Buick engine and it rumbled to life. From the interior of the sedan, he looked at me standing alone at the edge of the driveway and gave me a big wink, which I pretended not to notice. With the edge of a handkerchief wrapped around her index finger, Mother dried the corners of her eyes and managed a faint smile and a wave. Dad eased the car forward, rolling it slowly down the driveway, until it reached the main road and disappeared.

chapter two

The meeting with Mr. Spencer was intended to acquaint new boys with the basic rules of the school. It was held in the school auditorium and the entire freshman class was there, most of them in heavy woolen sport coats they were expected to grow into, baggy khaki pants, and ties that were much too long for young bodies that were still filling out. A few seemed to have been dressed by custom tailors, in Harris tweed jackets or navy blazers with gold buttons and gray wool trousers that fit perfectly. And everyone was wearing wide-eyed looks of fresh-scrubbed, pink-faced, beardless innocence that would disappear forever by the end of the school year. The rest of the audience was composed of new students like me, who looked older and were scattered around the room, dressed like the freshmen, in jackets and ties.

I took a seat near the back, to be as inconspicuous as possible. I still hadn't met any other new students, but I was content to be by myself. Most of the new students were gathered in seats near the stage, from which they would steal furtive looks in my direction until the meeting began.

"Is this seat taken?" someone asked. I looked up and saw a homely white boy in a tie and jacket looking down at me with dark, beady eyes and a wide, lopsided smile. His dark brown hair was thick and straight and slicked down, with a part on the side, but the most memorable feature of his face was his skin. It was pockmarked and oily, and inflamed with acne. Of course, he was not the only student in the auditorium, let alone the school, with skin trouble, but his was worse than anything I had ever seen anywhere, and in the limited environment of Draper, the eye of the casual observer was as likely to be drawn to that face, I assumed, as to the color of my own dark brown skin.

"Nope," I said, removing from the seat next to me the books I had just purchased in the bookstore.

"My name's Vinnie Mazzerelli," he said, extending his hand and shaking mine as he sat down. "Guess you're new here, too. What grade you in?" He was speaking to me in a whisper, his mouth shielded by the back of his hand, while onstage, Mr. Spencer welcomed everyone in a silken voice, reminding us how fortunate we were to have the privilege of a Draper education.

"Sophomore," I whispered back, with my eyes still focused on Mr. Spencer, who was standing behind a lectern with a complacent expression on his face.

"You are among the most intelligent, most gifted members of your generation. You come from the finest families and the finest traditions, and many of you will go on to positions of great leadership, to lead our industries, our banks, our armed forces, our government, while our job during your years here at Draper is

14

to prepare you to assume these positions of great influence, so that you are qualified, both intellectually and morally, to hold them." Spencer spoke to us with matter-of-fact candor, and as I listened, I felt the power of his message relaxing my concerns about being the only colored student in the school, about speaking differently and looking different from everyone else, about doing well and finding understanding at Draper. It seemed that I was being given access to virtually everything I would need in order to overcome the shortcomings of my youth and to find success in my adult life. All I needed to do was perform.

"Where you from?" whispered Vinnie. I was having a hard time dividing my attention between Spencer's exhortations and Vinnie's questions, but I felt I couldn't ignore Vinnie altogether.

"Virginia," I whispered out of the corner of my mouth, hoping my one-word answer might cause him to lose interest.

"No kidding!" he exclaimed softly. "My sister's down there now. She's a junior at Hollins." I greeted this news with silence and intensified my concentration on Mr. Spencer's remarks.

"Of course, with leadership comes responsibility, and an important element of responsibility is knowing the rules. So one of the first things I want you to do before the end of the day is to read the Draper School handbook. It contains all of the rules you will be expected to obey during your years at Draper." And without missing a beat, his tone shifted, from silken to imperious. "Read it and read it well." On the stage, the headmaster had removed a copy of the handbook from the inside pocket of his brown tweed jacket, and was holding it before him like a hymnal, reading selected portions to the audience through half-moon spectacles perched on the tip of his long, aquiline nose. Everyone, even Vinnie, seemed to be listening.

"There are four offenses at Draper," intoned Mr. Spencer, "for which the punishment is immediate expulsion. They are: the use of tobacco, in any form; the use of alcohol; cheating; and the commission of any act recognized as a crime by the laws of the state of Connecticut." He cleared his throat, and concluded: "As I have said, gentlemen, a Draper education is a privilege and one that must be guarded with the utmost care. If you work hard and live within our rules, you will discover, upon your graduation, that the world will open up for you like an oyster. And the pearls of life will be yours for the taking. Good luck to each of you, and welcome to Draper." As the new boys filed out of the auditorium, Mr. Spencer stood alone on the stage, smiling at his new charges, none of whom, it seemed, bothered to smile back.

"You headed back to the dorm?" asked Vinnie as we left the auditorium.

"Yes," I said. "I want to get unpacked and look at my assignments. What about you?"

"I'm unpacked already, but I'll walk back with you," he said. "What floor are you on?"

"Third. What about you?"

"Second. One flight down. I've already met some of the guys. They seem pretty nice. What time is dinner served around this place?"

We were walking across the campus to the dormitory, as the late afternoon sun burnished the edges of the trees and the brick surfaces of the buildings with golden light. The brilliant green lawn surrounded us like the sea, filling the air with the fragrance of freshly mowed grass. It was as though I had been deposited at a resort or a country club, neither of which I had ever visited, to spend the next three years of my life. I was in awe of my good fortune. Oh, I knew there would be adjustments to make, both on my part and on the part of the school, but, as I made my leisurely way across the campus with Vinnie, I thought I could feel the past slipping away. I was shedding like an overcoat the image of myself with which I had been raised, of the good colored boy brought up in a proper colored home to serve the needs of the race during its sojourn in captivity, treading the narrow line separating them from us, with proper manners and diction and the refinements of general appearance (natural or self-imposed): proper skin color, hair texture, and dimensions of lips and nose. Even the Church, into which I had been recently baptized, seemed to lose any claim on my thoughts. Like Joe Louis, I had escaped the harsh and final judgments of the South. I was free to become whoever I wanted to become. I had only to avoid his mistakes. My success would be my contribution to the race.

As Vinnie and I were about to enter the dormitory, the front door swung open, and a group of students emerged in dress shirts, open at the neck, and khakis, engaged in a noisy discussion.

"The Browns are gonna walk away with it."

"G'wan. Nobody's gonna beat the Giants. Conerly to Gifford. Can't be stopped."

"Anybody ever heard of the Colts?"

"Aw, you're just saying that 'cause your old man owns a piece of the team."

"So? Mara's father owns all of the Giants. Why do you think he's picking them?"

Everyone laughed, including me.

"You're new, aren't you?" said a large, freckle-faced boy with long red hair that looked as though it had just been combed into a wet pompadour. I had seen the style on the street at home on young white men wearing jeans and white T-shirts, sometimes with a pack of cigarettes rolled into one sleeve, revealing a blue tattoo. They were usually loud and up to no good. He looked at me with mischievous eyes and a roguish grin and said, "What's your name?"

"Garrett," I said. "Rob Garrett. What's yours?"

"Mike Sargent. But most people call me Carrot," he said, squinting through a miniature thicket of copper-colored eyelashes, and he proceeded to introduce the others in his group. They all had blue eyes and distant half-smiles that seemed to be intended more to please the headmaster than me. "Where're you from?" he asked. I told him. "That's a pretty part of the country down there. What made you want to come up here?"

"Same as you, I guess. Trying to get the best education I can, so I can better myself," I said. It was a stock answer, the identical one I had given when a Draper alumnus had come to our house to interview me the year before.

"This guy sure has you figured out, Carrot," said Rolf Schroeder, a slim blond boy with a deep tan. "He knows exactly why *you're* here." Everyone laughed again except Vinnie and me.

"I don't understand," said Vinnie with a confused look. "Isn't that why we're all here? I mean why else would you come to a place like this?" The laughter abruptly stopped. The smiles disappeared and the mood outside the dormitory entrance, still washed in afternoon sunlight, became chilly.

"Who's he?" said Carrot, looking at me and nodding toward Vinnie.

"That's Vinnie," I said. "He's new, too."

"Vinnie, huh? Vinnie what?" said Carrot, this time looking straight at Vinnie.

"Vinnie Mazzerelli," said Vinnie, in a good-natured voice.

"Where ya from, Vinnie?" said Carrot. "You from Virginia, too?" I could feel something building, but I wasn't sure what it was.

"Me?" said Vinnie. "I'm from New York," and he pronounced it in a way I had never heard before: "Nooo Yawk."

"I thought so," said Carrot, with a hint of a sneer. "Tell me, Vinnie, what does your father do down in New York?" he added, making a crude attempt to imitate Vinnie's pronunciation. "Does he make spaghetti or drive a cab?" Carrot and his friends exploded in laughter. Even Vinnie laughed, although his face was flushed. I was speechless. I had always thought of prejudice

19

as exclusively a matter between black and white. Of course, I also knew what it meant to be treated unfairly by my own people, some of whom regarded me as spoiled or stuck up because of the circumstances of my birth or the fact that I did well in school, but these exceptions paled before the lengths to which white people were willing to go to maintain the myth of their superiority. It seemed Vinnie was being gored by the same ox. And he was a white boy.

"He's actually a cardiologist," said Vinnie when the laughter had died down.

"Where's his office?" said Peter Holcomb, a short boy with a crewcut who had been silent up until then. "The Lower East Side?" Carrot and his friends were doubled over in laughter. Vinnie was now red as a beet, his acne suddenly less apparent, but his face still managed to hold on to a tight, goofy little smile, despite the insults.

"He's got two offices," said Vinnie, with forced good humor. "One on Park Avenue and one at Mount Sinai."

"Oh, really?" said Carrot. "Is he a Jew, too?" And the group dissolved in laughter again at Carrot's rhyming.

"Hey, look, fellows," said Vinnie in a limp voice. "I don't know how this got started, but it's getting close to dinnertime and I want to wash up. So, if you'll excuse me," and he pulled open the dorm door to enter.

"Don't scrub too hard," said Rolf. "You might bleed to death." Snickering, the group strolled away.

I followed Vinnie into the dormitory. The first-floor hallway had dark mahogany paneling and a tile floor. The lights were off, but in the shadowy coolness, I could see that his cheeks were wet, although he tried to wipe away the evidence with his shirtsleeve.

"How come they jumped on you like that?" I said in wonderment. "They really had it in for you." I thought that Vinnie might have offended one of them earlier in the day, or perhaps there was a feud between Vinnie's family and one of their families, like in *Romeo and Juliet*.

"God, I don't know," he said. "I've never seen any of them before. I don't know what set them off, but they were pretty rough. I can take it, though. I've heard that kind of stuff before. I'll be all right."

I told Vinnie I would see him later, and went up to my room to stretch out on my bed. It was still light out, and, as I lay on my back, I could see the tops of the trees turning dark green against the pale blue sky. I thought about where my parents would be by now. Somewhere along the Jersey Turnpike, I guessed, and then it would be nightfall, through Delaware, Maryland, and home, all the places I had left behind, that I had wanted to leave behind. It was too late to call them back to come and get me. They were returning home. I was going forward. But forward to what? Who was this new person I wanted to become, freed of the carefully articulated mold of the good colored boy that the South—and even my parents—had prescribed for me? I recalled what my mother had said just before she left. "They won't let you forget that you're a Negro." Perhaps she's right, I thought. Perhaps I can't escape the image that others have created for me, but if I don't try, I will never know if I can or not. And this could be my only chance. I thought about the friends I had left behind in the South and the cramped, sad lives they seemed destined to lead, the hollow trappings of maturity they would be expected to acquire, a sharp suit of clothes, a Sunday hat, to have a regular job teaching school or sorting mail at the post office or even, perhaps, to become a professional sitting behind their own desk in their own office in the colored part of town. The card parties they would attend on Saturday afternoon. The house parties on Saturday night. Church on Sunday morning. Dinner on Sunday afternoon. Their lives would be defined by the limits of their existence in the South, and those limits were absolutely fixed and utterly impregnable. I wanted to find my own way of life, one that did not depend on how well I fit the mold. I wanted to be myself, and if I did well, I thought Draper would give me that opportunity. But the incident with Vinnie troubled me. Suppose something like this happened again? And what if something like this happened to me? What would I do? How many others in the school were like Carrot and his friends? And what did they think of Negroes?

Weeks passed without another incident, although when I saw Vinnie, he would complain that the fellows on the second floor were giving him a hard time. Most of the time, I chalked it up to his tendency to exaggerate, like the time he told me Joe Louis was one of his father's patients.

"My dad said he's going to drive up one weekend soon with Joe Louis and take us all out to dinner," said Vinnie. Weekend after weekend passed, and they never showed up.

chapter three

I went to classes, went to meals in the dining room, and attended to my studies, and I found that, as Cousin Gwen had recommended, I was most comfortable when I kept to myself. That way, the differences I noticed between me and those around me—teachers, classmates, fellow students—were less obvious. I still spoke like a southerner, and a colored southerner at that, and despite my efforts to disguise my accent to make myself sound more northern, it was common for my roots to be exposed when I spoke. Asked to recite in class, I could sense amused glances being exchanged between my classmates as I labored to deliver my assignment in a neutral voice. At mealtimes, I ate and listened to the table conversation and was often the first to be excused.

The conversation in the dining room was usually dreary, concerned with subjects in which I had no interest at all—golf courses, New York society, or which towns in Florida had the best beaches—but occasionally it touched on something that caught my ear. A member of the senior class had been caught with gin in his aftershave bottle and had been sent home. The new French teacher's wife was spending an awful lot of time with Mr. Hall from the science department. They were often seen together around the campus, and one of the freshmen had overheard the French teacher, who was his dorm master, arguing about it with his wife late one night. "What do you expect me to do in this godforsaken place?" she was heard to have said. "Crawl into a hole?"

The subject of race, however, was never mentioned. Instead, the name of a well-known Negro athlete would come up, and everyone would agree that he was extraordinary. I had come from a community that regarded all sorts of Negroes as extraordinary— Dr. Carver, Dorie Miller, Marian Anderson, Father Divine—but none of them were ever mentioned. Nor was there any mention of Negroes like Emmett Till, whose name had been a household word at home after he was lynched. There was so much that they didn't know, so much, it seemed, that they didn't want to know. It was as though we didn't exist, except to provide them with entertainment, and it soon became clear that, among our people, white people admired the colored athletes above all others, if they even knew of any others. They preferred Willie Mays for his showmanship and his humility to Jackie Robinson, of whom, it seemed, they were wary. Nor was there much enthusiasm at all for Joe Louis, who was considered a god, if slightly tarnished, by everyone at home. For the most part, however, the conversation had little to do with me, and I had little to do with it.

And so I came to enjoy the privacy of my room. I understood that I was at Draper to work, and I had to do that on my own.

There were occasional visits from classmates, usually to get an assignment or to discuss an answer to a problem, but once the information was obtained, the visit was over and the visitor would depart. We received our first grades at the end of October and I nearly made the honor roll; however, Vinnie had not done so well. Nor had there been an improvement in his social life. He had become the butt of jokes on the second floor, some of which had to do with his skin condition and others with his heritage. On the second floor, Vinnie had become a pariah.

Vinnie was my only regular visitor. He would stop in for a social call, to fill me in on a recent development in his life or to ask my advice. I was usually working when he arrived, but he would tell me a joke or do an imitation of a teacher in the classroom, and it would be enough to get me to put down my book and laugh, which I did not otherwise have a chance to do. Nevertheless, he was struggling.

"You know what they've done now?" moaned Vinnie. It was a chilly afternoon in the middle of November, and the trees had been reduced to skeletons of trunks and bare branches, although the sun was strong and bright. He was seated on the edge of my bed while I was at my desk reviewing my history assignment. "They've put up signs."

"What kind of signs?" I said, looking up from my work and wincing. I knew all about signs. WHITES ONLY. COLORED. NIGGERS KEEP OUT. THIS ESTABLISHMENT RESERVES THE RIGHT TO SERVE WHITE PEOPLE ONLY.

"In the bathroom," he said. "They put one over a basin that

says VINNIE'S SINK and another on the door to a stall that says VINNIE'S TOILET." Up until now, Vinnie had been able, with effort, to maintain his composure in the face of such indignities, but I could tell from his voice that he was starting to unravel. His face still held the lopsided smile that he often wore and his skin still bristled with acne, but his small, dark eyes were desolate, haunted. "What did I do to deserve this? Rolf told me they had a floor meeting and decided to give me my own sink and toilet and I'm not supposed to use the others. What can I do?" he said, in despair.

"Did you call your folks?" I said.

"I call my folks every night. My dad has already talked to Spencer several times," he said.

"What did Spencer say?" I asked.

"'Nothing to worry about. Boys will be boys. Everything's under control.' Meanwhile, I'm a nervous wreck. My grades are terrible. They're tossing shaving-cream bombs into my room at three A.M., so I can't sleep. Nobody on the floor will speak to me, and the rest of the school thinks I'm impossible to get along with."

"I think your father ought to come up here and meet with Spencer face-to-face," I said. "That will get his attention."

"My father already suggested that to him," said Vinnie. "He even suggested a meeting with Spencer and him and all the kids on the floor to clear the air, but Spencer didn't want to do it. He said it wasn't necessary, and he didn't want to give the impression things are out of control. He said the school has traditions to maintain and a reputation to uphold, and then he said something that burned my father up. He said, 'We all experience challenges in our lives, and character is measured by how we face up to those challenges and overcome them. Vince'—he never calls me Vinnie—'should think of this as just another challenge along the road of life.' I guess my dad got really hot when he said that. He told Spencer if things weren't straightened out soon, he was going to talk to a lawyer."

I was intrigued by Vinnie's mention of a lawyer. We never put much faith in lawyers at home. If you needed to draft a will or pass papers on a piece of property, you would hire a lawyer, but if you were colored and had a serious problem that involved the law, you were better off handling it yourself. It was cheaper, for one thing, and for another, the white lawyers couldn't be trusted, and neither could many of the colored ones. The courts were the worst of all. The judges thought it was their solemn duty to preserve segregation, and that was all that mattered. I didn't know anything about lawyers or courts in the North at the time, but if Vinnie's father was going to talk to a lawyer, I thought he must know what he's doing.

The next evening I had returned to my room after dinner when there was a knock on my door. It was Dillard standing in the doorway with a broad smile.

"Got a few minutes?" he said.

"Sure," I said. "Come on in." Although I didn't have any classes with Dillard, I had seen him around the campus often since that first day, and he had always been friendly. He walked in, closed the door behind him, and took a seat on the bed.

"How's it going?" he said.

"Not too bad," I said. "Latin is a lot of work, but I'm starting to get the hang of it. And science is pretty tough, but everything else is under control." I was seated at my desk, and as I looked at Dillard hunched over on the edge of the bed, with his forearms resting on the tops of his thighs and his hands clasped between his legs, I began to wonder about the reason for this visit. "How about you?" I said.

"Pretty good. Team's doing pretty well. Made the honor roll." Could it be, I thought, that he still wants me to come out for the football team? "Say, you're a friend of Mazzerelli's, aren't you?" he said. I said I was. "Well, what's his problem, anyway?" Dillard was still smiling, but his tone of voice was hostile.

"I don't know," I said. "Seems like a regular guy to me."

"Well, a lot of the guys can't stand him. They say he's always talking about how his father is a big-time doctor, and who his father's patients are. Pretty obnoxious."

"I don't know. I never heard anything like that." I decided, for the moment, not to mention Joe Louis.

"Well, the fellows on the second floor want him to move, but the only way to get him out is to persuade him to switch rooms with someone else in the dorm. So far, nobody is willing to do it." There was a long pause. Dillard had stopped smiling a while ago. He took a deep breath. "Are you interested?"

"Not me," I said. I sympathized with Vinnie's plight, but not enough to become any kind of martyr. The only thing left for the fellows on the second floor to do to Vinnie was to set fire to his room.

"There's a rumor going around that his old man's going to sue the school. Can you imagine? I tell you, these people are always looking for an edge. Anything to knock you off balance so they can get the upper hand. They never do anything like gentlemen. That's why you never see them in any of the better clubs or restaurants or anything. They're so pushy."

Dillard was like most of the students at Draper, certain that the world, as it appeared through his bright, self-confident gaze, was a world his parents and grandparents and ancestors had bought and paid for, and, therefore, a world that he was able to see with unerring accuracy. And anyone who sought to be a part of that world required a pedigree. That left out Vinnie, and I suspected, me too. Dillard was like the white boys in the South who still believed in the legitimacy of the Confederacy, nearly a hundred years after the end of the Civil War. Boys whose heroes were Robert E. Lee and Stonewall Jackson, who considered Richmond the Capital City, and the South a land answerable only unto itself, with its own history and inviolate traditions. I had always felt like an outsider in that world, and now I was beginning to feel like an outsider in this one.

"What do you think is going to happen?" I said.

"I can't really say. I know Mr. Spencer's been spending a lot of time on it, but he says Vinnie's father is very tough to deal with. Very excitable. They say the Italians are all like that. Carrot said they'll try to blackmail you if you're not careful. He said his father had a run-in with one of them over some real estate deal, and the guy threatened to go to the papers if his father backed out."

I had seen Carrot around the campus after our first meeting, but I had avoided any direct contact with him. I was surprised to hear Dillard bring up his name, and I was curious about their relationship.

"Is Carrot involved in this, too?" I asked.

"Well, sort of," said Dillard. "A lot of the guys on the second floor look up to him, so Mr. Spencer asked him to have a word with them to get them to back off of Vinnie, until something could be worked out. Carrot's a good man. He just wants to do what's best for the school."

"Did he talk to them?"

"Yeah. He talked to them a couple of days ago, and things have been pretty quiet since then."

The silence that followed gave each of us a chance to consider this last statement. Dillard had obviously offered it as proof that Vinnie's situation, with Carrot's intervention, was under control. But after seeing Carrot in action, I had my own ideas about what he had said to his friends on the second floor.

"Have you seen the signs?" I asked.

"Signs? What signs?"

"In the bathroom on the second floor. There's one over a sink that says VINNIE'S SINK and one on the door of a toilet stall that says VINNIE'S TOILET. Rolf told Vinnie they took a vote and decided to assign Vinnie his own sink and toilet. He's the only one who's supposed to use them."

Dillard grinned. "You're kidding. Why, that's hilarious." He slapped his knee with his hand. "These guys will try to make a joke out of anything."

"I don't think Vinnie considers it a joke."

"Sure it is," Dillard shot back, with a smile of proprietary confidence. "Vinnie's problem is that he takes everything so seriously. He needs to relax and get rid of that chip on his shoulder." As simple as that.

It was a test of Vinnie's character, and I realized that my only hope of surviving in such a world was to be able to identify what I knew to be the truth, even though others chose to ignore it, and to find my own path through the wilderness.

"I'd better get back to work," I said.

"Let me know if you change your mind," said Dillard, still smiling as he left the room.

A few days later, I was walking alone to my room after dinner when Vinnie caught up with me. The Thanksgiving holidays were a week away, and everyone, including me, was looking forward to going home.

"You'll never believe what happened," said Vinnie. His hands were stuffed into his pants pockets. His head was down, and he was wearing an unbuttoned sport jacket as he walked beside me.

"Try me," I said.

"Now they want to move me into the infirmary. Spencer called me in and said he'd been thinking it over, and he thought I'd be a lot happier if I moved into the infirmary after the Thanksgiving break."

"What did you tell him?"

"I said I had to talk to my folks about it. It might be better. Less pressure."

"Don't do it, Vinnie. Don't agree to it. It's like . . . ," and for some reason I hesitated, perhaps because I had not used the word in months. "It's like segregation." We had reached the dorm and started up the staircase inside.

"I'll call my folks," said Vinnie, stopping at the second-floor landing. "I'll talk to you later."

A couple of hours later there was a knock on my door. It was Vinnie.

"I talked to my father, and he said I should give it a try. I don't know what to think anymore." Vinnie sat down on my bed and slowly shook his head, as though he was trying to take it all in. "I wish I'd never come to this place," he said. His head was bowed at first, but then he raised it, and I could see that his eyes were filled with tears. "I guess they got what they wanted after all," he said.

Every Sunday afternoon since I had arrived at Draper, I had called my parents to tell them how I was doing. I had mentioned Vinnie's problems, but because the problems didn't involve me, they seemed unconcerned. Now I wanted to call them and tell them everything, about the slurs and the harassment and the signs and Mr. Spencer's refusal to do anything except put Vinnie in a segregated room, and I wanted to ask them to come and take me home, but I knew I couldn't. I couldn't because I had no place to go. I had made my decision to abandon the South, to escape the web of its myths, and I was now discovering what the rest of the world was like. And my parents had paid for the ticket, not me. For me, the journey was just beginning.

"Can I help you move your things?" I said.

Vinnie nodded. With his hand, he wiped away tears that were rolling down his cheeks. "I wish I didn't have to do this. They're just going to make fun of me even more." He sighed heavily. "But maybe I can at least get some rest."

"When do you want to move?"

"Soon as possible." He sounded as though it was resolved. "Tomorrow morning."

The following morning, when I knocked on Vinnie's door, was the first time I had been to his room in weeks. He usually came up to my room to talk, to give himself a breather. On the door, someone had posted a sign that said QUARANTINE: ENTERING THIS ROOM MAY ENDANGER YOUR HEALTH, and below it was a crudely drawn picture of Vinnie with slicked-down hair and red dots all over his face and a large X drawn through it. I opened the door and entered. Vinnie was still packing. The odor from the shaving-cream bombs was everywhere and there were traces of shaving cream in every corner, but there was another odor that was just as strong but nauseating, repulsive. I recognized it immediately as dog feces.

"Vinnie," I said, "have you checked around your room? It smells like dog shit in here."

"I know," said Vinnie. "I smelled it last night when I came back from talking to you, but I looked everywhere and I couldn't find anything. If you see something, let me know, will you?"

Vinnie had packed his suitcases, and he was putting the rest of his belongings in cardboard boxes. "I'll start to take things down," I said, and I picked up two leather suitcases and walked down the stairs to the dorm entrance. I started to leave the suitcases at the front door, and then I thought about what had been happening to Vinnie and decided to take a short walk over to the infirmary and leave them there. When I entered the infirmary, a nurse was standing inside the door with her hands clasped, a pleasant older woman in a white uniform and a white nurse's cap who seemed to be waiting for me. The interior of the infirmary was quiet and shadowy. It had the feeling of a rest home.

"Well, Vincent," she said. "We're so happy you're going to be staying with us." She was smiling broadly.

"I'm not Vincent, ma'am," I said. "I'm Rob Garrett. I'm just helping Vinnie move."

"Well, when you see him, tell him we're waiting for him." She spoke like a character out of a storybook, a fairy godmother, and as I walked back across the campus to the dorm, I thought maybe this wouldn't be such a bad move for Vinnie after all.

When I got back to Vinnie's room, the boxes were in the hallway, packed and ready to go. I walked inside. The room was just about empty. His record player was packed up and sitting on the floor next to his laundry bag, which was almost full. Vinnie was sitting on the side of the bed, and he looked up with an expression as disconsolate as the one he had worn the night before.

"I just talked to the nurse at the infirmary," I said. "She seems pretty nice. She said to tell you they are looking forward to having you." Vinnie looked up at me. He was completely unmoved. His eyes seemed lifeless, flat.

"You know that smell we tried to find?" he said. He nodded toward the laundry bag. The top of the laundry bag had been drawn tight. I went over to it and opened it. Resting on top of a white oxford cloth shirt was a large mound of dog shit. I quickly drew the bag shut.

"Oh, God," I said. "This is awful. C'mon, Vinnie. Let's get out of here." I went over to Vinnie and pulled him up. "Take this," I said, handing him the record player. "We'll leave the laundry bag." We walked out into the hallway and picked up the remaining boxes. One or two students on the floor were standing in the doorways of their rooms, silently watching. No one offered to give us a hand. "Wait a minute," I said to Vinnie, and I put my boxes down, walked back to the door to his room, and ripped down the poster and tore it into pieces, leaving them in the doorway. I picked up the boxes again, and Vinnie and I headed for the infirmary.

chapter four

After breakfast on the day before Thanksgiving, I boarded a bus that was waiting on campus to take Draper students to the local railroad station. Only a week had passed since I had helped Vinnie move into the infirmary, and I was still troubled by the events that had led up to it. I would have preferred to sit by myself, but the bus was filling up quickly, so I took a seat next to an upperclassman named Burns, a tall, thin, strawberry-blond fellow with pale skin and long, delicate fingers. I had heard that he liked to play the piano in the common room of his dormitory and that when he did, a crowd would sometimes gather to listen. He was staring pensively out the window and barely seemed to notice when I took the seat next to him. When there were no empty seats left, the driver shut the door and pushed the gearshift forward, and the bus slowly headed down the main driveway. It was a gray morning, and the air was moist and chilly. Filled with Draper students—"the most gifted members of your generation," Mr. Spencer had called us—the bus ferried us away from the campus as though we were a group of Boy Scouts departing on an excursion. Everyone was looking forward to the break from classes, and the bus was humming with talk of social plans, real and imagined.

"Hey, Cartwright, are you going to the Plymouth Rock Ball on Saturday? There are supposed to be a lot of girls from Miss Daggett's on the list."

"I got an invitation, but I haven't decided."

"It should be swell. It's at the Carlyle again."

"It's *always* at the Carlyle, you numbskull. Did you get an invitation?"

"Not yet."

"You shoulda seen her. Long red hair. Bazooms out to here. She was having dinner at the Yale Club with this old silver-haired guy wearing an ascot and a blazer. He looked like he was her father. My brother, Chris, has seen them there before, and he says this guy was her *boyfriend.* Chris said they come into the club for dinner all the time. She doesn't like to cook. The old guy works downtown at Brown Brothers. Manages her trust fund. He's a Yalie. Class of twenty-four. You wanna meet me at the club sometime this weekend? Maybe she'll show up."

During all the talk about vacation plans, Burns and I sat quietly. I never expected to be invited to the social events that my classmates attended at home, although it was inevitable that I heard about them—the coming-out parties at country clubs, the formal dances at big-city hotels where everyone would get dressed up in tuxedos and ball gowns so they looked twice their age and a society band would play those bouncy show tunes and everyone would dance the fox trot and stand around smoking cigarettes and drinking whiskey from silver flasks. Invitations to these events were much coveted, and I suspected that Burns had a few tucked away in his coat pocket. I was looking forward to spending my vacation at Cousin Gwen's apartment in Harlem. I had reading to do for school, and I was going to see my parents for the first time since September. I was also hoping to explore a little of Harlem on my own, since I was now old enough to attend school away from home.

"Wonder what *Burns* is gonna do this weekend?" shouted someone from the back of the bus, followed by hooting and raucous laughter. Burns continued to look out the window of the bus, as though he hadn't heard anything. I thought I recognized Carrot's voice, but I didn't bother to turn around.

"Probably going to a concert," said someone else. "Arthur Rooobinstein." There were more hoots and giggles.

"Or a bar mitzvah," said the first voice, and the bus rocked with laughter. Burns and I remained silent, but I noticed that his ears and the skin on his neck had turned bright red and his lips were pursed into a thin pink crease. As the bus rumbled along to the railroad station, everyone's attention was quickly diverted elsewhere, but I was puzzled that the comments about Burns had evoked such laughter.

"You're a friend of that Mazzerelli kid, aren't you?" said Burns, turning away from the window.

"Yeah," I said.

"It's a shame what has happened to him," he said. "This

place sucks." He turned back toward the window. Brightly colored leaves littered the sides of the road and the surface of nearby fields like confetti.

I had never really talked to an upperclassman before. I assumed they were as unmoved by Vinnie's plight, if they were even aware of it, as the members of my own class, and I was surprised to hear Burns express sympathy for Vinnie.

"It's been pretty bad," I said. "And the worst part is, nobody seems to care."

Then Burns turned toward me, lowered his head, and spoke in a confidential tone. "You know why that is, don't you?" His green eyes were riveting, as though he possessed a family secret he had sworn not to reveal. I shook my head in uncertainty. "It's because the ringleaders are all from families that have sent boys to Draper for years. Sargent. Holcomb. Schroeder. Their fathers and uncles and cousins are all Draper men, and a lot of them are still around. There's only one reason that Spencer hasn't stepped in and cracked the whip." Burns stopped for a moment, with a dramatic pause.

"What's that?" I said. I was bursting with curiosity. Burns had suddenly given me a different outlook on Draper, and I was eager to hear more.

"Money," said Burns. "They have a lot of it, and they give a lot to the school. They also know how to raise it." Burns was smiling mysteriously. "And don't forget, Sargent's father used to be on the board of trustees."

So that was it, I thought. Vinnie never had a chance. The

deck was already stacked against him. I decided to take the seat next to Burns on the train down to New York, if I could. I wanted him to tell me more about the world of Draper behind the scenes, as well as the wider world beyond.

The train had already arrived and was sitting on the tracks when the bus pulled into the parking lot next to the station. There was a rush to get off and find your bag among the pile that had been stuffed in the luggage compartment beneath the bus and get on the train before it pulled away from the station. I managed to find my bag quickly; however, Burns was still searching for his, so I offered to save him a seat and headed for the train. I entered a coach and found two empty seats, put my suitcase onto the overhead rack, and sat down. A few minutes later Burns appeared, wilted and holding his suitcase. His face was flushed and his blond hair was falling into his eyes. He tossed his bag up on the luggage rack and collapsed on the seat next to me.

"Whew," he said as the train jerked and moved slowly forward. "I didn't think I was going to make it. I couldn't find my suitcase at first. Somebody had taken it by mistake." And then in one smooth motion, Burns reached into the pocket of his sport coat, produced a pack of Lucky Strikes, gave it a flick of his wrist so that two cigarettes emerged, and offered me one. I was astonished. In his remarks to incoming students, Mr. Spencer had made it clear that all forms of tobacco were forbidden at Draper, and here was Burns, not thirty minutes away from the campus, offering me a cigarette from a pack that was by no means full.

"No, thanks," I said. "I don't smoke." I confess I was tempted by his offer. Tobacco was big business in Virginia and it seemed that nearly everyone in the state smoked, but both of my parents disapproved of the practice: my father didn't like the stains cigarettes left on your teeth and my mother didn't like the smell they left in the house. She never put ashtrays in the living room. But I was still curious about the cylinders rolled in white paper that seemed to give people such pleasure, and were it not for the fact that I felt an obligation not only to myself but to my family and the race to avoid unnecessary risks, I would have gladly taken Burns up on his offer.

Burns shrugged and took out one of the cigarettes, held it up to his lips with two long fingers, and lit it. No one else in the coach seemed to notice. In fact, I saw a few other students smoking in the rear. He leaned back in his seat, crossed his legs, and blew a cloud of smoke across the coach, which was now barreling down the tracks. In his wool sport jacket and gray trousers, he looked at least twenty and very worldly, and as I watched him holding the cigarette between his fingers, occasionally raising it to his lips, it began to dawn on me that there was more to Burns than I had realized.

"Are you from New York?" he said between puffs.

"Me?" I said. "Nope, I'm from Virginia. I'm just going to New York to stay with a relative for the holidays. She lives in Harlem."

"No kidding!" said Burns. "I go up there sometimes. Does she live near any of the clubs? Small's Paradise? Minton's? They used to get some pretty good groups up there, but these days you usually have to go downtown to Fifty-second Street for the best jazz, or all the way to the Village."

I listened to him in silence. I had vaguely heard of Fifty-second Street and the Village, and I could remember reading something about Small's Paradise in *Jet,* but they meant nothing more to me than that. I was tempted to ask Burns what went on at these places, but rather than appear naive, I decided to simply nod, as though I knew exactly what he was talking about.

"Do you ever go to any of the jazz clubs in Harlem?" said Burns, mashing his cigarette into an ashtray embedded in the armrest.

"Not really," I said. "I'm not old enough." In New York City, you had to be eighteen to enter a nightclub that sold liquor.

"Oh, that doesn't matter. You could easily pass for eighteen." I suppose he had a point, but I had never thought about it before. I was tall and I had begun to shave every morning. When I wore a jacket and tie, I probably did look eighteen, especially to white people. White people, I had discovered, had the annoying tendency to overlook the distinguishing features of my face and only see my color. At least once a week, since I had been at Draper, someone would tell me that I looked just like Willie Mays or Floyd Patterson or Sweetwater Clifton. At first I tolerated the comparisons, telling myself they were really compliments, until I finally had to admit that they were merely evidence of the inability—or unwillingness—of white people to see me for who I really was. Of course, they had displayed a similar blindness toward Vinnie, but without comparing him to a popular athlete. At Draper, Vinnie's fate was to be seen as a pariah, for whom there were no comparisons.

"Where do you live?" I said.

"On the Upper East Side," said Burns. "My folks have a duplex on Park Avenue, but we usually spend the summer in the Adirondacks." It sounded as though Burns also came from money, like a lot of the students at Draper, but he seemed different, not only because of his sympathy for Vinnie, but because he knew about the world. He was the only person from Draper I had met who knew anything about Harlem.

"How do you manage to get into these clubs?" I was pretty sure Burns wasn't yet eighteen, and I figured he must have a fake ID or at least a fake mustache.

"It's easy. I just show up, like everybody else. With all the competition from downtown, the clubs in Harlem are glad to let you in, no questions asked."

"And what do you do when you go?"

"Oh, mainly I go to see the musicians and listen to the music. New York has the best jazz in the world. It used to be in Kansas City, but not anymore. Do you know anything about jazz?"

"I can't say that I do," I said. "At home, we listen to rhythm and blues. A lot of folks at home think jazz is the devil's music. I'm talking about older people, churchgoing people. As far as they are concerned, you're committing a sin if you go anywhere near a nightclub where jazz is playing. We mostly listen to

Johnny Ace, Little Esther, Shirley and Lee, people like that." I leaned back in my seat for a few minutes to close my eyes, and I thought of home. Except for gospel music, which I thought was terribly old-fashioned, the only music played on the Negro radio station at home was rhythm and blues. White people called it race music, and I suppose it was, in the sense that the musicians were always colored and, as far as I knew, so was the audience, but I'm sure that wasn't how the white people meant it. They meant it as a warning to other whites, especially the young ones.

"One time," I said, "my friend Russell and I went to this big rhythm and blues concert. It was at this theater in town called the Majestic." I paused for a moment, deciding whether to explain to Burns that the Majestic was segregated and that Negroes had to sit in the balcony. I decided to skip that part for now.

"Oh, really," said Burns. "Who was in the show?"

"Ruth Brown *and* Joe Turner," I said proudly. "Ever hear of them?"

"Oh, sure," said Burns. "They're on the radio all the time."

"On the afternoon of the show, I was sitting on the porch. I had already been dressed for two hours in a starched white short-sleeve shirt and khakis I had ironed myself, and I was whiling away the time before leaving for the Majestic by listening to the local Negro radio station. Leon the Lover Anderson, king of the local disc jockeys, was touting the show in his inimitable style. 'It's gonna be a *baaad* mamma jamma, ladies and gents, boys and girls. Ruth Brown *and* Joe Turner on the same stage at the Majestic Thee-a-ter. Now, can you top that? You know you can't beat it with a stick. If ya wantcha wontcha, then why in the world dontcha? Awri-i-ight. Sendin' this one out for Haywood and Pearl and Tiny and Eulamae. They gon' be there tonight. Don't you miss it! Big Joe Turner singing "Shake, Rattle, and Roll."'"

"Well, how was the show?" said Burns. I smiled at his question.

"The show was terrific. We had a ball. But first we had to get there." I decided that this was as good a time as any to find out how much Burns knew about the South. "My folks didn't want me to go at all, because the Majestic is segregated. You know what that means?"

"Sure," said Burns. "They have it in Florida. I've seen it when my family goes down there for vacations. They don't let Negroes stay in the hotels or eat in the restaurants, and they can only sit in a certain section of a theater."

"Well, I finally got my parents to let me go. Russell came over and we started to leave and my dad asked us how we were going to get to the Majestic. I told him we were going to catch the bus and he said, 'Look, it's bad enough that you're going to a show in a segregated theater. Why do you have to go in a segregated bus?'" I chuckled at Dad's line, but Burns was silent.

"You mean even the buses are segregated?" he said. He seemed surprised.

"The buses. The schools. The restaurants. The movie theaters. The swimming pools. The water fountains. The bathrooms. Every-thing is segregated in the South," I said. "So Dad drove us to the show and picked us up afterward. Russell and I went inside and climbed up to the balcony, which was the only place we were allowed to sit, and we found a couple of seats. The balcony was packed, but after a few minutes everybody around us started rushing for the door. They were going downstairs to the white section on the first floor, which was empty except for a handful of white kids. Russell and I went down with the others and found seats in the white section, and pretty soon the curtains opened and the lights went up and Ruth Brown came on the stage wearing this red-sequined dress that was so tight she could barely walk. Have you ever seen her?" I said. Burns shook his head, but I could tell he wanted to hear more. "Well, she's sorta short and chunky," I said. "But on the stage, she's a real live wire. So the audience was yelling for her, everybody on their feet calling, 'Ruth Brown, Ruth Brown,' like they knew her, and she just stood there with this big grin on her face, enjoying the attention. And then all of a sudden, she grabs the microphone and lets loose with 'Momma, He Treats Your Daughter Mean,' shimmying and shaking in that red dress. It brought down the house. There were people jumping on the seats. Dancing in the aisles. Some were even trying to climb up on the stage. It got so crazy that a white fellow in an usher's uniform started walking up and down the aisles with a flashlight saying, 'Just cause we let y'all down here, don't mean y'all can tear the place up. If y'all keep it up, you gonna have to go back upstairs where you belong,' but nobody paid him a bit of attention."

"Wow," said Burns. "That sounds really exciting." His eyes were shining and, for a moment, I thought I'd made a convert to rhythm and blues, but he lit another cigarette and resumed his look of cool sophistication. "That stuff's okay," he said. "But you haven't heard anything until you've heard Lester Young play the saxophone." He took a puff of his cigarette and released a stream of smoke toward the ceiling. "Look, if you're not doing anything this weekend, maybe we can take in a show together at one of the clubs. Uptown or downtown, somebody's bound to be around." I was eager to take Burns up on his invitation, but I could just imagine what my parents would say, not to mention Cousin Gwen, if I told them I was going out to a New York nightclub with a schoolmate. It would be enough for my mother to withdraw me from Draper on the spot and bring me home for good. And yet I didn't want to say no.

"Sounds like a great idea," I said, "but I need to find out what my parents have planned."

For the rest of the train ride, I thought about how I could get out of Cousin Gwen's apartment for one night without arousing my parents' suspicions. I decided I would tell them that I had been invited to Burns's home for dinner. My father would offer to drive me to Burns's home and I would decline, but if he insisted, I would let him drop me off near the entrance to Burns's building and meet Burns nearby.

I was intrigued about jazz. I had no idea what it sounded like, but I had heard it sometimes referred to as "Negro music," and I wondered what that meant. Burns had called it "the freest music there is," which made me even more curious. And the fact that churchgoing people were against it made me want to hear it all the more. Burns seemed to know a lot about jazz. He could name all the greats, Bud Powell, Dizzy Gillespie, Thelonious

Monk, Coleman Hawkins, and someone named Bird. He would casually work their names into our conversation, as though he was on a first-name basis with all of them.

"Bud Powell is the greatest jazz pianist in the world," he said flatly, as the train was nearing Grand Central station. "Maybe he's in town. If he is, you ought to try to hear him. He's a genius." When the train arrived at Grand Central, we exchanged phone numbers and walked down the platform with our bags. The lobby of the station was huge, bigger than any place I'd ever seen, big enough to hold three or four Majestics easily, with an enormous, vaulted ceiling and marble everywhere. It was swarming with people, nearly all of whom were white, except for the self-important redcaps, who were strutting around, pushing their carts laden with luggage, as though they were in service to royalty.

"Is your friend going to meet you here?" said Burns. Cousin Gwen had sent me careful directions for taking the subway from Grand Central, but I still needed to find the subway entrance.

"I'm going to take the subway," I said. "Do you know where I catch it?"

Burns motioned for me to follow him and we walked outside onto Forty-second Street, where he pointed down the block. It was early afternoon, overcast and gray, with great streams of cars, trucks, and taxicabs moving along the street in both directions. "How are you getting home?" I said.

"I could easily walk it from here," said Burns, "but my father insists on having our chauffeur pick me up." At that moment, a long black limousine pulled up to the curb and a dark-skinned man in a dark suit and a chauffeur's cap got out and hurried over to Burns. "Well," said Burns, "speak of the devil. How ya' doing, Tyrone?" Tyrone made an obsequious half-bow. He was clean-shaven and stocky, with close-cropped hair, a thick neck, and ebony skin. He looked as though he could have been an athlete at one time.

"Jes' fine, Mr. Gordie," he said, with a broad, toothy smile. "Sho' is good to see you. How you been?"

"I've been fine, Tyrone," said Burns. "I want you to meet a friend of mine. This is Rob Garrett. He's in school with me at Draper." Tyrone's eyes narrowed as he looked me over, and his smile disappeared. "Rob, this is Tyrone Gaskins. Tyrone has worked for us for many years. He's like a member of the family."

"How you doin'?" Tyrone muttered without looking at me, as he bent over to pick up Burns's suitcase. Suddenly he added, "What sports you play up there?" giving me a wary glare.

"I didn't play any sports this fall," I said. "I decided to concentrate on my schoolwork." Tyrone looked skeptical.

"You didn't play no football? How they let you get away with that?"

"It's simple, Tyrone," said Burns. "It was Rob's decision. He didn't want to do it." Tyrone continued to look me over as though I was a species of Negro he had never seen before. He even seemed mildly resentful. I picked up my bag to walk down the street to the subway.

"I'll give you a call," I said to Burns. "Maybe we can do it on Friday evening."

"Friday might be a problem," said Burns. "Saturday would be better."

"Saturday's fine," I said, thinking it would give me an extra day to spend with my parents and in case they became suspicious.

"Say, why don't we give you a lift to the subway entrance? It's a bit of a walk, and it won't take us out of our way," said Burns.

"I wouldn't mind it."

"Okay, let's go!" said Burns. I could see Tyrone stiffen as he opened the door to the limousine for us. Burns climbed in first. I put my bag inside and got in behind him. Tyrone shut the door with a thud and went around to the driver's side. "Times Square is probably crowded," said Burns. "Why don't we drop Rob off at Fiftieth Street?" Tyrone murmured his assent and quickly pulled into the traffic, snaking between cars and accelerating in the open lanes at breakneck speed. I had never ridden so fast in such heavy traffic, and I had little time to appreciate the luxury of riding in a limousine. Before I knew it, Tyrone had pulled the limo up to a corner curb.

"There's the entrance," said Burns, pointing to a dirty concrete structure that looked like a bunker. Tyrone remained behind the wheel, so I got my bag and opened the door myself.

"Thanks a lot for the ride," I said, loud enough for Tyrone to hear me, but he seemed not to. "I'll give you a call on Friday, Gordie."

"Okay," said Burns, "but be sure to call before sundown." He used such a natural voice that I thought nothing of it at the time, but as I stood on the platform waiting for the train, I thought it seemed a little odd. As the train rolled into the station, however, I concluded his family had probably made plans for dinner on Friday evening, and I thought nothing more of it.

I boarded the train headed uptown and found a seat. The doors closed and the train accelerated quickly, barreling through the tunnel so fast that every passenger, even those who were seated like me, had to hold on to something to avoid being thrown to the floor. Eventually, I found the rhythm of the train's movement and began to look around at the other passengers. A well-dressed Chinese couple—at least I thought they were Chinese—were seated across from me, studiously avoiding eye contact with anyone except each other. There were several white people on the train, most of them elderly and simply dressed. The women wore hats and the men needed a shave. The whites were either talking to each other or reading the paper or looking at the advertisements that were posted in the train. And there were several colored people, seated apart and looking out the window at the switching lights or dozing with their heads bowed as the train sped through the tunnel. As we headed north, the Chinese couple and the white people got off at various stops and were replaced by more Negroes, until the train reached 110th Street and it looked as though we were traveling through the South in a segregated coach.

chapterfive

Instead of going directly to Cousin Gwen's, I decided to get off the train at 125th Street. For as long as I could remember, I had heard people at home talk about 125th Street as though it was the eighth wonder of the world. "The big time," "the crossroads of Negro America," they called it—but on the few occasions when I had visited New York with my parents, I had only glimpsed the street in passing, on our way to Cousin Gwen's apartment. Now that I had some time of my own, I decided to see what all the fuss was about. I knew Cousin Gwen was expecting me, so I couldn't stay for long, and, although my suitcase wasn't very heavy, I still had to carry it. But for the moment, I was free to see Harlem for myself.

I emerged from the subway at the corner of 125th Street and looked around. There were shops and businesses, stretching as far as I could see. With my bag in hand, I started to walk. Along both sides of the street, there were banks, restaurants, theaters, supermarkets, pawn shops, even a department store right in the middle of a Negro community. Eventually I reached Seventh

Avenue, which was lined with large apartment buildings, some as much as a block long and ten stories high, and big churches as well as little storefronts, flanked by funeral homes, nightclubs, doctors' offices, beauty parlors, bars, and liquor stores. The traffic light was green, and the people around me were crossing, so I crossed with them, looking around in amazement at the sights. Diagonally across the street was the Hotel Theresa where, I had heard, a lot of Negro entertainers liked to stay. Both streets seemed as broad as highways and clogged with traffic, taxis, delivery trucks, brand-new Cadillacs and Lincoln Continentals, even a few prewar Packards, Fords, Dodges, and old jalopies, all, it seemed, driven by Negroes who were honking their horns at once. The sidewalks were as wide as some streets at home, with Negroes moving up and down them in both directions, more Negroes in one place than I had ever seen before.

"Whatcha looking for, son?" said a high-pitched voice I didn't recognize. I looked around and saw a short, light-skinned old man in a jacket and tie. He was wearing a little gray Persian lamb cap that resembled a fedora without a brim and tortoise-shell eyeglasses, which gave him a somewhat scholarly air.

"Nothing, really," I said. "I'm just looking."

"It's a sight to behold, ain't it?" said the old man, smiling. "All these African people in one place."

"Why do you call them African?" I said. It seemed obvious to me that the people on the street were American Negroes, as was I, and as he gave every appearance of being. He cocked his head to one side and squinted at me with one eye nearly closed.

"Boy, where you from?" he said, with an edge to his voice.

"I'm from Virginia."

"What you doin' up here?"

"I'm going to school."

"I thought so," said the old man, his voice now a mixture of self-satisfaction and contempt. "What school you going to?" he said, as though he knew the answer already.

"Draper." I was a little uneasy about telling him, but I decided to anyway.

"Where is *that?*" he shot back, apparently unfamiliar with the name but relishing the role of inquisitor.

"It's in Connecticut. It's a boarding school."

"You mean to tell me you going to a big-time school like that and you don't know you an African?" he said. "What they teachin' you up there anyway?" I was taken aback. Because he was an old man, I felt I should defer to his age, but I found his premise preposterous. There was no question that our ancestors, his and mine, were African slaves, but so much had happened in between to dilute our African ancestry, it seemed absurd to call either of us African. What purpose could it possibly serve, I thought, except to fuel the ravings of an eccentric? Indeed, as I looked at the old man, who was several shades lighter than I was, I could not help but think how ridiculous it was for *him* to call himself an African, since it was obvious that he had a good deal more white blood than black blood in his veins.

I looked around and I realized we were standing in front of a building that was unlike any other in the area. It was a small brownstone apartment building, four stories high, located on the northeast side of Seventh Avenue, a few doors up from 125th Street. From the second floor down to the street, the building's exterior was covered with signs, the biggest of which identified it as THE HOUSE OF COMMON SENSE AND PROPER PROPAGANDA. Underneath, in much larger letters, was printed,

> WORLD HISTORY
> BOOK OUTLET ON
> 2 , 0 0 0 , 0 0 0 , 0 0 0
> (TWO BILLION)
> AFRICANS AND NON-WHITE PEOPLES

Around the perimeter of the sign were hand-painted portraits of colored leaders from around the world, Haile Selassie of Ethiopia, Tubman of Liberia, Jomo Kenyatta of Kenya, Nasser of Egypt, all of whom I had heard of, as well as someone named Garvey, whom I didn't recognize. On the sidewalk, there were other signs, one of which said,

> REPATRIATION HEADQUARTERS
> BACK TO AFRICA MOVEMENT
> REGISTER HERE!

The signs were professionally lettered and the overall effect was similar to what you'd find at the Believe It or Not tent at a traveling circus. And there were tables on the sidewalk piled with books and pamphlets and newspapers, all on racial themes.

"You need to get yourself a *real* education," the old man said, "instead of filling your head with white ideas." He picked up a newspaper from a nearby card table. "Read this," he said, handing the paper to me, "instead of that trash the white man has been feeding you. You need to know your *own* history before you take up all those European subjects they been giving you up there. The Europeans want you to believe civilization begins and ends with them." He made a face like a child who has just been given a dose of castor oil. "Nothing but foolishness," he sputtered. "Utter nonsense. And don't you be stupid enough to fall for it. You must have a good mind or you wouldn't be up there in the first place. You don't need the white man. Stay with your own people. Anytime you want to learn more about yourself, you know where to find me. I'm here seven days a week," and he handed me his business card. I was fascinated and a little discomfited by what he had to say. His point of view was so different from anything I had been exposed to in the South. I was inclined to linger and find out more about him, but since I didn't have much time, I decided to keep moving. I thanked him for his advice, put his card in my pocket, and said goodbye.

With the newspaper tucked under my arm and my suitcase in my hand, I fell in with the waves of people moving west with the green light across Seventh Avenue. When I reached the sidewalk on the other side, I stopped and looked back, as the crowd swept past me. As I stood against the tide, I looked across the street, searching for his tiny figure, and after a moment I found him, standing on the sidewalk in front of his bookstore, shielding his eyes with one hand. When he saw me turn around, he waved his hand briefly, like a grandfather watching his grandson cross a busy street, and then he turned and disappeared inside his store.

By then, I had only seen one police car. It was parked on 125th Street, a few doors down from the House of Common Sense, under a NO PARKING sign, with two white policemen in dark blue uniforms seated in the front. They were the first white faces I'd seen since emerging from the subway, and all they seemed to be doing was watching the traffic, which was heavy and at a standstill. The windows of the police car were rolled up tight, and the policemen made no effort to get out and wade into the intersection to get the traffic moving. Perhaps, I thought, they didn't want to risk getting run over.

I decided to follow the crowd that was headed along 125th Street. The broad sidewalks were swollen with colored people moving in both directions, and I felt as though I was being swept along by the dark mass of humanity into which I had entered, as though I was immersed in a river, carried by its current toward some inevitable destination. I was exhilarated to be there, to be surrounded by so many brown faces at one time. And so I wandered down the street with the rest of the crowd, occasionally nodding at the colored men coming my way, when our eyes would meet, acknowledging the unspoken bond between us. But where, I thought, is everyone going? Up ahead, I could see a theater marquee hanging over the sidewalk with the word APOLLO in huge letters above it, and below, the words RHYTHM AND BLUES REVUE. It immediately brought to mind the Majestic, but when I reached the marquee, there was no crowd lingering underneath waiting to be admitted, just a slim, sable-colored man with a mountainous process—a glossy arrangement of straightened hair crimped in waves that covered his head. He was wearing a silver tuxedo jacket and black stovepipe trousers, a pale pink shirt with a thin black tie and shiny black shoes with long, pointed toes. He glanced several times at his watch and looked up and down the street without noticing me, although I was only a few feet away. There was something familiar about him. I was certain he was an entertainer, dressed like that and standing in front of the Apollo, and I thought he might be someone famous. I stopped to get a good look, and when I did he gave me a hard stare at first, but, slowly, his face softened into dim recognition.

"Don't I know you from somewhere?" he said with a wrinkled brow, looking me over carefully. I couldn't place him either. He didn't look much older than me, but he seemed a lot older.

"I don't know," I said. "Could be."

"Where you from?" he said. His eyes narrowed, as though he was on the verge of a discovery.

"Virginia," I said, and a broad smile split his face.

"Booker T. Washington Junior High School," he said with a grin, pointing at me with a long brown finger. "Am I right?" I chuckled and nodded my head in agreement.

"Did you go there too?" I said.

"I was a couple of years ahead of you, but I dropped out in the eighth grade 'cause they kept holding me back. Anyway, it turned out to be the best thing for my career. I used to see you in the library, looking at all them books. I used to wonder why you was in there looking at all them books." And slowly it began to dawn on me. I was talking to Willie Maurice Bowman, of Willie Maurice Bowman and the Rainbows, the hottest local singing group in my hometown when I was younger. They used to win all the talent shows.

"Aren't you Willie Maurice Bowman?" I said. His smile widened.

"That's me," he said. "But for reasons of show business, I don't go by Willie no more. Peoples just call me Maurice now. I didn't catch your name?"

"Rob. Rob Garrett."

"Oh, yeah, I remember. You're Doc Garrett's boy. Your daddy fixes my momma's teeth. What *you* doin' up here?"

"Going to school," I said. Willie Maurice looked puzzled. "What for? Wasn't you going to school at home?"

"Yeah, but this school isn't segregated. My folks thought it would be better for me."

"You like it better?"

"I can't say yet. I just started."

"Where's it at?" said Willie Maurice.

"Connecticut," I said. He gave me a curious look.

"Nothin' but white people up there."

"I know. I'm the only colored student in the whole school."

"Damn!" He looked as though I had just told him I had gone over Niagara Falls in a barrel. "Man, you got a lotta nerve." I decided to change the subject.

"What about you?" I said. "What are you doing up here?"

"Me? I'm still workin' on my act, tryin' to make it as a singer," he said, running his thumbs up and down underneath the lapels of his tuxedo jacket, and occasionally patting his process with the palm of his hand. "I was just in here auditioning for a spot on the Rhythm and Blues Revue."

"How did it go?"

"'Wait and see, wait and see.' That's what they all say. Not as bad as how the crackers put it back home. 'Go home, nigger. Don't bother me,' that kind of stuff, although it works out about the same." He seemed dejected. "It's a rough business." Then his mood brightened. "But I ain't gonna let nothin' stop me. I'm just waiting for a break."

"And the Rainbows?" I said. "What happened to them?"

"I wish I could tell you, man," he said, slowly shaking his head. "They came up here with me. We was all in it together, but I'm the only one that's still singing. Alvin is in prison for robbing somebody 'cause he needed something to eat. Eugene is walking around Harlem somewhere right now with a needle in his arm. Jimmy Bivens got married. He got three kids already and another on the way. He's working in a factory over in Queens somewhere. And Tonto, you remember Tonto? He was part In-

60

dian. Choctaw. Handsome as a motherfucker. Couldn't keep the girls off him. Tonto got killed in an apartment down on 116th Street over some broad. Her old man caught him in bed with her and shot 'em both. Boom. Boom. Just like that. Shot 'em both right through the heart. Blood all over the place. I had to go down to the morgue to identify the nigger's body. He looked like Crazy Horse after the soldiers caught up with him."

"Damn," I said. "That's terrible. I had no idea." I was beginning to see Harlem in a different light. Not only as a place of danger, but as a place where dreams became unraveled and abandoned. I was glad to run into someone from home, but Willie Maurice's story was unnerving, and I was becoming concerned about the time. I decided to head to the subway.

"Look, Maurice," I said. "I gotta be going, but I hope things work out for you, man." Shrugging his shoulders and jabbing his elbows against his waist, he looked as if he had just taken the stage, his thin brown face a mask of synthetic invincibility, the pink-yellow palms of his hands open toward me, massaging the air like a spiritualist calling up the dead.

"All I need is a break, man," said Willie Maurice. His face slowly dissolved into a tiny smile. "I hope things work out for you up there at that school. You must have a lot on your mind, bein' around nothing but white folks every day." We consoled each other with a pat on the shoulder, and I turned and headed for the subway. It was beginning to get dark and I knew Cousin Gwen would be worried. On my way to the train, I looked behind me for a moment. Willie Maurice was still standing in front of the Apollo, checking his watch and patting his process.

As I stood on the subway platform waiting for the train, I thought about the old man outside the bookstore. I still had his card, and I reached into my pocket and took it out. It said LEWIS MICHAUX, FOUNDER AND PROPRIETOR, NATIONAL MEMORIAL AFRICAN BOOKSTORE. And then I unfolded the newspaper he had given me. The masthead at the top of the front page said MUHAMMAD SPEAKS, oddly printed in prim, Old English type, but the headline underneath was bold and unmistakable, like the signs in front of Michaux's store. It read, WE MUST HAVE JUSTICE! and at the bottom of the page was an article about a Negro who had been beaten by the police and a photograph of a light-skinned colored man with a boy's skinny haircut. He was wearing a suit and tie and he was looking directly at the camera with an expression of barely contained fury, and he wore eyeglasses with dark plastic frames and metal around the bottom of the lenses, but his eyes were so magnetic, so intense, the demure eyeglasses seemed like a mere prop, like the eyeglasses Clark Kent used to wear to disguise a much more powerful being behind them. The caption underneath the photograph said "Malcolm X, Minister, Muhammad's Mosque No. 7." "We're not interested in white justice," read the quotation under the caption. "We want justice for the black man. If this sort of thing doesn't stop, we'll have to stop it ourselves."

The train arrived, stuffed with Negroes, and I squeezed myself on. The doors shut and I held on to a pole with several other passengers as the train accelerated, and I thought of my encounter with Michaux and his exhortations of Africa. The anger he expressed was not unfamiliar to me. At some point, every Negro wants to scare the wits out of the white man, but I had never heard the anger expressed so openly. As the train hurtled forward, it occurred to me that Michaux had no interest in the integration of the races, which I had been brought up to believe was the ideal for every Negro, the same ideal that Jackie Robinson and Dr. Du Bois and the NAACP had fought for. For Michaux, integration was not an ideal at all, but rather a threat to the future of our people.

chapter six

When I reached Cousin Gwen's apartment, she immediately took me to task. "Boy, where have you *been?* I been worried sick about you. I called the school and the train station. What took you so long?"

I was ready for her. "I decided to walk over to Times Square to look around," I said, trying to appear as unruffled as possible. "I must have lost track of the time." After admonishing me to remember to call if I was going to be late again, she told me to put down my bag and come into the kitchen.

"Are you hungry?" she said.

"I could use a little something," I said, glancing at my watch. It was almost five o'clock.

"How about a ham sandwich? When you finish it, you can help me get dinner ready for tomorrow." Cousin Gwen took a large baked ham and a jar of mayonnaise from the refrigerator and put them on the kitchen table, and with a big carving knife she sliced several thick slices of ham from the bone, spread mayonnaise on two slices of Sunbeam bread, and made my sandwich. With the wrinkled brown hands that had made the ham sandwich with such care, she placed it on a plate and presented it to me. "Here. Don't eat too fast."

"Thank you." I took the sandwich and began to devour it.

"Would you like a glass of milk to go with that?" said Cousin Gwen.

"Yes, m'am," I said. When she placed the glass of milk next to my plate, I felt a warmth and security I had not felt in many months. I could have been seated in the kitchen at home.

"Well, how are things going," asked Cousin Gwen, in her familiar coy voice, "now that you've been up there for a while?" There was something about her tone that made me uncomfortable, as though she already knew the answer to her question and just wanted me to confirm it. She sounded like a gossip columnist for a newspaper.

"It's okay," I said. "I almost made the honor roll last marking period."

"Well, now that's a pretty good start," she said. I was sure she wanted to know more. "How are you getting along *socially?*" It sounded as though she wanted to hear about Vinnie's travails, which I suspected she had learned about from my parents, but I was in no mood to talk about them.

"I've met a few fellows," I said, "but mostly I've kept to myself. Like you told me to do."

Having taught for many years, she must have sensed my reluctance, because she abruptly changed the subject. "Well, we'd better get started on this dinner for tomorrow. Your parents should be here by three o'clock, and I'm sure your father will be hungry."

As much as I looked forward to seeing my parents, I still felt the same sense of distance from them that I had felt in September when they were about to leave me at Draper, and I felt it at that moment in the kitchen with Cousin Gwen. They were all residing in the past, living with their memories of encounters with white people that had accumulated over the years, encounters still tainted with humiliation and bitterness, with insults and intimidation. I had already discovered that Draper was not immune from bigotry, and I wasn't certain what my own future would be like. But I knew that I did not want it to be divided by race like my life in the South had been.

I thought about my encounter with old man Michaux and my fleeting introduction to Malcolm X on the subway. The starkness of their vision of the future was like the negative print of a photograph, a vision of racial separation in reverse, but one that also seemed to be rooted in the past. I wondered if that vision would be my future, if I could ever escape history. I was intrigued by Michaux's exhortations to study our African heritage. I didn't know much about Africa and I wanted to know more, but I was not prepared to drop all of my courses to concentrate on an area of study that Draper didn't offer. And the tone of belligerence both Michaux and Malcolm X adopted seemed hopelessly self-defeating, although reminiscent of language I had heard before, used by angry colored men at home on street corners or at sporting events or in parking lots, arguing with each other about a woman or the result of a ball game or the meaning of a passage of Scripture. It was the voice of anger at the cards that life had dealt.

I got up from the kitchen table and walked over to a window. The sun was setting and the sky was bright red, but below the streets were dark, the paths of the maze deep in shadow. The globes of streetlights, the lighted windows of shabby tenements, the neon signs of shops and bars and the lights of cars and trucks were beginning to illuminate the darkened streets. And I felt once more the urge to wander through that maze, to understand why, in the largest Negro community in the world, there were so few white people. Harlem was in the North, not the South, but when I walked down 125th Street earlier in the day, it seemed like a bigger version of home.

"Can you chop me some onions?" said Cousin Gwen. She removed my empty plate and replaced it with a wooden cutting board, a carving knife, and a bowl with three large yellow onions. I had not been assigned a task like this since leaving home.

"Sure," I said. "I'll just wash my hands." I washed up quickly in the kitchen sink and returned to the table. "What's this for?" I said as I began to peel the onions.

"Collards," said Cousin Gwen. "Collards are tough, so I cook them for a long time over a low flame with onions and smoked ham hocks and water. I'll cook them for a while tonight and finish 'em off tomorrow morning." Cousin Gwen's thin arms were covered with flour and buried in an enormous blue mixing bowl.

"Are you making bread?" I said as she kneaded a pale ball of dough in the bowl.

"Rolls. I'll let this rise overnight and they'll be ready for the oven in the morning."

I started to chop the onions and, as I did, I remembered why I always hated the job. My eyes were filling with tears from the onion fumes. "This is killing me," I said.

Cousin Gwen looked at me and smiled. "You look like you just got a whipping. Take that cutting board with the onions over to the sink and keep the water running while you finish chopping." I was ready to try anything, so I did what she said and it worked.

When I finished chopping the onions, Cousin Gwen put them into a pot with the smoked hocks and the collards that were sitting on the stove, and turned on the burner underneath. "How about peeling and coring some apples for an apple pie?" she asked, handing me a big blue bowl of red apples. She had already begun to make the crust, so I got right to work. As we worked in silence at the kitchen table, I began to think about Harlem. I wondered how much it had changed since Cousin Gwen had arrived. She had lived there for more than forty years, so I asked her, "What was Harlem like when you moved here?"

At first she didn't answer. I thought maybe she didn't hear me, but when I looked at her, I could see that she was concentrating on the pie crust, folding ice water and pieces of lard into the flour. Then she mixed it into a ball and started to roll it out with a rolling pin.

"It was wild. The streets were ruled by bootleggers and racketeers who were paying everybody off. I wasn't twenty-five at the time. I had finished college and managed to find a job teaching school, and I thought I was pretty hot stuff. You could walk down 125th Street and see James Weldon Johnson and Dr. Du Bois and Langston Hughes all on the same afternoon. And Garvey's people would be out, dressed up in those fancy military uniforms and marching up and down Seventh Avenue like they were about to take over the world. I tell you, it was wild." She shook her head slowly, smiling as she recalled the days. "Of course, during the Depression, there was a lot of suffering. I was lucky enough to have a job, so people would come to my door begging for food and I'd give them what I could. Everybody did. You'd see them dressed in rags out on the street holding a sign, WILL WORK FOR FOOD. Little children holding up a piece of cardboard. It was painful to watch, but people managed to get through it. Prohibition was over, so the bootleggers were not as prevalent, but the numbers runners were around and there was plenty of good music in the clubs. Harlem has always been a lively place."

"Who was Garvey?" I said, peeling the red skin from an apple. Cousin Gwen had rolled out the pie crust and folded it carefully, and was unfolding it in the pie pan. I remembered Garvey's picture on the sign in front of Michaux's bookstore.

Cousin Gwen began to crimp the edges of the pastry in the pie pan. "I guess you don't hear that much about Garvey in the South. Garvey was a West Indian, a black nationalist. Heavyset, dapper, and black as coal. He believed we should all go back to Africa and he started his own organization, with a steamship line to take us back. He called it the Universal Negro Improvement Association. It had a newspaper and it would hold parades with people marching up and down the street in uniforms, and Garvey himself would ride in the back of a big convertible like the biggest politicians—FDR and La Guardia—used to ride in, and he would be all dressed up in a military uniform like Napoleon, with gold braids and medals on his chest and a plumed hat. It was all for show, but he could give quite a speech and, of course, the West Indians loved it. Everybody loved it. Oh, he was something, chastising the white man, spinning out his dream of taking everybody back to Africa to a packed hall with that singsong voice of his. He knew how to draw a crowd." Cousin Gwen began to core and peel the last apple and then she sliced it into the big bowl with the others. "But when Dr. Du Bois and James Weldon Johnson and the leaders of the NAACP saw how big Garvey's audiences were, they had a fit. They publicly attacked him for leading the race down the path of destruction. Of course, they were advocates of integration, and Garvey didn't want to have anything to do with integration. Unfortunately, Garvey wasn't much of a businessman. The steamship company failed and the prosecutors got involved and Garvey ended up going to prison for fraud." Cousin Gwen stopped slicing the apple for a moment and looked at me. "Why is it our people always fall for these charlatans?" she said, and she shook her head and resumed slicing. "Anyway, that was the end of him, although there are still a lot of people in Harlem who admire Garvey and what he stood for."

Cousin Gwen mixed the sliced apples with sugar and spices and then poured them into the pastry shell. She dotted the apples with butter and carefully placed a covering of pastry on top, fitting the edges into the grooves of the crimped pastry already in the pan. There," she said, admiring her handiwork. "I'll just put this in the oven. It'll be ready in about an hour." She opened the oven door and a gust of warm air enveloped us as she put the pie in the oven. "I'm going to stay up and wait for this pie to finish. The collards won't be done by then, but they'll have a good start." The heavy odor of the collards hung in the air.

"You must be tired," said Cousin Gwen, walking into the living room. I followed her and walked over to the front window. The immense darkness was spread before me, studded with lights, as though all of Harlem was awake. I wanted to linger at the window even though Cousin Gwen had suggested that I turn in. "There's a clean towel and a washcloth on the day bed in the study," she said. "That's where you will sleep. You know where the bathroom is. Now don't stay up too late. We've got a full day tomorrow." To my surprise, she gave me an affectionate pat on the arm and smiled. Cousin Gwen rarely displayed physical affection, and her manner was often so sharp that I some-times wondered whether she liked me at all or merely tolerated me to preserve her relationship with my parents. But this gesture was so spontaneous, so natural that it caught me by surprise, and I was forced to reconsider how I felt about her and what she had to say.

I said good night, washed up in Cousin Gwen's spotless white tile bathroom, and retreated to the study. It had indeed been a long day, and my mind was spinning as I thought again about the day's events. At last I had seen Harlem with my own eyes, but I wondered what more there was to the place, beyond the huge buildings and the wide streets and the sidewalks flooded with Negroes. There was danger here, I knew from talk-ing to Willie Maurice and reading the newspaper, but I had yet to encounter it. I thought about Garvey, and I wondered if he had been flawed like Joe Louis, losing his way perhaps as only a colored man can. Both were tragic figures, but it seemed odd that Harlem, for all its grandeur and presumed sympathy, could not save them. I was exhausted. In Cousin Gwen's study, I was surrounded by bookcases stuffed with books I was too tired to examine, so I put on my pajamas, switched off the light, and slipped between the covers of the day bed, where I instantly fell asleep in the darkness.

chapter seven

On Thanksgiving, my parents arrived at Cousin Gwen's early in the afternoon. They had left Virginia in the Roadmaster the day before and stopped to visit friends in Delaware, where they spent the night, arising early the next morning to begin the last leg of the trip. By the time they arrived, dinner was almost ready. Cousin Gwen had made candied sweet potatoes, assigning me the responsibility of placing marshmallows on top of the dish and running it into the oven just before serving. Basted, browned, and swollen with stuffing, the glistening turkey rested on top of the stove as Cousin Gwen was busy making the gravy. I had already set the dining room table with Cousin Gwen's finest tableware, long-stem crystal water glasses, Copeland china, and silver flatware she had inherited from her mother, everything arranged according to her precise instructions on a lace tablecloth of white Irish linen. Outside there wasn't a cloud in the sky, and sunlight was pouring in through the dining room windows.

"Well, well, well," said my father with a grin as he shook my hand and threw his arm around my shoulder. "You're looking pretty good, I'd say."

"I'm doing okay," I replied. I didn't want to say any more. I wasn't prepared, at that time, to discuss the details of my experience at Draper with Vinnie or the events of the day before, even though I knew they wanted very much to hear about them. As far as I was concerned, these were private matters, like my decision to go to a nightclub with Burns, and the less my parents knew about them, the better.

"You mean you're not ready to come home?" said my mother in mock surprise, wrapping her arms around me. I knew she was kidding, but I wondered if there was something more to her question. Since I had arrived at Draper, the thought of returning home had occurred to me more than once, but I had clung to my resolve to remain. Despite moments of great uncertainty, I was determined to finish what I had begun, to prove that I had the will to survive and find my way through the wilderness.

Cousin Gwen's Thanksgiving dinner was predictably sumptuous. The turkey was moist and perfectly done, and she had stuffed it with cornbread, grated orange peel, and country sausage, which gave it a wonderful aroma. The giblet gravy she had put together made the turkey even more succulent. The collards were tender and smoky from the ham hocks. I had put the sweet potatoes in the oven at the last minute and they were now on the table with the marshmallows, crispy brown and puffed. There were slices of baked ham, and homemade cranberry sauce, and, of course, Cousin Gwen's incomparable hot rolls. It was a feast, and as the deep blue sky began to take on a rosy hue, we ate ourselves silly, helping ourselves to seconds, and in my father's case, to thirds. And to top it off, when dinner was finished, Cousin Gwen brought out the apple pie, which she had warmed in the oven.

"My goodness, Cousin Gwen," said my father when he finished dessert. "If you keep feeding us like this, the boy won't want to go back to school."

"Oh, he's going back, all right. Nothing would stop that." She looked at me with a knowing smile. Even though I hadn't discussed my reservations about Draper with her, I had the feeling that somehow she knew my initiation had not been without incident.

"Well, there's a lot going on back home," said my father. "After that big Supreme Court case the NAACP won in 1954, all the schools were supposed to open right up for us, but the whites have been resisting it bitterly. They say they will fight it to the last man, just like the Civil War. People are starting to wonder if we'll ever get integration." My father leaned back in his chair. "I guess it just proves that we made the right decision in sending you to school up here."

I let my father's words hover over the dining room table, and I thought about old man Michaux and his distaste for integration. I wondered if what was happening at home was simply a confirmation of his view of the world.

"Some of the young people at home are starting to get organized to protest the situation," said my mother. "They've put a little group together, but I'm not sure just what they intend to do. They are still in the talking stages, but several of your friends are involved. Roosevelt Tinsley, Sylvia Newsome, and Russell. Russell Woolfolk." For the first time since I had arrived at Draper, I felt something more than a twinge of longing for home. If this activity of my friends actually came to something, I thought, they could have a role in bringing segregation to its knees. And meanwhile, I would be safely tucked away in a boarding school in Connecticut, where I could read about it in the papers. "It's mostly college students," said my mother, "but there are also quite a few high school students participating. It will be interesting to see if they can get something done. People are tired of waiting."

After dinner, we cleared the table and my mother helped Cousin Gwen wash the dishes. I sat with my father in the living room while he read the newspaper and probed the spaces between his teeth with a toothpick. I could hear conversation coming from the kitchen. My mother and Cousin Gwen were talking about me and, at one point, my mother confided to Cousin Gwen that she was concerned about me being under "pressure." "He's the only one of us up there, you know," she said.

"I know, Clarissa, but that pressure is no different from what he'll face if he gets out into the world and becomes a doctor or a lawyer. The boy's got to learn how to stand on his own two feet," said Cousin Gwen. "Look at these youngsters in Harlem spending all of their time with each other, and most of them aren't going anywhere. When they're around the whites, they clam right up. The colored kids only talk to each other, and half the time you can't even understand what they're saying. And if they eventually do talk to a white person, it's usually a policeman or somebody who is telling them what to do. They don't have any idea what it's like to talk to a white person as an equal, much less a white person sitting next to you at the dining room table. I know it's worse in the South, but this is *not* paradise. If you want to amount to something today, you have to broaden your reach. You have to look beyond what's familiar to you, beyond what's comfortable to you, no matter what color you are."

I was emboldened by Cousin Gwen's words. I had no idea she thought that way. From what she said, it sounded as though she wouldn't disapprove of me going out one night with Burns to hear jazz in a nightclub. Once again, she had surprised me by revealing something about herself that I had never suspected. Across the room, my father rustled the newspaper. I was certain he was also listening to the conversation in the kitchen.

"He wasn't sent up there to be a guinea pig, you know," said Mother. "We sent him there to get the best education we could provide, to get him ready for college. But if he's going to have problems because he's the only one there, well, I don't have to put my child through an ordeal just to give him an education. It isn't worth it. I'll bring him home."

"Honey, he's going to have problems with white folks anywhere he goes," said Cousin Gwen. "Even in a school like that where they claim to want him so bad, he's bound to have problems. And he's going to have problems with white folks for a long time to come. They sure don't seem to be in any hurry to treat us as true equals. But that doesn't mean we have to accept it. That boy can handle anything they throw at him. He's already proved it, but he needs you to stand by him."

As the words drifted from the kitchen into the living room, I thought about how I had been taught to give whites a wide berth whenever I was in their presence, to be suspicious of anything they said or did. Those feelings hadn't vanished at Draper. My experience with Vinnie had confirmed what I had been taught. My conversation with Michaux in Harlem had evoked it as well. But then there was my encounter with Burns, and the thrill of making secret plans to go out to a nightclub together, of gaining each other's confidence. It seemed, at least between the two of us, that it didn't matter what color we were, and I wondered if this was the way it was supposed to be when integration finally arrived.

My father rustled the newspaper again. "Have you thought about what you'd like to do while you're here?" he said. "Is there anything you need? We could do a little shopping if you need something." This was as good a time as any to make a move, I thought.

"I don't have any plans for tomorrow," I said. "But a friend from school has invited me to his house for dinner on Saturday evening." I held my breath, waiting for Dad's response.

"That's nice, son," he said, without taking his eyes away from the newspaper. "Where does he live?"

"Park Avenue," I said. Dad put the papers down abruptly and looked across the living room at me.

"Park Avenue!" he exclaimed. "You traveling in some mighty fancy circles for a colored boy, ain't you? Who is this fellow?" I could tell he was suppressing a smile.

"Gordie Burns," I said. "He's in the class ahead of me."

"Burns, huh?" said my father. "His people must be from Scotland. 'Man's inhumanity to man. Makes countless thousands mourn.'" I gave him a puzzled look. "That's Robert Burns, Scotland's greatest poet," he said with a wink. "All right. Your mother and I were going to take everybody out to dinner on Saturday, but if you have a social engagement, I guess we'll just have to make other plans."

chaptereight

At breakfast the next morning, my mother brought up my plans for Saturday. "I understand you have a dinner invitation for tomorrow night," she said, excavating a wedge from her grapefruit. I did my best to appear nonchalant.

"A friend from school asked me to dinner at his house," I said.

"And he lives on Park Avenue?" she said, obviously impressed.

"That's what he said. I don't have his address. I have to call him," I said. I wasn't sure what the fuss was about. I assumed Burns came from money, with a chauffeured limousine and all that, and I'd heard about Park Avenue, but I'd never seen it. Although Cousin Gwen seemed interested in the discussion, she remained silent. The reactions of my parents, however, made me curious.

"Well, we have to hear all about this," said my mother. "What time are you supposed to be there?" I was becoming concerned, wondering if my parents would take me to Burns's house and park the car on the street to wait for me until dinner was over.

"I don't know," I said. "He wants me to give him a call today."

I knew I had to make that call when no one else was around, and I began thinking about how it could be orchestrated. I decided it might be best to go for a walk and call Burns from a pay phone. I could even take a subway down to 125th Street and make the call from there.

"You know your father and I were planning to take everyone out to dinner on Saturday," said my mother, pausing for dramatic effect. She finished her grapefruit and rested her spoon on her plate. "But I suppose we can just as easily go out tonight," she added, with a sigh. "That is, if everyone is available."

"I'm free," I said. "I've got some reading to do for a class and I might want to go out for a walk a little later, but other than that, I'm available."

"Me too," said Cousin Gwen. "I'd love to go out to dinner tonight."

"Well, that settles it," said my father. "Let's plan to meet here at six o'clock, and we'll get ready to go to a restaurant. Gwen, you got any ideas about where we should eat?"

"You can get a pretty good meal at Lucille's down on 125th Street," said Cousin Gwen. "That's about the nicest place around."

"Sounds good enough to me," said Dad. "Clarissa, why don't we go out for a drive this morning? Gwen, you're welcome to come along. We can leave the socialite here to do his schoolwork before his engagement tomorrow night." Dad laughed good-naturedly, and everyone at the table joined in.

"Just give me a moment to get my things together," said

Cousin Gwen, and she rose from the table and went off to her bedroom.

"What do you have to read, son?" asked my father.

"American history," I said. "Right now, we're reading Tocqueville's *Democracy in America*. It's pretty interesting. Have you read it, Dad?"

"I can't say that I have. What's it about?"

"Well, this Frenchman came to the United States in the eighteen hundreds and spent almost a year traveling around the country and making notes about what he saw. The book is about his observations of the United States."

"I don't suppose he has anything about Negroes in there. For most of these white historians, we don't even rate a footnote."

"You'd be surprised, Dad. There's quite a bit about slavery, and about the treatment of the Indians as well as Negroes. There's even a section on mulattoes and the friction between light-skinned Negroes and dark-skinned Negroes. It's quite interesting."

"Is that so? And have you discussed any of this in class?"

"So far, we haven't," I said, and it occurred to me that we might not discuss it at all.

Wrapped in a stole of muskrat pelts and wearing a black felt hat with a long pheasant feather, Cousin Gwen returned to the front room. "Well, I'm ready when you are," she said. She stood before a hallway mirror adjusting the feather at a dashing angle. The pelts covered her shoulders and arms so conspicuously, she looked like a trader from the Northwest Territories, but I thought better of mentioning it.

"Well, come along then," said my mother. "We should be back in a couple of hours, son." As soon as the door closed, I felt a wave of excitement at being left alone in Cousin Gwen's apartment. Not only would I be able to call Burns and make arrangements to go out on Saturday night; if I was careful about the time, I could even browse through the books in Cousin Gwen's study or go for another walk to see more of Harlem. But I knew if I went out and returned too late, my parents would be worried and it would be much more difficult to sneak away with Burns the next day.

I found the piece of paper on which Burns had written his telephone number, and I went into Cousin Gwen's bedroom to call him. It was a small, cluttered room, with dark drapes and a double bed covered with a pink spread. Next to the bed, the telephone was sitting on a night table surrounded by bottles of pills, a small tin of hard candies, a half-filled water glass, a jar of cold cream, and a small ceramic vase filled with dusty plastic flowers. On the same side of the bed were books stacked in piles on the floor and a large wicker basket filled with newspapers and magazines, some of which I knew, like *Our World, Sepia, The Afro-American,* and the *Amsterdam News,* and others, like the *Liberator,* the *Nation,* and the *New Masses,* that I had never heard of. The television sat on a table in a corner of the bedroom opposite a large, stuffed lounge chair, with a notebook lying on the seat cushion. Cousin Gwen spent most days in her bedroom watching television, hoping to see a colored face. Every so often, but rarely more than once a month, she said, a Negro entertainer like Rochester or Peg Leg

Bates or a singing group like the Mills Brothers or the Ink Spots, or sometimes just an unknown, rubber-legged tap dancer with straightened hair, would appear like magic on the television screen and Cousin Gwen would pick up the notebook and make an entry, recording the entertainer's name, the show, and the date, time, and channel. Even though the drapes had been pulled back, the room, which looked out on the back of the building, seemed dark and heavy with the musty smell of old clothes, barely disguised by the fragrance of moth balls emanating from the over-stuffed closet.

I picked up the receiver and dialed Burns's number.

"This is the Burns residence," said a voice at the other end. It was the voice of an older woman, chilly and formal, with a vaguely European accent. "With whom do you wish to speak?" Suddenly I was at a loss for words. Even though I had never met her, the mere sound of the woman's voice made me freeze.

"Hello? Hello?" said the woman. "Is anyone there?" I struggled to speak and finally managed to get a few words out.

"Gordie," I said, haltingly. "Gordie there?" I could just imagine what she must have been thinking, but her icy voice never lost its formality.

"One moment, please," she said.

After a moment, Burns got on the telephone. "Garrett?" he said. "I thought it might be you. Are you all ready for tomorrow night?" He sounded as excited as I was.

"Yeah," I said. "But I still have to work out a few details. I have a feeling my parents are going to want to drive me down to Park Avenue and drop me off at your place. I told them that I was invited to your house for dinner, but I think they are going to insist on bringing me."

"That's okay," said Burns. "I'll tell the doorman to expect you, and the elevator boy will bring you right up as soon as you get here. You can meet my parents. Just don't tell them we're going to a nightclub. Say we're going to a movie."

"Sounds all right with me. Say, Burns, who was that woman who answered the phone?"

"That was Hildegarde, my mother's secretary. She always answers the phone. Why do you ask?"

"Oh, I don't know. She just sounded so formal. I wasn't expecting it."

"Yeah," said Burns, with a snicker. "She thought you sounded a little strange too. She almost hung up on you." We both laughed.

"What club are we going to?" I said.

"Jinxie's. It's uptown, on Seventh Avenue. Coleman Hawkins is playing there this weekend. He's always good. It's a nice place."

"What time should I plan to get to your apartment?"

"How about seven o'clock?" said Burns. "That way we can be uptown by eight, in time for the first show." My heart was starting to pound again. This was going to be great. An adventure cloaked in secrecy. Going to see Ruth Brown at the Majestic would seem like child's play compared to this. I got his address and said goodbye to Burns, put down the receiver, and sat on the side of Cousin Gwen's bed. I wasn't sure when my parents and Cousin Gwen would return.

To distract myself, I went into the study. There were books everywhere, in bookcases surrounding the day bed, in piles on the floor, stacked in the windowsill, and on top of a desk. I chose a bookcase at random and began running my finger along the titles on the spines. *Little Women. Great Expectations. Call of the Wild. Moby Dick.* All familiar, although the only one I had read was *Great Expectations.* I moved to another bookcase. *Cane. Home to Harlem. Black Boy. Their Eyes Were Watching God.* The only one I recognized there was *Black Boy,* and that was because I knew the name of its author, Richard Wright. Wright also wrote *Native Son,* which my parents had lying around the house for a while, but for some reason, they always managed to keep it away from me. I decided to move to a third bookcase. *The Negro Labor Vanguard, International Socialist Review, Black Bourgeoisie.* Cousin Gwen certainly had a broad appetite for books, but now I was lost. There was nothing familiar to me here at all; however, my curiosity about the last title led me to take out the book and open it. It was new, written by someone named Frazier, and it had that wonderful, fresh smell that new books have. I turned to the table of contents and noticed a chapter titled, "Behind the Mask." A statement at the beginning of the chapter caught my eye. "There is an attempt on the part of parents in middle-class families to shield their children against racial discrimination and the contempt of whites for colored people." Boy, did that sound familiar, so I skimmed the page until I saw another sentence that gave me a start. "Despite such efforts to insulate their children against a hostile white world, the children of the black bourgeoisie cannot escape the mark of oppression." *The mark of oppression.* I had never heard the term before and I wondered exactly what it meant. It sounded awful. Did I have the mark of oppression, I wondered. And if I did, what was it like? Could it be seen?

It was getting late and my parents would be arriving any minute with Cousin Gwen, so I replaced the book on the shelf, went over to the day bed, and fumbled through my bag until I found my copy of *Democracy in America.* I took it into the living room and sat down on Cousin Gwen's worn and faded sofa, opened it to the bookmark, and read until my eyes fell upon the following words: "In one blow oppression has deprived the descendants of the Africans of almost all the privileges of humanity. The United States Negro has lost even the memory of his homeland; he no longer understands the language his fathers spoke; he has abjured their religion and forgotten their mores. Ceasing to belong to Africa, he has acquired no right to the blessings of Europe; he is left in suspense between two societies and isolated between two peoples, sold by one and repudiated by the other; in the whole world there is nothing but his master's hearth to provide him with some semblance of a homeland." Could this be the mark of oppression, I thought, the absence of any sense of one's humanity? If so, I was certain it did not apply to me, although I lingered over the part about being 'left in suspense between two societies and isolated between two peoples.' I already felt suspended between two societies, but, I told myself, this notion came from a book that was written by a Frenchman more than a hundred years ago. Lots of things had changed since then. Or had they? Certainly not, according to Lewis Michaux. He could have written that paragraph himself. And yet, despite our resentment at the oppression we had suffered in this country, every Negro I knew still considered it home. We paid our taxes, served in the military, recited the Pledge of Allegiance, and wondered when things would get better.

chapter nine

By Saturday afternoon, I was more excited than I'd ever been. The sky was cobalt blue and cloudless and, under a brilliant afternoon sun, Harlem shimmered like a mirage. During dinner at Lucille's the night before, to my relief, no one had mentioned my upcoming visit to Burns's apartment, and now I was doing my best to appear composed by sitting on the sofa in the living room and reading *Democracy in America.* At one point, Cousin Gwen came in and sat down in the wing chair across from me to read one of those magazines I had never heard of, the *Negro Vanguard,* and I found my thoughts drifting away from my book and toward Cousin Gwen. She seemed so wise, wiser than just about anyone I'd ever met. Maybe her wisdom was the result of owning all of those books, but to me those books on the *masses* and the *vanguards* seemed pretty boring. I didn't bother to look at them. I had the feeling they could get you into trouble, even though Lewis Michaux was selling them out in the open on Seventh Avenue, with a police car right down the street. And then it occurred to me how different Cousin Gwen was from the rest of my parents' friends. She was unconventional. She spoke her mind regardless of what others might think. And she had a library filled with books. I had visited the homes of most of my parents' friends and there might be a few dust-covered volumes on a shelf next to some bric-a-brac, but no one, not even my parents, had a library. It was as though they had stopped thinking about ideas, about the world and how to change it. Obviously, Cousin Gwen hadn't.

"I'll be interested to hear what you have to tell about your trip to Park Avenue," Cousin Gwen said, looking up from her magazine as she spoke. "It's a different world down there, you know. *Big* money. Not a colored face anywhere in sight, except for the cooks and chauffeurs and the cleaning ladies, and, of course, they all use the back entrance. I don't suppose they'll make *you* use the back entrance, but if they try, you say '*No, thank you. I'm a guest of the*'—what did you say that boy's name was?" she asked.

"Burns," I said.

"Oh, yes, the *Burns* family," she said. "Sometimes these wealthy white people like to change their names when they come into a lot of money. As though anyone can shed the past and take on a new life." Cousin Gwen was looking directly at me now as she spoke. "But it's not that easy to take on a new life, is it?" she said. "Even with money. You can't change your past, no matter how hard you try. When I came here, I thought I had reached the promised land. I thought I had said goodbye to race prejudice and I was free to start a new life. I thought I could do whatever I wanted to, become a different person, but I soon discovered that it wasn't that easy. I couldn't find an apartment downtown no matter how hard I looked, but I easily found one in Harlem. If I went downtown to a restaurant for dinner with a friend, we'd have to wait forever to get seated, and then they'd stick us in the back somewhere, behind the coat rack. I applied for a teaching job and they sent me straight to Harlem. And even now, when I'm downtown and I need to get home, I don't bother to try to get a cab. The cabdrivers take a look at you and assume you're going uptown and they drive right past you. So it isn't that easy for us to take on a new life, no matter how badly we might want to."

I thought about what Cousin Gwen had said, but I didn't care if Burns was Gordie's real name or not. I was just happy to find a friend at Draper. Gordie was interested in the same things I was interested in. He seemed to feel the same way I did about a lot of things, like what had been done to Vinnie. And he had also a sense of adventure. What difference did it make what his father's name might have been.

By now the sky was the color of violets and in the distance, the moon hung like a silver disc above the rooftops. My father came into the living room. "Well, it's getting close to five-thirty," he said. "You don't want to be late." Being late, of course, would be an unpardonable sin, since it would confirm a stereotype that, in our minds, all white people held of us: the belief that colored people are perpetually late.

"I'll be ready in just a minute, Dad," I said, getting up from the sofa. I went into Cousin Gwen's study to put on a fresh white shirt, a tie, and a tweed sport coat to go with my chinos, and returned to the living room. My mother looked me over. "Did you wash up?" she said. "Let me see those fingernails." I held out my hands, which she inspected to her reluctant satisfaction. "What about deodorant?"

"*Mom,* I used it this morning," I said, groaning at her interrogation.

"He's just fine, Clarissa," said my father. "Let him be."

"Well I don't want him to find himself in an embarrassing situation when he gets down there at the dinner table with all those white folks and somebody says 'Please pass the potatoes,'" she replied.

"Couldn't be any more embarrassed than he is right now," said my dad.

My mother, father, and I left Cousin Gwen with her pad on her lap sitting in front of her television, and we climbed into the 'oadmaster and drove south, taking 110th Street across to Park nue and then heading down.

'n in the dark, I could see that the buildings along this he avenue were rundown, with metal fire escapes hang-
' front, little shops with signs in Spanish painted on ws, clusters of brown-skinned men with curly hair ber eyes standing on corners under streetlights in their pockets, and lots of kids running in and I couldn't believe this was the same street

where Gordie lived. But suddenly, as the Roadmaster continued to roll along, the streets became cleaner, the sidewalks became deserted, and the buildings became tall and grand. As we rode by, you could see inside their lighted lobbies, huge pots of flowers standing at each side of the door. Awnings began to appear on the sidewalks and doormen in brass-buttoned uniforms and white gloves patrolled the entrances. We were in another world.

The gray stone building where Gordie lived took up an entire block and looked more like a bank than an apartment building. A long, dark blue awning ran from the curb across a huge sidewalk to large, double glass doors with brass kickplates and brass handles polished to a high gloss. Through the doors you could see tapestries hanging from beige walls and a spectacular cut-glass chandelier suspended over a table with a large vase containing an explosion of red roses.

When my father pulled up to the curb, my mother rolled down the window. The doorman, a tall, strapping white fellow, walked over to the Buick and leaned over to the door. "Can I help you?" he said. He sounded impatient, as though we were taking him away from something much more important.

My mother relished such situations, enlisting her best classroom voice to deal with them. "Yes, you can," she said. "Our son is having dinner with the Burns family this evening. We're just dropping him off, but there's no need to park the car."

"Are you sure you have the right place, lady?" said the doorman.

"This *is* the Burns residence, isn't it?" said my mother, doing her best to control her indignation.

"That's right," he said. "But I don't know anything about a colored boy visiting the Burns family this evening." He was wearing a dark blue uniform, the coat bristling with gold braid and buttons, and a cap like policemen wear. His black shoes were gleaming. Change his color and give him a plumed hat, I thought, and he could pass for Marcus Garvey. He had obviously been hired to discourage intruders. With his hands resting on the Roadmaster's passenger door as if to keep my mother from getting out, he leaned over and took a long look inside the car, staring first at my folks and then at me seated in the back. I felt as though we were about to be charged with a crime. I had to think of something fast or my plans for the evening would be wrecked.

"Look! Would you just give the Burns apartment a call?" I blurted out. "Gordie's expecting me."

"Gordie, you say?" said the doorman, raising his eyebrows. "What's *your* name, anyway?"

"Rob Garrett," I said. The doorman reached inside his coat pocket and produced a crumpled piece of paper, squinting to read it in the darkness. Then he folded it and put it back inside his coat.

"Okay," he said. "Yer awright." He opened the back door of the car and held it, standing stiffly at attention, as I climbed out and walked over to the sidewalk. He shut the door firmly. "Come right this way," he said, escorting me up to the entrance doors and holding one door open. Before entering, I stopped and looked back at my folks, who were still parked at the curb in the Roadmaster. Even at a distance, I thought I could sense their anxiety. Or was it their anger at our humiliation?

"Don't worry about me," I called. "I'll just take the subway home." I strode into the lobby as though I had been visiting Park Avenue for years.

"Take Mr. Garrett up to the Burns floor," said the doorman to a silver-haired white man wearing a gray cotton jacket. The old man struggled to his feet from his seat, and I followed him into the elevator. We rode up in silence on a carpeted floor, surrounded by panels of richly inlaid wood. In the back of the elevator was a folding bench, which I badly wanted to try, but we were slowing down and I didn't want to do anything to offend the attendant. He opened the door at the twenty-first floor and said, "Burns to the left." I thanked him and stepped into a large hallway with recessed lighting and a mirror on the far wall. On a table underneath the mirror, another bouquet of fresh flowers perfumed the hallway. The only other door was far down the hall to the right, at the opposite end from the Burnses' apartment. I glanced at the mirror to check my tie and noticed how confident I looked, as though I had passed some test with flying colors. I rang the doorbell and a colored woman who seemed to be about my mother's age opened the door. She was thin and brown and wore a black maid's uniform with a little white cap and small white apron. At first she seemed startled to see me, but she quickly composed herself. "May I help you?" she said in a drawl so southern, I knew she had to be from somewhere farther south than Virginia.

"Is Gordie in?" I said.

"Who shall I say is callin'?" she asked.

"Rob Garrett," I said. She was standing in a grand foyer with Persian carpets, antiques, and paintings in carved gold frames. I was still in the doorway.

"I'll tell him you're here, sir," she said. "Won't you have a seat?" She motioned to a settee in the foyer made of slender pieces of wood. It looked much too old and fragile for me to sit on.

"That's okay," I said, stepping inside. "I'll stand." The woman closed the front door and disappeared into another room. I felt as though I was in a museum. The apartment was cavernous. From the foyer I could see into the living room, which had high ceilings, long, dark velvet drapes, and tall windows with dramatic views of the city at night. The living room floor was covered with the biggest Persian rug I had ever seen. Heavy wood frames holding two portraits of old men with beards and sober expressions, dressed in black suits and little black hats, were hanging from the walls. Sofas and lounge chairs upholstered in a fringed red fabric looked very expensive, and large potted plants looked like small palm trees. Mahogany bookcases stuffed with books lined two walls, and in a far corner of the room, a big arrangement of purple and white flowers in a large green vase sat next to an unusual brass candelabra on top of a black grand piano. The candelabra had holders for seven candles, six on a lower row and a seventh on the top. Supporting each of the candleholders was a brass hand, each one in the shape of a palm print, open the same way Willie Maurice's palms had been open just before I left him standing in front of the Apollo. It was strange. I had never seen anything like it before.

"Well, Garrett, are you ready to go?" Gordie had come into the foyer dressed as I was, in a tie and jacket. "Before we leave, why don't I introduce you to my parents? Have a seat in the living room. I'll go and get them." He disappeared to another part of the apartment, and I sat on a sofa and took a closer look around. The brass candelabra caught my eye again, and I noticed writing on one of the open palms, but I couldn't make out what it said. Seated in the Burnses' exotic living room high above the city, surrounded by the potted palms and the antiques, I felt far removed from the rest of the world. I could imagine living like this one day myself.

I heard a door open and Gordie returned with his parents, escorting them into the living room, trailed by the faint scents of cinnamon and licorice. "Mother, Dad," he said, "I'd like you to meet Rob Garrett. Rob's a friend from Draper." Dressed in a blue silk smoking jacket and wearing bedroom slippers, his father was older than I expected, but his dark eyes twinkled mischievously as he held out his hand to me. I rose from the sofa to shake it.

"It is a pleasure to meet you, young man," he said, with an accent that sounded French to me. He was tall and lean like Gordie, but his skin was a shade darker and his thin hair was beginning to gray. He was wearing a little black cap like the Jewish people wear. And then it suddenly came to me like a bolt of lightning: Mr. and Mrs. Burns were Jews. And Gordie was a Jew, although I would never have known it, since I thought all the Jews were named Goldberg or Cohen. I didn't know much about the Jews. You hear things, of course—that they have money, that they keep to themselves, that they are "sharp," "slick," "greedy"—but you hear things about Negroes too, and most of it's trash. People are people, in my book, and you have to size them up one at a time.

There was a Jewish man at home, a shopkeeper who used to sell dental implements and equipment. His name was Mr. Cohen and he had a little store that my father would sometimes visit when he needed to replace things. Dad used to say that Mr. Cohen was the only white man he knew who wouldn't make him wait. He would treat Dad like he was any other customer. If a white man came in after Dad, that white man would have to wait his turn.

"And this is my mother," said Gordie. "Mom, Rob Garrett." Mrs. Burns extended her pale hand theatrically, and I shook it. She had long, flaming red hair that she wore in an old-fashioned style, piled on top of her head, and she was wearing a dark green dress that fell below her knees. She seemed much younger than her husband.

"Very nice to meet you," said Mrs. Burns. "Now, Gordon, I'd like you to be back home by eleven. Is that understood?" She sounded just like my own mother.

"Okay, Mom," said Gordie. "I'll be here."

"Tell me, young man," said Mr. Burns, "are you from Manhattan?"

"No, sir," I said. "I'm from Virginia."

"Virginia!" he said. "Well, I'll bet you're glad to be up here in New York."

"I'm getting used to it, sir."

"Well, you two go off to the movies and enjoy yourselves," he said. Gordie and I headed straight for the door. As soon as we left and were in the hallway, I told Gordie about the doorman. "'I don't know anything about a colored boy visiting the Burnses' apartment,'" I said, mimicking the doorman. "If I hadn't mentioned your name, he would never have let me in, and that would have ruined everything."

"Charlie's not the worst guy in the world," said Gordie, "although he can get carried away sometimes. I don't know why he had to bring up the fact that you're colored, though. When I get back, I'll tell my father about it. He'll have a word with him. It won't happen again."

The elevator arrived and with a yawn the old man opened the door and took us down to the lobby. As we entered the lobby, the doorman appeared, in full regalia. "Yes sir, gentlemen. Would you like a cab?" he said.

Gordie glanced at his watch. "That's not a bad idea," he said. "Oh, Charlie, did you meet my friend, Rob Garrett?"

"Why, yes," said Charlie, "we met earlier when he arrived."

"So you did," said Gordie, in a cool voice. Charlie's face turned beet red.

"I'll get you a cab," said Charlie, and he walked out to the sidewalk to hail a taxi. Soon thereafter, he stopped a yellow cab and opened the door for us to climb in. We both thanked him, and Gordie pressed a small piece of money into his palm as we got in.

"Thank you, sir," said Charlie. "Have a pleasant evening." He shut the door with a thud and we headed for Jinxie's.

chapter ten

The sign, which was attached to the roof of the club, consisted of one word, JINXIE's, in tall letters outlined with incandescent light bulbs against a dark blue background that seemed to merge with the surrounding darkness. The club itself was a squat, brick one-story fortress, with small windows that seemed to be painted over to block the entry of light from outside. As we walked to the door, I could hear the growl and moan of a saxophone and I tried to contain my excitement. I wanted to act as though going to Jinxie's was something that I did every day. A dark-skinned Negro man with a moon face and wearing a tuxedo greeted us at the door. "Good evening, gentlemen," he said, smiling. "Table for two?"

I let Gordie do the talking.

"Two will be fine," said Gordie, and the doorman led us across the floor to a table right at the side of the bandstand. The thickly shadowed room was crowded with colored patrons seated at a jumble of tables and chairs. Colored men in suits and ties leaned back in their chairs with their jackets open and their suspenders exposed. Others were in sport shirts and sunglasses. A few colored women were wearing fancy print dresses and hats, but most wore blouses and skirts and saddle shoes or loafers. As we were being led to our table, I glimpsed one or two white people in the crowd. A well-dressed white woman sat at a table holding hands with a dignified-looking colored man in a dark suit. A young white man wearing sunglasses and a loud sport shirt sat with his arm around a colored woman, her straightened hair pulled back in a bun. I tried not to stare, but I had never seen anything like it. I had always understood that these relationships were taboo, scorned by both whites and Negroes, and yet no one in the club seemed to be paying any attention to them. I decided not to either.

On the bandstand, perspiring heavily under the spotlights, stood an older, light-skinned colored man with a carefully trimmed mustache and regal bearing. He was elegantly dressed in a dark, tailored suit, a white shirt with French cuffs, and a dark tie, and sported a charcoal gray fedora. He stood at the front of the bandstand playing a gleaming tenor saxophone, his body rigid, his shoulders hunched as if to brace himself against a strong wind, his eyes completely closed. The notes spilled out in bright, intricate spurts at first, his smooth yellow cheeks ballooning with air, his long yellow fingers flying up and down the keys of the instrument until the air in his cheeks was spent and he would take a deep breath and begin again. Eventually the spurts lengthened into one long, seamless stream, meandering invisibly through the forest of the darkened room. Three younger colored musicians were behind him, one hunched over a piano, running his fingers up and down the keys, another standing, plunking a big bass violin, and the third, sitting amid a dazzling array of drums and cymbals, repeatedly striking a large cymbal with one wooden drumstick to keep time and tapping a snare drum between his legs with another. The drummer's head was turned away from the audience as if he couldn't care less what we thought. Occasionally he would wildly flay his drumsticks against the cymbals and drums in a brief, flamboyant solo. But my eyes kept returning to the older man with the saxophone, wearing the dark fedora with the brim flipped down as though he was about to leave for a business meeting. For one thing, he was the only man in the club wearing a hat, and I had always been taught that gentlemen removed their hats in a room where ladies were present, but it suggested to me an inner confidence, an independence of mind that I admired. What attracted me most, though, was the sound of his instrument, which was, in the shadowy intimacy of the club, immense and mesmerizing.

"That's Coleman Hawkins," whispered Gordie, nodding at the saxophonist. "He's been playing the sax for over thirty years. It's a tough instrument to play. He was the first jazz musician to really master it. Some people even call him the Father of the Saxophone, but in the last few years, there have been so many great sax players to come along, he's been overlooked." With an elaborate flourish, Hawkins finished the piece, rapidly fingering the keys to produce a warm, fluttering sound, then releasing the saxophone to hang free from a cord around his neck, letting it dangle like an outrageous piece of jewelry before tucking it under his right arm as if for safekeeping. The audience burst into applause. Some people stood as they clapped. Others cheered, but he barely acknowledged any of them, merely nodding and touching the brim of his hat, before picking up a copper-colored drink in a highball glass from a little table at the rear of the bandstand. He drank it down in one gulp and then took a few moments to consult with his musicians, as the audience, which had been silent during his playing, began to chatter freely.

"Can I get you fellows anything?" said a slender, coffee-colored waitress standing over us. She had large, beguiling eyes, her hair was cut in a pixie style, and she was wearing a black turtleneck blouse with a little red skirt and high-heel pumps. Her legs were long and shapely in fishnet stockings. In the darkness, I couldn't make out her features that well, but from what I could see, she looked awfully pretty, as pretty as any colored girl I'd seen since leaving home. She reminded me of Delores Winbush, who lived down the street from our house. Delores was the daughter of the principal of the colored high school and she was a couple of years older than I was. Every boy I knew wanted to go out with Delores, but nobody had the nerve to ask her for a date. We would see her in the hall at school or walking down the street and wave at her or smile with embarrassment if she noticed us, but the mere thought of having a conversation with her was paralyzing. She was tall and willowy, with skin the color of vanilla extract, and she was an excellent athlete. She loved to go to the municipal swimming pool, the colored pool, which was always crowded with glistening brown bodies during the summer. In the neighborhood, it was rumored that on summer mornings, Delores would get up early and show up at the pool to swim when it opened at 7:00, and I sometimes imagined her in a pure white bathing suit, lowering herself into the turquoise pool, which was sure to be empty at that hour, to swim laps by herself, her lean brown limbs in constant motion, slicing the clear, shiny surface of the water with barely a splash, while high above her, seated in a tall ladder chair, a lifeguard, bronzed and naked to the waist, watched her.

"I'll have a Rheingold," said Gordie.

"Make it two," I said, with all the confidence I could muster. My eyes followed the waitress as she disappeared into the far shadows of the room. Although things had gone smoothly so far, I was still concerned about being underage in a nightclub. The musicians were getting ready to play another number. With glassy eyes, Coleman Hawkins put down his drink, placed the mouthpiece between his lips, and launched into a torrent of notes, rearing back and forth with his eyes squeezed shut as the music seemed to explode from inside of him. He was joined immediately by the other musicians, as though all of them had suddenly plunged together into a lake and were being kept afloat by the turbulent force of their rhythms. The audience was elated by the vigor of the music. Several people responded by shouting as though they were in church—"Get away, Hawk, get away!" "Talk to me, Bean! Go 'head now. Preach!"—and Hawk and his sidemen seemed propelled even faster by the shouts. Burns whispered to me that in addition to Hawk, Coleman Hawkins was also called Bean. The waitress brought our beers and poured each into a glass. Gordie and I pooled our money and paid her. We left her a generous tip, which she didn't even seem to notice, and then she moved away to another table and I lost sight of her. I had hoped to strike up a conversation with her, as I had with Lewis Michaux two days before, but the music was loud and she was busy. It didn't seem possible. She was really good-looking, but I thought she was probably older than I was.

"Well," said Gordie, "what do you think?" By then, like most of the people in the club, he was smoking a cigarette, and billows of smoke were circulating in the spotlights above the bandstand. The musicians were taking a break. The drummer, the piano player, and the bassist were sitting in the audience talking with patrons, but Coleman Hawkins had disappeared. I took a swallow of my beer. It was the first beer I had ever tasted, and I kept waiting for it to knock me for a loop, but it didn't seem to bother me. I reached for Gordie's package of cigarettes, which were lying on the table, and I took out a cigarette and held it between my fingers.

"This is fantastic," I said, "and Hawk is unbelievable! I've never heard anything like this." Gordie was smiling proudly, even a bit smugly.

"What did I tell you?" he said. "You'll never hear anything like it at Draper." With a knowing smile, he held up his beer glass and tipped it in my direction, and I picked up mine and tipped it toward him, and we both took another sip of our beers as though we had just pulled off a great caper. "You'd better figure out what you want to do with that thing," said Gordie, nodding toward the unlighted cigarette I was still holding between my fingers. I laughed and handed it to him to put it back in the pack.

Coleman Hawkins had now returned to the stage, hat firmly in place, with another drink in hand. He was thumbing through sheet music, with a brooding expression, like a banker examining ledgers. It occurred to me that because he was a man of great presence, everyone in the club was keeping their distance from him, whereas his musicians were seated at tables being lionized by the audience. He seemed sad, as he stood by himself on the bandstand with a drink and wearing that hat, in a roomful of adoring admirers. After a few moments, he looked out into the darkness of the club, searching for his musicians as if he needed company, and, once he had found them, he gave each of them a look that made it clear he was ready to start playing again. We were seated only a few feet from the bandstand, and, when they had all returned to the bandstand, I could hear him scold them gently, in a voice so deep it seemed to rumble up from the underworld. Then the sidemen took their positions, and with several quick stomps of his foot he set the beat for the next tune, and they all took off, soaring, with Hawk in the lead, upward like a rocket, right through the nightclub ceiling, passing the bright lights of the Jinxie's sign and the rooftops of nearby tenements, and on and on, into the infinite darkness. I didn't know the name of any of the tunes they played, but it didn't matter. I was riding with them, and I was willing to go as far as they would take me, but after listening to Hawk for a while, I began to recognize snatches of familiar tunes that he was weaving into what he was playing, "Jeepers Creepers" and "A Foggy Day," but mostly there were stretches, especially in the slow numbers, when all I could hear was what sounded to me like loneliness.

I had forgotten all about the time, and when I glanced at my watch I was horrified to discover that it was already 11:00 P.M. "Gordie," I said, "we're late." But he was still soaring with Hawk, and to bring him back to earth, I put my wristwatch right in front of his eyes.

"Holy shit!" said Gordie, looking at my watch. "We'd better get going."

"I know," I said, "but why can't we stay until the end of this set?"

"It's okay with me, but who knows how long it's going to be?" said Gordie. "It could go on for a half-hour or more."

I imagined my mother standing at Cousin Gwen's living-room window with her arms folded, looking up and down Edge-combe Avenue for any sign of me. And then I remembered I was on my own. "Look," I said, "let's stay for a little while longer. We can always say we got caught in traffic or something." Gordie didn't need a lot of persuading.

"Why not?" he said with a laugh. "And as long as we're at it, we might as well have another beer." He held up his empty glass and motioned to the waitress, and she came over.

"Another round, fellows?" she said. I looked up at her and she seemed amused, although her eyes were cast downward. "Sure," I said, with a grin. With the music from Hawk's sax floating around us, she wiped the tabletop and picked up the empty glasses, but just before she turned to leave, she looked straight at me, holding me in her gaze, her wide eyes luminous through the smoke and the darkness, as though she had something private to tell me. I didn't know what to do. It was such a long look that it made me think we might really have something to say to each other after all. And then she turned on those long brown legs covered with the fishnet stockings and strode off through the crowd. When she left, I thought about what my mother would say about her. I could hear my mother's voice cutting through the music that filled Jinxie's like a buzz saw. "You say you met her in a nightclub? What was she working there for? And wearing that little skirt and those stockings? You can do a lot better than that, son."

"Not bad," said Gordie, when the waitress had disappeared. He was looking at me with a mischievous smile.

"I know," I said. "She's cute."

"She certainly is," said Gordie. Hawk was winding down the last number of the set, leaving a trail of softly diminishing notes punctuated by takes from the piano player. At the end of the tune, everyone in the club was on their feet clapping and cheering, including Gordie and me, until Hawk and the others had left the stage. I was afraid to look at my watch. "I think we better get the check," said Gordie, waving the waitress over to our table, and we watched as she worked her way toward us through the crowd.

"May we have the check, please?" said Gordie when she arrived. She quickly added up the bill and handed it to him, and looked straight at me again. I was nervous. I could feel her eyes on me but I didn't know what to say.

Eventually, I mumbled, "How much do I owe you, Gordie?" as he reached for his wallet, took out a twenty-dollar bill, and handed it to the waitress.

"Don't worry about it, Rob," he said. "We'll settle up later." She took the twenty and started to give him the change, but Gordie said, "That's okay. Keep it," and we quickly headed for the door. I didn't bother to look back.

Outside the club, it had gotten chilly. Burns and I were having a short discussion on the sidewalk about how we were each going to get home when a tall, light-skinned Negro in a dark suit and tie and a black raincoat approached me. "Say, young brother, can I have a word with you?" said the man. He took me by the elbow and firmly steered me away from Gordie, as though he wanted to speak to me in private. He had reddish, close-cropped hair and a sober expression, and he was wearing those severe eyeglasses that schoolteachers wear, the ones with dark plastic frames and metal under the lenses. I had a feeling that I had seen him somewhere before, but I couldn't place him. Something in his manner was imperious, and it made me cautious, although I went along with him. "Look here, young brother, you know you're too young to be in an establishment like that," he began, once we were out of earshot of Gordie. "You got to be eighteen years old to be hanging out in a nightclub, and I *know* you ain't no eighteen yet. Am I right?" His voice had a soothing, streetwise pitch, a door-to-door salesman's voice, and he gave me a quick, disarming smile, as though he already knew the answer to his question.

"No, sir," I responded.

"Well, let me make a proposition to you. Why don't you meet me at the mosque down on Lenox Avenue tomorrow morning. We're holding some classes on the problems of the so-called Negro in relation to the white man, and what's the best way to deal with him. You look like an intelligent young brother. You'd probably like these classes. We got classes on self-defense, African history, Arabic, and the teachings of the Honorable Elijah Muhammad. What do you say?"

"I'd like to," I said, trying to sound as sincere as I could, "but I have to go back to school tomorrow."

"What school is that?" he said, raising his eyebrows.

"Draper," I said. He seemed puzzled.

"Draper what?" he said.

"Draper School. It's a boarding school in Connecticut."

"Well, look," he said. "If you give me your name and address, I'll see that you get a copy of the paper every week. Won't cost you a dime."

I didn't know what to say. I wasn't sure what paper he was talking about. "What paper is that, sir?" I said. He gave me a stern look.

"The voice of the messenger, of course. *Muhammad Speaks.*"

"I'll have to think about it, sir," I said. "Do you have an address where I can write for it?"

"Hey, Rob!" called Gordie, "we better get a move on or we're really going to be in trouble," and he walked out to the street to hail a cab.

"He's right," I said to the man wearing the black raincoat and the schoolteacher eyeglasses. "My folks were expecting me half an hour ago. You'll have to excuse me." And as I moved away from him, I heard a loud voice coming from a group of men standing around a dark sedan parked down the street. It was a voice I was sure I knew from somewhere.

"Don't waste no more time with him, Minister Malcolm. He ain't black. He just a so-called Negro, wantin' to be a white boy." I wasn't sure just what it meant to be a "so-called Negro," but the accusation that I wanted "to be a white boy" stung as soon as I heard it. I had never had my racial identity challenged before, and immediately, I wanted to confront the person who was responsible. I looked down the street toward the group to try to identify the speaker, but from that distance, the men were indistinguishable, all thick-necked, young colored men in dark suits, white shirts, and dark clip-on bowties, heads shaved just like Tyrone's. *Tyrone!* Of course. It had to be Tyrone. Although I couldn't make him out in the darkness, I noticed one member of the group lurking behind the others in the shadowy street, hunched over like a running back waiting for the play to begin. I wanted to tell Burns what Tyrone had said, so I walked over to him. He was still standing in the street futilely trying to flag down a cab. "Gordie," I said. "I think your chauffeur Tyrone is over there with those men on the sidewalk."

"Where?" said Gordie, looking around quickly. "Maybe he can give us a lift."

"Over there, near that sedan," I said, pointing to the group of five or six men around the car. Although they were dressed up, they stood grim-faced under the streetlights, looking as though they were spoiling for trouble. "He just shouted something that he must have wanted me to hear. He must not like me."

"What did he say?" said Gordie.

"He said I wanted to be a white boy," I said.

Gordie looked surprised. "Tyrone said *that?*" he said. "Are you sure it was Tyrone?"

"It sure sounded like him," I said.

"Come on," said Gordie. "Let's see if we can find him." We walked over to the group around the sedan. A couple of them, who were leaning against the car, stood up with the others when they saw us approach. A few were wearing dark glasses, and they all had their arms folded across their chests, forming a small phalanx that took up most of the sidewalk. A couple of the men were dark-skinned, others were brown or lighter, each one dressed like a beefy funeral director, standing motionless, expressionless, on the sidewalk. "Do any of you know Tyrone Gaskins?" said Gordie when we reached the group. "He works for my family and I'd like to speak with him for a minute." There was no response. Gordie began to inspect them, walking along the front of the phalanx like a foreign dignitary as they stood at attention, but Tyrone wasn't there.

"I don't see him," said Gordie, turning to me. "You must have heard somebody else."

"I'm sure it was Tyrone," I said. "I don't know where he could have gone." Suddenly Minister Malcolm rushed over, the tails of his black raincoat flapping behind him. "What's going on here? What are you doing with my men?" He sounded indignant.

"We're looking for Tyrone Gaskins," said Gordie. "He works for my family, and my friend here, Mr. Garrett, thought he saw him a moment ago standing over here with your men."

Malcolm smiled. "The only Tyrone we have is Tyrone 27X. I don't know nothin' about no Gaskins. Maybe that's his slave name," he said. "We don't recognize the names that were given to us by our slave owners."

"Well, where is *he,* sir?" said Gordie. "I'd like to have a word with him."

"He's in the car," said Minister Malcolm, still smiling, as though he had been harboring a secret, nodding at the darkened sedan whose windows were rolled up tight. Indeed, as I peered through the windows, I could see a burly figure in the darkness sitting motionless behind the steering wheel. "That's my driver," said Minister Malcolm, proudly. "He drives for a white family downtown during the day and he drives for me at night."

"Well, can I talk to him?" said Gordie, moving suddenly toward the car to open the passenger door. In a flash, Minister Malcolm's smile disappeared, replaced by an angry frown.

"Don't you touch that door, white boy!" he shouted. He was infuriated, although managing to control himself, but his hazel eyes

114

were hard as agate. "Don't you *dare* put your hands on that car without my permission," he said, spitting out his words. For the first time, I saw a glimpse of the rage I had observed in the photograph of Minister Malcolm on the front page of the newspaper, and I knew this was a man who was capable of exploding when provoked.

Gordie froze and then stiffly backed away from the car, his face ashen. The minister's men were still standing in formation with their hands behind their backs, nodding at each other with knowing smiles and murmurs of approval. A little audience of bystanders was beginning to form a semicircle around us to watch what was going on, while, standing next to the sedan, Minister Malcolm smoldered, his hazel eyes blazing behind his schoolteacher glasses.

Gordie walked over to me and whispered nervously, "What do you think? Maybe we should just leave." I wanted to leave, but I was still smarting from Tyrone's insult, and I was convinced it was Tyrone who had spoken. I wanted to see him face-to-face, to confront him and get an explanation, but it was obvious that I needed the minister's cooperation.

"The only reason we came over here, Minister Malcolm, is because the man insulted me," I said. "We're not looking for trouble, but I don't like somebody calling me something I'm not, and I have a feeling you wouldn't like it either." He gave me a wry smile, as though I had struck a chord somewhere inside him, and then he walked around the car to the driver's door and opened it. The driver was still seated inside, staring straight ahead.

"If you wasn't black, young brother, I wouldn't be doing this," said Minister Malcolm, and he told the driver to get out of the car. We were half a block away from Jinxie's, so the light wasn't perfect, but as soon as the driver got out, I knew it was Tyrone. At first I could only see his back, as he and Minister Malcolm were quietly talking back and forth, but the height was right and the neck and shoulders were broad enough and he was dark enough, and then, slowly, he turned around to face us over the hood of the sedan, and there was no question it was he. It was like being in a cop movie, when the cops show the suspect to the victim for the first time.

"Tyrone?" shouted Gordie immediately. "Why didn't you come out? I was standing right here next to the car. You must have known it was me. We just wanted to talk to you. I just wanted to get a ride home." Tyrone stared straight ahead, his face a mask of cool indifference, as though Burns wasn't even there. Gordie was shaken by Tyrone's refusal to recognize him.

"Tyrone?" called Gordie across the hood of the sedan, as though the chauffeur had not heard him the first time. But Tyrone remained impassive. "Can't you at least look at me?" said Gordie. He was pleading, as he would to a friend, but Tyrone continued to stare blankly ahead. It was apparent that in Tyrone's mind, at least in this setting, Burns had ceased to exist. He had become invisible, like a magician's assistant at the circus, and Gordie seemed stunned by his inability to get Tyrone to look at him. "What the hell is happening?" he cried. He was becoming agitated, as though he had been somehow betrayed. I saw a smile briefly flicker across Tyrone's face, a cruel smile, like the ones the boys at Draper flashed when Vinnie and I were standing outside the dormitory. The bystanders on the sidewalk were becoming loud and their number was beginning to grow.

"What's goin' on, anyway?" said a bedraggled old colored man in a worn, smelly overcoat. He was using a cane, walking all around, asking others in the audience the same question.

"Nothin', old man," said one of the minister's men, fiercely. "It ain't *nothin'*."

"Look like somethin' to me," said a middle-aged Negro woman in a sweater and a housedress. "Why is that white boy upset like that? What did them Black Muslims do to him?"

"Who is that fellow standing over there with Minister Malcolm?" said one voice.

"Anybody call the cops?" said another.

I couldn't be silent any longer. "What you got against me, man?" I yelled at Tyrone across the sedan. He gave me a baleful stare. His eyes had become slits. "I never did anything to you. You don't even know me. So how come you want to call me out of the race, telling the man I want to be a white boy? I don't want to be nothin' but myself, *nigger*," and as soon as I uttered the word, I could see his face light up like the sign at Jinxie's. Minister Malcolm was leaning into him, holding the lapels of his suit coat to restrain him, murmuring softly to him, but Tyrone was built like an ox and Minister Malcolm, though tall, was lean. I could see them struggling on the other side of the sedan, and the bystanders in the audience were beginning to cheer.

"Get in the car," ordered Minister Malcolm as Tyrone broke away, trying to feint around him and get to the other side of the sedan. "That's an order," said Minister Malcolm emphatically. "Get in the car." But Tyrone was in no mood to obey. He looked at me across the sedan with a malevolent frown. "How you sound, motherfucker, callin' me a nigger! You Jew-lovin' dog. You must be a Jew yourself," and he threw himself on the hood of the sedan to try to scramble across and reach me. I froze with fear.

"Grab him," Minister Malcolm shouted to his men, "and put him in the car," and they swooped down on Tyrone, who was by now spread-eagle on the hood of the sedan, and hustled him into the back seat of the car. Two men climbed in the back on each side of Tyrone and slammed the doors. Minister Malcolm took the wheel and they sped off rapidly into the night, followed by a second car carrying the others.

Gordie was slumped against a light pole, quietly sobbing. Most of the crowd had disappeared, but a few people walked over to him, examining him with curiosity, as he had examined Minister Malcolm's men earlier.

"What he do to you?" said an older colored woman with gray hair. Gordie just shook his head and looked away, wiping his tears with his bare hand. "Musta done somethin' terrible to get you all upset like this," she said, patting him on his shoulder. "Don't worry, son. The Bible say, 'Weeping may endureth for the night, but joy cometh in the morning.'"

It was after midnight. I knew I was late returning to Cousin Gwen's, but I couldn't leave Gordie in that condition. "Come on," I said. "Let's go for a walk," and I took him by the arm and led him down Seventh Avenue. We were both still trembling. Even at that hour, there were people sitting on stoops and on the fenders of parked cars, and they silently watched us as we made our way down the street. "You gonna be all right?" I said.

Gordie nodded. "I'll be all right," he said, but I could see he was still shaken. After a couple of blocks, he seemed to loosen up. He took out a cigarette and lit it, and his face was illuminated in the Harlem darkness. In that moment he looked like an old man, as though the incident with Tyrone had suddenly aged him.

"Let's go back," I said, and we turned around and headed toward Jinxie's. Gordie seemed much calmer after lighting the cigarette, so I decided to have one myself. "Let me try one of those," I said, and he handed me the pack and the lighter without a word. We stood on the sidewalk and I took a cigarette and placed it between my lips, letting it droop slightly, the way I had seen the detectives do it in the movies, but as I tried to click the lighter, the cigarette drooped so much that it fell from my lips onto the sidewalk before I could get the lighter to work. Gordie laughed and I laughed and it was good, because we both realized that despite what had just happened, life would go on. I quickly bent over to pick up the cigarette and put it back in my mouth, while Burns expertly clicked the lighter and produced a flame.

"Just stick it in the flame and take a puff," he said, and I followed his instructions, or at least I thought I did. With the cigarette in my mouth, I held the tip against the flame until it started to glow bright orange and I inhaled deeply, so deeply that my

lungs filled with smoke and I choked. I was seized with a coughing spell that bent me in half for several minutes. Gordie was
laughing uncontrollably. "I said take a *puff*," he said. "That's all
you need. You're not supposed to smoke the whole thing at
once," and he whacked me on my back a couple of times to help
me stop coughing. Eventually I came out of it, although my
lungs continued to burn. I decided to give it a final try. I was still
holding the lighted cigarette between my fingers and I brought it
up to my lips and took a small puff, so small that I could barely
see the smoke leave my mouth when I exhaled, but it was a start.
We headed back up the street, and despite the incident with Tyrone and the irritation in my lungs, I felt almost jaunty as I took
my first real puffs from a cigarette and blew out the smoke.

When we reached Jinxie's, there were several taxicabs
double-parked in rows. People were still leaving and entering
the club and you could hear Hawk flying high inside every time
the door opened. It was nearly one o'clock and I knew my parents would be ready to call the police. I said goodbye to Gordie,
who seemed to have recovered from the initial shock of the encounter with Tyrone. Gordie said goodbye and climbed into
one of the waiting cabs, which made a U-turn and disappeared
down Seventh Avenue, and I climbed into another.

"Four oh nine Edgecombe," I said, settling back in my seat. I
was two hours late.

chaptereleven

"Well, how was your evening?" said my mother, who was standing in Cousin Gwen's doorway when I arrived. Her voice was as frosty as a cold root beer, but I acted as though there was nothing out of the ordinary, and I strolled into the apartment with my hands in my pockets to disguise my lingering nervousness. Without saying anything else, she closed the door and followed me into the apartment. My father was sitting in the living room reading a newspaper, but Cousin Gwen was nowhere to be seen, and the door to her bedroom was closed.

"You're over two hours late," said my mother in a voice that cut through the air like a razor blade. She was standing in the living room with her hands on her hips, and she seemed to be close to tears. "Why didn't you call? You're in a strange city. Did you ever stop to think we'd be worried about you? And what have you been doing anyway? You smell like you've been smoking cigarettes."

Dad put down his paper and gave Mom a quick look of disapproval. "Clarissa, Clarissa. It's all right. He's back now and he's fine. You've made your point. Now let it rest." He ruffled his newspaper for emphasis and then looked at me. "How was it, son?" he said. And deep inside I had the feeling that he knew everything, that he knew the story about dinner with the Burns family had been a fabrication, that he knew I had been out on the town and he was trying to give me cover, and I even thought that at some point I might like to tell him what the evening was like. But I decided to think it over first.

"I had a good time," I said. "His folks were nice. Big apartment they have," and I pretended to yawn. "I'm tired. I think I'll turn in." I just wanted to be by myself. I didn't want to answer any more questions about my evening or the Burns family or what I had for dinner, even though I knew they were probably dying to hear about all of it. "See you in the morning," I said.

I went into Cousin Gwen's study and closed the door without bothering to turn on the light, and I lay on my back on the day bed. I could see moonlight framing the study window and the dark sky and the glimmer of a few stars in the distance. My body was still trembling imperceptibly from the confrontation with Tyrone. As I lay there, I repeated his poisonous words out loud: "so-called Negro," "Jew-lover," words that had never been spoken to me before. My ears rang when I said them. I couldn't imagine why he would say such things about me, since he didn't know me. Maybe he thought the only way for a colored boy to succeed in the white world was to become an athlete, and when I told him

I wasn't playing sports, he must have thought I was weak, "trying to be white." A lot of Negroes have disdain for studying and prefer to cast their lot with sports, but I couldn't figure out what this had to do with Burns. Why had Tyrone been so cold, so indifferent toward him? I remembered Tyrone's smile from the other side of the sedan, as though he was enjoying the sight of Burns breaking down. Was it because Gordie had stumbled upon Tyrone's secret, his affiliation with Minister Malcolm and the Black Muslims? That must have been it, I thought. Tyrone's secret had been revealed. His mask had been removed and his façade was no longer necessary. And once it had been cast aside, Tyrone was free to declare himself, which he did in his angry words to me, words that were probably meant as much for Gordie's ears as for mine. I doubted if Gordie really knew much about Tyrone, although Tyrone had worked for his family for years. I was sure he didn't know that Tyrone was a Black Muslim or a chauffeur for Malcolm X. But he knew Tyrone well enough to expect him to help tonight, and he fell apart when Tyrone acted as though he didn't know him. It was all very strange, different from anything I had seen before. Very strange and very sad.

I could hear sounds outside the door to the study, footsteps padding in and out of the bathroom, and my parents' voices as they prepared for bed. It occurred to me once again that I was still the embodiment of my parents' dreams, and even more so, I suspected, after this visit, but what they could not know was that deep inside I had begun to have misgivings about Draper and whether I should remain there. As my mother had warned, even at Draper, where I had been left alone for the most part, I could not get away from prejudice. Willie Maurice was surely right—being around nothing but white folks every day puts a lot on your mind. And even in Harlem I felt uneasy. Except for Willie Maurice, who was, after all, from home, nobody I met on the street seemed at all interested in how I felt about things. Everybody was trying to prove they were tougher and angrier than the next person. Nobody bothered to look inside the heart, mine or anyone else's.

In the darkness, I went over to the window and looked across the rooftops of Harlem, the battered contours washed in steely moonlight. So much was happening, so much was changing inside of me, around me. I could feel it all revolving, and I was struggling, groping to find a place for myself on the slippery walls of the world, and suddenly, my eyes began to fill with tears, blurring my view of the moonlit rooftops and the distant stars, and I returned to the daybed and buried my face in the pillow to muffle my sobs, and cried myself to sleep.

chapter twelve

At the breakfast table the next morning, my mother spoke of going to church, but my train was scheduled to leave at 1:00 P.M. and I didn't want to be trapped in a church service with the choir whooping and clapping and the minister shouting and carrying on, and then have to get up and walk out in the middle of it all.

"You're right," said Cousin Gwen. "You get in there, you'll never get out." I had a feeling Cousin Gwen wasn't much of a churchgoer. When we were in the kitchen talking about Marcus Garvey, at one point she muttered under her breath that Garvey was "no better than these jack leg preachers we have to contend with." And among all the books she had in her apartment, I couldn't recall seeing a single one about religion. Not even a Bible. "You'll be much better off if you get on that subway at eleven thirty and get down there to the station with time to spare," said Cousin Gwen.

"Well, I can drive the boy to the station," said my father. "I don't have to go to church. I don't know any of these churches up here anyhow."

"You know Abyssinian," said my mother.

"*Everybody* knows Abyssinian," he said. "And everybody will probably be there, but I can skip it."

We cleared the breakfast dishes and I went into the study to strip the daybed and pack. It was a beautiful day. The sun was streaming into the study window, filling the room with light. There were books everywhere and, in spite of my insecurity about Draper and what to do with my life, I felt comforted by being in a room that was filled with books. I wanted to read what Cousin Gwen had read, to find the ideas that her books contained and to use them to help me find my way. I felt that they were my only hope, that without knowing what was in the books, without at least understanding the ideas of others, I was lost, as lost as Joe Louis and Marcus Garvey had been, as lost, in my own way, as Vinnie.

When I finished packing, I went into the living room with my suitcase. Cousin Gwen was wearing a housedress and was curled up in a wing chair, with a coy smile that could have been mistaken for a wince. "Did you have a nice time last night?" she asked.

My parents were still in the guest room packing, and I was tempted to tell her about our trip to Jinxie's. I don't think she would have disapproved, but I didn't have the nerve. "It was okay. I had a nice time."

"Your parents said there were a few words with the doorman when you arrived," said Cousin Gwen.

"Yeah. At first he didn't want to let me in the building. When I mentioned Gordie's name, he changed his tune. It was like you said. I don't think they have too many colored people show up at the front door."

"Well, that's how it can be up here, sometimes. The whites can be downright nasty, and they don't even realize it. The same thing happened to me once. I was going to a meeting at the home of an acquaintance on the East Side and the doorman told me I couldn't be admitted to the apartment building. I knew the hostess had given him my name, but he didn't bother to ask me for it. I just walked right past him. 'You'll have to get a ball and chain to stop me,' I said. He came running after me. 'Wait, wait!' he said. 'What's your name, madam?' When he said 'madam,' I knew I was in control, but I still had to be careful. So I told him my name and he checked the list and found it, and he became a different person altogether, charming and polite, like he should have been in the first place. But so often, we don't get that far. They take one look at you and they think they have all the answers they need. And that's when the trouble starts. Of course, it's different in the South. Down there, they think they have the right to do whatever they want. They don't have to ask you your name, because as far as they are concerned, you don't *have* a name."

We were silent for a moment. There was something on my mind. I wasn't sure how to say it, but I finally did. "Cousin

Gwen, did you ever think about how much Negroes talk about race? I mean we talk about it nearly all the time. From the minute we get up in the morning until we go to bed, everything we say ends up becoming a discussion about race. It gets tiresome after a while."

"We are all a product of our experience, and our experience in this land has not been a happy one, even though it's our country. Because of what has happened in the past, we have to be vigilant. Always. That's why we talk about race so much, because we have to consider all the angles in everything that goes on around us. Once you have been defined as a second-class citizen, white folks feel free to treat you any way they please. I hope it won't always be this way, but until we truly get treated like everybody else, we can never let our guard down." Cousin Gwen paused. "I know what you mean, though. Talking about race all the time can make you weary, but things should get better one day. I just wish I knew when."

"You ready to go, son?" said my father. He had come into the living room holding his suitcase.

"Ready when you are," I said. I got up and went over to Cousin Gwen and gave her a kiss on the cheek. I felt much closer to her than I ever had before. "Thanks for everything, Cousin Gwen. I'll be back to see you before long."

Cousin Gwen beamed. "I'm always here," she said. "Come anytime." And then I went out into the hallway and pushed the button for the elevator. My folks were still saying goodbye to Cousin Gwen when the elevator arrived, and I got on with my suitcase and held the door for them. We rode the elevator down-stairs in silence. I was thinking about Burns and wondering if he had said anything to his parents about the incident with Tyrone. And I wondered what my own parents were thinking. I had cut off any discussion of last night's events by going into the study and shutting the door, but I knew they had not forgotten about the fact that I was so late returning. We loaded the luggage into the back of the Roadmaster and headed downtown, following the same route we had taken the night before, across 110th Street and down Park Avenue, passing through the Spanish area, until awnings and doormen and freshly swept sidewalks gradually came into view, and suddenly, there was Gordie's building with a doorman in a dark blue uniform standing outside.

"Isn't this the building where we dropped you off last night?" said my father, slowing down the car.

"It sure is!" said my mother. "And look! There's that door-man. I ought to go over there and give him a piece of my mind right now." As the Buick continued slowly down Park Avenue, we stared across the street at the doorman. I could see it was a different person, and I wondered if Gordie had said anything to his parents about the incident with Charlie the night before. I thought perhaps I might see him coming out of the building, and we could give him a ride to the train station in the Road-master, and I could introduce him to my parents, but he never appeared, even though I continued to look for him out the back window until we were far down the street.

"You know we tried to get in touch with you last night, when you weren't back on time," said my mother. "Dad was going to drive down here to pick you up, but these people don't have their telephone listed, and you didn't leave us the number." I breathed a sigh of relief. I could just imagine the conversation between my mother and Mrs. Burns, once they discovered that they had both been hoodwinked. For the rest of the way, I sat quietly in the back of the car, as we passed the towering buildings and broad sidewalks, empty but for an occasional fellow selling Sunday papers on the sidewalk or a well-dressed couple, headed, perhaps, for church.

When we reached the train station, I got my suitcase from the trunk. In spite of my misgivings about Draper and the turbulence of the events the night before, I was eager to return to school. I was beginning to get used to the idea of being on my own and thinking for myself, and as long as I could do those things, I felt I was free. As I stood on the sidewalk waiting for my parents to leave, my mother rolled down the car window. I leaned in and gave her a kiss and reached across to shake my father's hand. In the midst of the uncertainty swirling around me, it occurred to me that the one thing I could count on was their love.

chapter thirteen

Inside the enormous station I stood on the train platform looking for Burns, but he never appeared. While I was waiting, several fellows from Draper came by and I asked if anyone had seen
him, but no one had, and when the conductor called, "All
aboard!" I stepped onto the train and found an empty seat. I
rode back to school alone. It was a long ride, and I slept most of
the way. There were a few fellows from Draper in my coach, but
we barely spoke. When the train finally reached the stop for
Draper, it was almost dark and the streetlights were on. Still
groggy from my nap on the train, I slumped into the first seat
available on the bus that was waiting in the parking lot. I was sitting next to the window, watching passengers get off the train in
the purple dusk, when someone said, "Is this seat taken?" I
looked up, and it was Burns.

"Gordie!" I exclaimed. "What are you doing here? I stood on
the platform in New York for half an hour looking for you. I
thought you'd missed the train." He was all dressed up in a dark

blue suit and white shirt with a red silk tie, and he reeked of cologne.

"My father took us to breakfast at his club this morning and we were having such fun, we lost track of the time. I almost missed it. I was running down the platform as the train was pulling out of the station, and I barely managed to hop on the last coach; then I found a seat and did my math homework until I fell asleep. I'm still tired," he said with a yawn. "Some night, huh?" and he grinned at me, at first, but then his face became serious. "I haven't figured out how to tell my parents about Tyrone. Remember, they thought we were going to a movie. But I guess I've got to say something. It felt really strange today when Tyrone drove me to the railroad station. He was in such a mood. Usually, he's kidding around, you know, and has a lot to say, but not today. He wouldn't even look at me. What do you think I should do?"

"I think you should call your parents and tell them what happened as soon as we get back to Draper," I said, in a low voice. "I think the guy is dangerous. I wouldn't want him around me." Gordie seemed surprised.

"Aw, come on, Rob," he said. His voice was softly pleading. "He's not that bad. He just got a little upset, that's all." I couldn't believe what he was saying.

"Did you hear the things he said last night, about me being a Jew-lover?" I said. "That was vicious. And did you see the way he tried to climb across that car to get at me?" We were both speaking quietly, our voices nearly drowned out by the groaning motor of the bus.

"Yeah, but that was you," said Gordie. "He was angry because of what you called him. I'm telling you, I've known Tyrone for years. He's a part of our family. He just had a bad night, that's all."

"There's a difference between me saying the word and you saying it, and he should know what it is. He shouldn't lose control over something like that. I'm telling you," I said, "I think he's dangerous. Didn't you notice? Even Minister Malcolm couldn't control him." It was clear that Gordie didn't want to accept the idea that Tyrone was dangerous, but what really surprised me was the ease with which he was willing to overlook what Tyrone had said.

"Tyrone loves my family," Gordie insisted. "He knows we're Jews. For God's sake, he drives us to services at synagogue every week and takes us home afterward. Are you saying he's an anti-Semite?"

"If someone called you a nigger-lover because they saw us together, what would you think?" Gordie seemed stunned and leaned back in his seat. For the rest of the way, we listened to the drone of the bus motor without speaking.

When the bus arrived at Draper, everyone got out and stood around while the driver unloaded the luggage compartment. It was dark and chilly, and, as we waited for our bags with our hands in our pockets, the steam was pouring from our nostrils as though we were a herd of cattle in a corral waiting to be released. I found my suitcase and Gordie found his, and silently we walked across the campus together until we reached the fork in the footpath that led to each of our dormitories.

"I've thought about what you said," said Gordie. "I'm going to call my father as soon as I get back to the dorm," and he walked down the path toward his dormitory until he disappeared into the darkness.

The next morning after breakfast I saw him in the hallway on the way to class. "I spoke to my father last night," he said. He seemed proud to give me the news.

"Did he say anything about our trip to Jinxie's?"

"Not after I told him what happened. He's going to have a word with Tyrone." I was puzzled.

"Is that all?" I said. "What do you expect Tyrone to say?"

Gordie seemed nettled. "How do I know? Look, I talked to my father and now it's in his hands. I can't do any more than that." I suppose it was easier for me to make a judgment about Tyrone than it was for Burns or his father. After all, they had known Tyrone for much longer than I had. But it seemed obvious to me that Tyrone had changed since joining the Black Muslims, changed in ways that he had kept to himself, and in ways that he knew his employers would not approve of. It also seemed obvious to me, from the events on the sidewalk that night in Harlem, that Tyrone was a man who was capable of great rage, toward me, to be sure, and toward anyone who angered him, even

Minister Malcolm, and I wondered if Gordie or his father had given it any thought. I decided not to discuss the matter with Gordie again unless he brought it up. I had said my piece, and it was clear that he was uncomfortable discussing the subject.

There were only a few weeks to go before Christmas vacation, when I would return home for the first time since the beginning of school. I had not seen Vinnie around and I wondered how things were going in the infirmary. I was still spending most of my time in my room studying when I wasn't in class, but I reminded myself to go over and visit Vinnie before long. We were near the end of the marking period and I had a good chance to make the honor roll, so I worked as hard as I could, and sure enough, one morning I checked my mailbox and found a slip with my first-semester grades and congratulating me on making the honor roll. I wanted to call home and tell my parents right away, but I knew they were both at work. I knew once I told her, however, my mother would circulate the news right away, so that everyone would know by the time I got home.

chapterfourteen

Christmas vacation was approaching and I found myself looking forward to returning home, even though I expected to find things pretty much the same. I was curious about the student group that my mother had mentioned and whether they had ever gotten beyond the talking stage. I wanted to see Russell and the others to find out if they were serious about doing something and what their plans were. I didn't know if I could participate from Connecticut, but I was willing to give it a try.

One evening before dinner, I ran into Gordie in the hallway outside the dining room. The dining room doors had not been opened, and other students were slowly arriving, filling up the hall. While I had seen him around the campus, I hadn't spoken with Gordie since we had returned from New York. My misgivings about his defense of Tyrone and the way his father had chosen to deal with the situation had not changed, but I still considered Gordie a friend, and I was glad to see him.

"Are you going to be in New York over Christmas?" he said.

"I thought maybe we could get together and take in another jazz club, if we can both manage to get out of the house." We laughed uproariously, savoring the memories of our secret night on the town. Our schoolmates were staring at us, as though they were missing out on something. "You know that waitress we had was really cute," said Gordie.

"She sure was," I said. "If we'd had more time, I would have liked to get to know her."

"Too bad," said Gordie. "Well, if you're in New York over Christmas, maybe we'll go back to Jinxie's and try to find her." The hallway continued to fill up with students waiting for the dining room doors to open, closing in around us until there was little room to move.

"I won't be going to New York," I said. "I'm going home." And it occurred to me that for all its faults, life for me at Draper was still an improvement over life in the South. In the South, I could never stand, as I stood then, in the midst of a group of white people without a prickly feeling that my presence was considered offensive, or worse, that I was in imminent danger. I would have to take the greatest precautions to avoid touching them, not even brushing against their clothing, for fear of being accused of an impropriety or subjected to an act of violence. "What's that I smell?" "Well, I never. Boy, what in the *world* do you think you doin'?" "You are getting out of line, nigger," the words uttered with eyebrows arched in high indignation or with a slap or even a punch, knocking you to the floor, where you lay humiliated, wondering what to do next, suppressing your rage, as you calculated the consequences of unleashing it. By December, I still felt a sense of unease with the students at Draper, as well as the teachers, but I had to admit that it did not come close to how threatened I felt around whites at home.

The dining room doors opened and everyone rushed in to find a table. Gordie and I took seats at the table of my history teacher, Mr. McGregor, a shy, aging bachelor, tall and slender, with a thin face and sad gray eyes. McGregor was a demanding teacher. My first papers were returned awash with his unflattering comments scribbled in red ink, and I had to work as hard to decipher his handwriting as to understand his comments. Gradually I got the hang of his approach, and I earned an A for the first semester.

As usual, Mr. Spencer said grace before we all sat down. Most people bowed their heads when grace was said, although I never did and neither did Burns, and when I looked around I noticed that Mr. McGregor didn't bow his head either. We took our seats and our waiter, a senior named Goodlow, went into the kitchen to get the food. Goodlow was not considered a brilliant student. Burns, who had had a mathematics class with him a year earlier, once confided to me that Goodlow used his fingers for the simplest computations. Goodlow was, however, a stalwart member of the hockey team, and it was apparent from the way he swaggered off to the kitchen in his white waiter's coat that the hockey season had begun. A few minutes later he returned from the kitchen with a metal tray laden with dishes of steaming food. Although no match for Cousin Gwen's or even my mother's, the food at Draper wasn't bad and there was usually enough for seconds. The serving dishes were placed in front of Mr. McGregor and he filled each plate except his own with string beans and mashed potatoes and a slice of roast beef. On his own plate, he dropped a modest serving of mashed potatoes and a few string beans, passing up the meat altogether. Once everyone was served, we ate. At Mr. McGregor's end of the table, an upperclassman named Knowles was bending his ear about the League of Nations, eliciting a bemused look from the teacher, who picked at his dinner but ate little, and at Goodlow's end the discussion never ventured beyond the schedule for the Dragons hockey team. Burns and I were seated in the middle, listening to the others.

"Wilson was a great president, wouldn't you say, sir?" said Knowles. Mr. McGregor smiled and fed himself half a string bean with his fork without responding. "Maybe the greatest of the twentieth century," Knowles continued. "I mean, to come up with the idea of the League of Nations at that time was incredibly farsighted. He must have been really brilliant to come up with an idea like that, with everything that was going on at the time." Woodrow Wilson was from Virginia, from the same part of the state as my mother's people, and I grew up hearing stories about him. When he was president, he made sure everything in Washington was segregated. He even told jokes about Negroes, referring to us as "darkies."

"Wilson was a segregationist," I said. Everyone at the table suddenly stopped talking and looked at me. Mr. McGregor was smiling, with a twinkle in his eye.

"So what?" said Knowles. "That's what the people wanted, and a lot still do. You can't blame him for respecting the will of the people. He was still a great president and a great leader of the country."

"A great leader isn't afraid to stand up for what is right," I said. "Even when it's unpopular." There was an edge to my voice, and although the dining room was humming with conversation, our table seemed strangely silent.

"How do you know what's right?" said Knowles. "In a democracy, it's what the people want." He looked at Mr. McGregor for support. "Isn't that so, sir?" Mr. McGregor furrowed his brow.

"In theory," he said, "you are quite correct. That is what Plato said." Knowles wore a smirk as he listened. "But history has given us countless examples of how the majority can become tyrannical. Consider Athens in the time of Socrates. Or Germany's recent treatment of the Jews, for instance."

"Or the South's treatment of the Negro," I said.

"Hey, wait a minute," said Knowles. "You can't compare the two. The South didn't exterminate six million people, for God's sake."

"They just kept us in chains until the Civil War forced them to release us," I said. "And even now they treat us like dogs." Knowles looked deflated, as though his final line of argument had been exhausted, and an uneasy silence seemed to settle over the table. Goodlow got up to clear the plates. I felt exhilarated. I had spoken my mind at the dining room table, taking on an upperclassman, no less. I would never have spoken up before, but I couldn't allow Knowles's adulation of Woodrow Wilson go unchallenged. The table was cleared.

"Dessert, anyone?" said Mr. McGregor.

"What is it, sir?" asked Edwards, a classmate seated across from me who had been closely following my debate with Knowles. Everyone looked at Goodlow with anticipation.

"Jell-O," said Goodlow with a frown. Our faces fell in disappointment. There was a chorus of "May I be excused, sir," and the table emptied. Gordie and I walked out of the dining room together. Although I had promised myself not to bring it up with him again, I was still anxious to know what had happened with Tyrone.

"How did things ever turn out with Tyrone?" I said, hoping the passage of time had eased Gordie's sensitivity about the subject. We walked out of the hallway onto the darkened campus. The stars were out, shimmering on an indigo plain. We walked quickly, with our hands in our pockets, taking the lighted footpath that led back to the dormitories.

"Dad had to let him go," said Gordie solemnly. "He tried to find a way to keep him, but it was no use. He knew Tyrone had a hard life. Dad had a hard life too, so he called him in and asked for an explanation, but Tyrone just sat there breathing hard and glaring at my father, as though my father had done something wrong. Even though they used to talk all the time, Tyrone never said a word during the meeting. For years, Tyrone would take Dad someplace and they would talk about everything in the limousine. But my father said it became clear when he spoke to Tyrone in the study that the old Tyrone had left us and he didn't recognize the new one, so it would be better, he said, for the new Tyrone to find a position elsewhere. Tyrone took the news without any display of emotion. Dad gave him two month's wages, and Tyrone just handed him the keys to the limousine and walked out the front door without even saying goodbye. Dad said that after Tyrone left, he went into his study and shut the door and cried." Perhaps I had misjudged Gordie and his father, I thought, mistakenly interpreting their earlier reluctance to act decisively with Tyrone as a lack of backbone. Backbone, my parents always insisted, was essential for dealing with white folks. But his story made me realize that sometimes compassion can accomplish as much as backbone, if not more.

chapter fifteen

On the day that Christmas vacation began, I took the train with a group of schoolmates down to New York, where I was going to catch a Seaboard Railway train to Virginia. Gordie and I sat next to each other as far as New York. His parents were taking the family to Florida for the Christmas holidays. His sister, who was a Vassar student, was studying in France for her junior year, but she was flying back to New York the next day to join the family for the trip to Florida.

"We're coming back home a few days before New Year's Eve," said Gordie as we were walking into the station carrying our suitcases. "If I get a chance, maybe I'll run up to Jinxie's one night to see if that waitress is around." I wasn't sure why he wanted to go without me, and then I thought, Maybe he wants to talk with her himself.

The train home was crowded. Before arriving in Virginia, it was scheduled to stop in Newark, Philadelphia, Baltimore, and Washington, and after my stop, it would continue south. I found an empty seat next to an elderly white woman wearing a black wool hat. "Excuse me, madam," I said. "Is this seat taken?"

She had been thumbing through a copy of the *Ladies Home Journal,* and when I spoke she looked up at me. She seemed startled by the question. "I don't s'pose it is," she said, in a deep southern drawl, and she went back to reading her magazine. When I sat down, she was careful to smooth the material of her skirt underneath her thigh, and she leaned against the coach window, with her elbow on the armrest, so that she was as far away from me as the seating arrangement would allow. After a while I simply ignored her, and, to my surprise, she fell asleep.

"Washington, Washington," sang out the conductor as he entered the coach. I had not seen him when we left New York more than two hours earlier. He was dressed in a rumpled navy blue suit shiny from wear, with a vest that had dull brass buttons down the front and a watch chain loosely draped between the pockets. As he walked slowly down the aisle, he was checking the tickets of the passengers. When he reached my seat, he first spoke to the old lady, who had been awakened by his announcement. "How far you going, ma'am?" he said, extending his hand for her ticket.

"Atlanta," she said, rummaging through her purse. She found the ticket and handed it to him. The conductor looked it over and handed it back to her with a nod. "End of the line, huh?" he said. She was fingering a plastic candy cane that was pinned to the front of her blouse. "Goin' home for Christmas?" he said.

"Well, you're partly right," she said. "Actually, I'm trying to get to Alabama. That's where I'm from. I'll feel a lot better when I get there, too." She quickly glanced in my direction. Again the conductor nodded, and then he looked at me.

"Ticket?" he said in an even voice, with his hand now extended toward me. He smelled of cigars and hair tonic and there were ashes on his coat sleeves. He looked at my ticket and then returned it to me. "You know, when we get to Washington," he said in a confidential tone, "you'll have to move to the back of the train." I knew what the rule was, and, in my heart, I yearned to refuse to obey it, the same way that woman down in Montgomery had refused to move to the back of the bus a couple of years earlier. I tried to recall her name. Miss Rosa something. I nodded to the conductor and he continued down the aisle, but the idea of refusing to move to the back of the train was taking root, and I sat there trying to imagine what would happen if I actually went through with it. The train would be stopped in the darkness in the middle of nowhere, and the sheriff would be called, of course, about some crazy nigger refusing to sit in the colored coach, and the deputies would show up, red-faced and impatient, in marked cruisers with their yellow lights flashing outside the coach's windows, and at least a squadron of perspiring, mostly overweight white men in uniform, a few chewing toothpicks, would climb onto the train and hustle their way down the aisle to surround me while I sat. Their first act would be to help the old white lady out of her seat. Trembling but mad as a hornet, wearing her hat awry, she would clutch her magazine, her purse, and a satchel with one hand and nervously finger the plastic candy cane with the other. "Has he got a gun?" she would ask repeatedly in a hectoring, impatient voice as she was escorted down the aisle and off the train. The police would then force me to stand and would search me thoroughly right there on the train, going over every inch of my body while the other passengers gawked, and, finding nothing, they would open my suitcase, empty the contents on the floor, and sift through the garments in search of any hard object they could call a weapon. Satisfied I was not armed, they would confiscate my schoolbooks and papers to be studied for codes or secret messages. And then, while I was still on the train, they would interrogate me. If I had made the mistake of sitting down, I would be required to resume standing.

"Get up, Nigger! Stand up when I'm talking to you!" my interrogator, a gaunt white man with hard eyes, smoking a Camel and chewing gum, would shout at me. "What are you trying to prove, anyhow?" He would inhale his cigarette deeply, expertly, and blow the smoke in my face, the way they do in the war movies when they catch a spy. "Are you one of them troublemakers the Communists have been sending down here to agitate? Where are you from anyway? What's your address? Phone number? Where are you coming from? What stop did you get on the train at? You ever been arrested? How old are you anyway? What school do you go to? Where can I find your momma? Your poppa?" The questions would come at me like a flock of starlings, quicker than I could hope to catch, until I gave up try-

ing, my only response a beatific smile, although inside, I would be preparing for the worst. I was, after all, a child of the South, and I was aware of the dark retribution it could impose. But I had made my point. I had refused to obey the rule and I was willing to accept the consequences, even though I had no idea what they would be.

The train lurched forward and we left the station. Most of the passengers in the coach had gotten off by the time we departed Washington, and there were lots of empty seats. The old woman had fallen back to sleep, snoring loudly this time, so that I was forced to move several seats away from her, a decision I was certain would please her when she awakened. It was dark outside. There were a few stars scattered far off in the sky, but no moon. As the train crossed the bridge that spans the Potomac River to enter Virginia, I looked down at the water and shuddered. It was pitch black, like a bottomless pit.

Eventually, the train began to slow down. The engineer blew the whistle several times, and up ahead I could see a clearing with a few streetlights and a little wooden building next to the tracks, and several buses parked in a nearby field. The buses were olive-colored, and on their side was painted UNITED STATES MARINE CORPS. As the train slowed to a stop, soldiers got off the buses wearing dark olive uniforms with tan shirts and tightly knotted tan ties and medals, and there were brightly colored battle ribbons pinned to their chests. On their shoulders they were carrying olive green duffel bags stuffed with God knows what, and they quickly climbed aboard the train, noisily filling the empty seats. By the time the train started to roll again, all the seats in our coach were taken. A dark-skinned soldier took the seat next to me, and two more colored soldiers were sitting across the aisle. I took a quick look behind me at the old lady to see who was seated next to her. A boyish white soldier had sat down and was talking to her, and as I looked around the rest of the coach, I could see that nearly half the soldiers were colored. Most were sitting with one another, but a few were sitting with white soldiers. I leaned back in my seat and closed my eyes and smiled.

"Tickets, please. Tickets," was the next thing I heard. I opened my eyes and saw a conductor slowly coming down the aisle. He was old and stooped, with a pinched pink face and white hair and steel-rimmed glasses on his nose. He sounded like an old-time southerner. As I watched him work his way up the aisle toward me, I could see he was giving the tickets of the white soldiers a quick once-over before returning them, but he examined the tickets of the colored soldiers like a jeweler appraising a gemstone. As he returned the tickets to the colored soldiers, he said something to each one and pointed toward the rear of the train. Most of the soldiers in the coach, colored and white, were only a few years older than I was, and, except for the military uniforms and the mixing of the races, they could easily have been mistaken for a high school football team headed to a game. There was lots of lively chatter and good-natured joshing, and a few card games had started up, but not a single colored soldier got up to walk to the back of the train. When the con-

ductor reached my seat, he examined my ticket slowly and returned it. "The colored section is yonder," he reminded me,
without conviction, pointing to the rear of the train, and that was
it. No order to get up and move, boy. No threat to call the police
or throw me off the train if I didn't move. No plea to cooperate
with a poor man who was, after all, just doing his job. "There it
is," he seemed to be saying, "if you want to take advantage of it."
He might as well have been pointing to the dining car.

"Ticket?" said the conductor to the soldier seated next to me.
He was a handsome fellow with a short haircut and mahogany
skin, clean-shaven, wearing cologne, with two olive chevrons on
a scarlet patch attached to his coat sleeve. Two rows of battle ribbons and a bronze star decorated his chest. He smelled like a
lady's man, but he looked like a real soldier. He was sitting
straight up in his seat, and when the conductor spoke, he reached
into a small canvas bag that was lying on the floor between his
well-polished shoes, handed him the ticket, and resumed his perfect posture, with his eyes looking straight ahead. The conductor
examined the ticket slowly and returned it to the soldier.

"I see you got that there medal on your chest," said the
conductor.

"Yes, sir," said the soldier, keeping his eyes straight ahead.

"Where'd you get it?" said the conductor.

"Korea, sir. Inchon."

"Is that so?" said the conductor. He stood looking down at
the soldier as though he had something more to say, although
the soldier kept his eyes straight ahead. "That's where my boy

was," said the conductor, his voice breaking. "Inchon. But he didn't make it back." His eyes welled up, and with his coat sleeve he wiped away a tear from his cheek. The soldier noticed the movement and looked up, then reached into his back pocket and took out a crisply folded handkerchief and handed it to the conductor.

"Sorry to hear that, sir," said the soldier. "We lost a lot of good men at Inchon." The conductor took the handkerchief, lifted his glasses, and wiped his eyes.

"Well, he was one of 'em," said the conductor softly, and he returned the handkerchief to the soldier. He stood there for a moment to steady himself, putting his hand on top of the soldier's headrest. "You know about the colored section?" he said quietly, nodding toward the rear of the train.

"Yes, sir," said the soldier, his eyes still dead straight ahead.

"Don't pay it no mind," said the conductor, giving him a pat on the shoulder, and he turned to the soldiers seated across the aisle and asked them for their tickets. As the train rolled along, I leaned back again in my seat and thought perhaps things really were changing in the South. The conductor moved on to the next coach. Nearby, someone had a portable radio turned up loud so that everyone in our coach could hear it. After a while, Clyde McPhatter and the Drifters came on the air. Clyde McPhatter was singing his silky, falsetto rendition of "White Christmas" and the Drifters were singing the background, and after a few bars, all the colored soldiers were singing along. "I'm—doop

doop—dreaming of a white—doop doop—Christ-ma-as, with ev-er-ry Christmas ca-a-rd I write." In their spit-polished shoes and their trim uniforms, some of the colored soldiers were even standing in the aisles and swaying back and forth, popping their fingers to keep time with the beat, and, as we barreled down the tracks in the darkness, it seemed that life in the coach had entered a state of temporary suspension. The rules had been relaxed and the burdens of history had been lifted. Those who could reach the high notes were singing the lead with Clyde McPhatter, rearing back and hitting them on the nose, while others were hunched over and singing background with the Drifters. Everybody, including me and the soldier seated next to me, and even some of the white soldiers, sang along, keeping time with the music, as though we were all in the show together, on the stage at the Apollo or the Majestic or on a corner under a lamppost. Everybody was keeping time with Clyde McPhatter and the Drifters, waiting for Christmas to arrive.

chapter sixteen

It was almost midnight when the train arrived in town. A few colored soldiers got off with me, although I didn't recognize any of them. I got my suitcase and stepped down onto the nearly deserted platform and started to walk toward the station. There was a fizz of steam escaping, and as I walked through the vapor and the lingering odors of diesel fuel and body sweat, I could see my parents up ahead, inside the station. They were standing next to each other, smiling and waving at me. When I entered the station, my mother rushed over and hugged me, and my father took my suitcase from my hand.

"Well, look who's here," he said, "finally come back home."

"Did you have a good trip?" asked my mother.

"It was okay," I said. "A lot of marines got on the train just outside Washington and they were singing and carrying on most of the way here. Quite a few of them were colored."

"Must have come from Quantico," said Dad. "Big marine base up there. Were they acting up?"

"No," I said. "They were fine. One of them had a portable radio and everybody was listening and singing along. Some of the white marines were singing, too."

"You don't say," said my father. "I never heard of *that* before."

"Did you have anything to eat on the train?" said Mother. "I've got some tuna casserole in the oven if you're hungry." We walked out of the station toward the parking lot.

"I had a quick bite in New York when I switched trains," I said. "I'll see how I feel when I get home." It was warm outside and a soft breeze was blowing through the parking lot. The cold weather had already arrived in Connecticut, and the warm Virginia air felt good. Dad opened the trunk of the Roadmaster and put my suitcase inside, and we headed home. Main Street was almost deserted but the streetlights were on, as were strings of Christmas lights, wrapped around the lampposts like glowing serpents. At the top of each lamppost was an illuminated lantern of the head of Santa Claus with rosy cheeks and a jolly smile, which seemed to be suspended in midair. A couple of old white men in shabby clothes were stumbling along and looking in the windows of storefronts, and in several of the windows there were big posters announcing a Christmas Eve rally at the fairgrounds.

COME ON OUT

TO THE STATE FAIRGROUNDS

TO SHOW YOUR SUPPORT FOR STATES RIGHTS!

The posters were printed in bold black letters with a big picture of the Confederate flag underneath and "Merry Christmas!" at the bottom. All along Main Street, there were beauty parlors and clothing stores and coffee shops that I had been told were forbidden territory, and as we continued, we passed Pritchard's, the biggest department store in town, with its display windows dressed for the Christmas season and a poster for the rally in the corner of each one. Finally, at the end of Main Street I saw the sparkling lights of the Hippodrome, the only colored movie theater in town. I spent many Saturday afternoons as a child seated in its clammy darkness, transfixed by second- and third-run films, biblical epics like *The Robe* and *The Ten Commandments*, Westerns during which we would always root for the Indians, and horror movies that made me afraid to leave my seat and go home in the daylight.

The streets were dark and empty when we arrived in our neighborhood. The colored lights and Santa Claus lanterns were missing from the lampposts and all of the shops were dark. There were lights on in a pool hall, however, and through the windows I could see a couple of fellows with cigarettes in the corners of their mouths, leaning over the tables with their sticks to line up shots, but otherwise it seemed that everyone had gone home for the night. I thought of Harlem and the stream of people flowing endlessly along 125th Street, the late-night crowd at Jinxie's listening to Coleman Hawkins blow the roof off the place, and that cute waitress working her way between the tables to take orders for drinks, and I wished that I, too, was there.

Dad parked the car in our driveway and we got out. I took my suitcase from the trunk and we entered our house, as usual, through the back door. It was a brick ranch house with an attached garage and a screened-in porch that looked out onto the back yard, which contained a picnic table and a patio and a brick barbecue pit and pink crepe myrtle trees and blue hydrangeas that my mother had planted. When we walked into the kitchen, Dad said he was tired and went off to get ready for bed, but my mother stayed with me. As I stood in the kitchen and looked around, it felt as though I had never left. The air in the kitchen was heavy with the smell of tuna casserole, and it seemed as though the fluorescent fixture overhead had frozen everything in place, the kitchen table and chairs, the refrigerator and the stove, even the salt and pepper shakers and the sugar bowl, all preserved in the lavender light.

"Son, are you sure you wouldn't like something to eat?" said my mother, removing the casserole from the oven with a hot pad. I always found it hard to resist my mother's tuna casserole. She made it with two kinds of melted cheese on top.

"How can I say no?" I said, taking my customary seat, which had already been set for me, in the middle of the kitchen table. I opened my napkin and put it on my lap, and my mother took a plate from the cabinet and served me a large helping.

"Anything to drink?" she said, setting the plate down between my knife and fork.

"I wouldn't mind a glass of milk," I said, and dug into the casserole. How many times had I sat at the kitchen table, anchored under my mother's watchful gaze, feeling the warmth of her love and the deep sense of security only her presence could convey. Even now, when I had broken away and had returned home for a visit, I could still feel the force of that presence. I wondered, for a moment, if my dislike of Draper and my thoughts of returning home were the result of no longer having her constant presence in my life or the result of my discovery that Draper was not everything I expected it to be. At the same time, I knew I could not be one of those sons who never leave home, like Sylvester Reese. Occasionally, my parents and I visited his home on a Sunday afternoon. Mr. and Mrs. Reese were old friends of my parents. They raised five children, all of whom, except Sylvester, were married with children of their own and living outside the house. Mrs. Reese was a spindly, light-skinned lady with gray hair who would greet us at the door and invite us inside to sit in the living room. She would bring out a pitcher of iced tea and water glasses, and she and Mr. Reese, a retired Pullman porter with a face the color of gingerbread, would make small talk about the heat, until an awkward moment when Sylvester, a grown man wearing pajamas and slippers in the middle of the afternoon, sporadically employed and devoid of prospects, would appear in the living room to pay his respects to the guests with a sheepish grin, before quickly retreating to his room like a house pet. After he had disappeared, his parents would resume talking about the weather, as though Sylvester was just visiting for a few days, when everyone knew he had never left.

"Tell me, Robby, have you thought about what you want to do while you're here?" said Mother. "A lot of your friends have been asking about you. I saw Roosevelt and a few others at church a few weeks ago and they wanted to know when you were coming back." She poured me a glass of milk from the bottle in the refrigerator and brought it over to the table and handed it to me.

"I'd like to see Russell and find out about that group he's working with," I said. "Have you heard anything more about them?"

"Haven't heard a thing," she said, raising her eyebrows and pursing her lips. "Nothing's changed around here. The white folks say they'll fight to the end to keep things just the way they are. The courts don't seem to be able to get them to change. I don't know what a group of kids can do."

I finished my casserole and my milk and washed the plate and glass and put them on the drying rack. I was dog-tired. "You haven't lost your touch with tuna casserole," I said, kissing her lightly on the cheek. She smiled and wrapped her arms around me, and I felt the way I did as a child, when I had come home with straight A's on my report card and she hugged me with joy, while I yearned to go outside and play before it got too dark.

"I'm so glad to have you home," she said as she hugged me. "It isn't the same without you."

It was as if I was caught in an undertow, and I felt myself drawing away from her. "What's wrong, son?" she asked.

"What do you mean?" I said. "Mom, I'm fine." I gently extracted myself from her embrace. Part of me didn't want to be at home at all, and part of me wanted to collapse into her arms and tell her everything, that Draper was not what it seemed, that the students were cruel snobs who tormented each other for fun while the faculty looked the other way, that the headmaster was a toady for the wealthy benefactors and, other than the names of a few well-known colored athletes, just as she had said, no one at school, except Gordie, knew anything about Negroes, or seemed the least bit interested in finding out about us.

"I don't know what it is," she said. "You seem different. Is there something on your mind?"

"Nothing's wrong, Mom," I said, smiling weakly. She looked unconvinced. "Everything's fine. I'm just tired. I've got to get some sleep." I retreated into my bedroom and turned on the light, and I had the strange feeling that my room had been pre-served under a glass dome. My bed was neatly made and still covered with a Brooklyn Dodgers bedspread. A framed picture of Jackie Robinson stealing home was still on my desk where I had done my homework. The knotty-pine paneling my father put up when I was in grade school was still on the walls. Like the rest of the house, the room was neat as a pin, not a speck of dust anywhere. My books were carefully arranged in the bookcase, the ten-volume *Collier's Encyclopedia* I used to write my papers for school, *The Almanac of Negro History*, the *Hammond Atlas of the World* I received from my parents as a present on my twelfth birthday, and the book *When A Boy Grows Up*, which they had given me on my thirteenth. Even some of the books my mother had read to me as a child, *Toby* and *Make Way for Ducklings* and *Hopalong Cassidy Rides Again,* were there. When I opened my bureau, I found all of the clothes I had left behind, most of which were too small for me now, neatly folded and arranged in the drawers. It was as if I had never left.

I went off to the bathroom and quickly washed up, and on my way back to my bedroom, I called out goodnight and received two muffled replies. The door to my parents' bedroom had been left open a crack, and I could hear them chatting softly, lying in the dark on their bed, into which I was sometimes admitted as a child, when a bad dream awakened me in the night or the sun in the early morning.

In my room, I switched off the light and climbed into bed. I thought again about telling Mom what Draper was really like, but I knew that if I did, she would tell my father to cancel his patients and she would call in sick at her school, and she and Dad would put me in the back of the Roadmaster and drive me back to Draper after New Year's Day, straight through the night if necessary, and when we arrived the next morning, she would lead the way, marching into Mr. Spencer's office unannounced, cataloguing my complaints and *demanding* an explanation, and Spencer would be seated behind his desk, unruffled, smiling and puffing on his pipe, as if he had expected us, and he would offer us seats across from him in grand wing chairs and patiently explain that the world of Draper is no different from the world at large. "We are in the business of developing character," he would say; "we offer our boys an opportunity to develop the inner strength to handle any situation they will encounter in life." And we would listen intently, and when the subject of "the Mazzerelli lad" came up, Spencer would decline to discuss the details "to protect the boy's privacy," but he would assure us that the situation was much more complicated than it appeared, and he would smile again, baring his crooked teeth, and offer us the use of his private bathroom, scented with the fragrance of sandalwood soap, to wash up after such a long trip, and each of us would gratefully accept, and when we were all seated once more across from him at his desk, a magnificent desk of carved walnut with brass fittings and a green leather top, my parents would look to me, at last, for my final decision on Draper. And what could I say? After everything they had done to get me this far, the matter of my leaving had already been decided. No, I couldn't tell my mother the truth, whatever that really was. And on that night, as I had on so many others, I pulled the blue covers over my shoulders like a cloak and fell asleep under the banner of the Brooklyn Dodgers.

chapter seventeen

"So how you like it up there, anyway?" said Russell. We were sitting in the kitchen at my house before noon on the day before Christmas Eve, drinking iced tea and catching up with each other. Russell and I had been good friends since grade school, although our parents didn't know each other well. Russell's parents were not professionals. His father owned a small variety store and a laundromat next door. His mother worked in the store behind the counter making change, and sometimes Russell did, too. Neither one of his parents had gone beyond high school, but they were hard-working people who had managed to save enough to buy a house a few blocks away from ours. Russell looked the same, lanky and brown-skinned with those hooded eyes and a wispy mustache that made it seem like he wanted to look older.

"It's okay," I said, in a noncommittal voice.

"Your mother said you're getting the grades," said Russell, rattling the ice cubes in his glass. Mom was somewhere in the house, but I could imagine her standing in the dining room with her hands behind her back, pretending to be looking out the window.

"I'm working at it, man," I said. "The schoolwork isn't the hard part. The hard part is just being there."

"You the only one of us up there, right?" said Russell.

"I'm the *first* and the *only*," I said.

"Damn!" said Russell. "That's a whole lotta pressure. You got any friends?"

"One," I said. "A fellow from New York. I have another one, but he's in a pretty bad way. He had to move into the infirmary."

"How come?" said Russell.

"The other kids made his life miserable," I said.

"What did they do?" said Russell.

"They made fun of him. Harassed him. He has bad skin, so they made fun of that. He's Italian, so they made fun of that. They threw shaving-cream bombs in his room in the middle of the night. They even set aside a special toilet and a sink in the bathroom in the dormitory and he was the only one that was supposed to use them." Russell drew back, astonished. Neither of us said anything for a moment.

"So what did the principal do? What did the teachers do?" asked Russell.

"Nothing, really," I said. "Their solution was just to move him into the infirmary."

"How do *you* manage?" said Russell. "Have you had to deal with any of that stuff?"

"Nah, nobody has tried to pull anything like that on me so far," I said. "But you never know. I'm trying to decide if it's worth it. To stay, I mean."

When I received my letter of acceptance from Draper and I realized that I would be the first colored student in the school's history, I was secretly thrilled. I was going to be another Jackie Robinson and break a barrier, to make history of a sort, and I couldn't wait to show up. After all, I thought, how many Negroes have a chance to be the first at anything. "The longer I'm there," I said to Russell, "the more I feel like leaving. Sometimes it's okay, and then something happens to make me want to pack my bags. Like the other night in the dining room, this upperclassman starts talking about Woodrow Wilson and what a great president he was, and finally I couldn't take it any longer. I told him, 'Wilson was a segregationist,' and you know what he said? He said, *'So what?'* Just like that. It's that kind of stuff that makes it hard to take."

"So what are you going to do?" said Russell. "Stick it out?"

"I don't know," I said, shaking my head. "I just don't know."

"We sure could use you back here," said Russell, putting his glass on the table. "We're still trying to figure out how to get rid of segregation. Every time it seems like it's gonna die, something happens to keep it alive. Even though they managed to integrate the buses in Montgomery and get those kids into the white high school in Little Rock, we can't seem to get anything going around here. The NAACP can't even get a meeting with the mayor. He says they're just a fringe group that's up to no good. And the courts are slow as molasses in the wintertime. Even though the NAACP won that big case in the Supreme Court a few years ago, the one that was supposed to integrate the schools, around here the whites are still riding high. We been trying to get the high school kids together to put some pressure on the situation and speed things up. We're not like our parents. We don't have anything to lose, no jobs, no car notes, nothing that the whites can use on us. The big thing is getting everyone to agree. You go to a meeting and every kid wants to do something different." Russell paused for a moment and gave me a sober look. "But I'll tell you one thing we all agree on: nobody is scared of the white man. And they know it, too. They know we're coming. I truly believe that." Russell's eyes were shining with the same gleam I had seen in Lewis Michaux's eyes as he lectured me in front of his bookstore, and in Minister Malcolm's eyes on the sidewalk in front of Jinxie's, and even in Tyrone's eyes, crazy Tyrone, when he stood on Seventh Avenue that night, screaming at me at the top of his lungs.

"How can you tell?" I said. "Everything here looks the same to me."

"I'm telling you, man, you can see it in their faces," said Russell. "You go into a store downtown. Used to be they'd look right through you, like you wasn't even there. But now they're skittish, watching you like they waiting for you to *do* something."

"So what does your group want to do?" I asked.

"Still trying to decide," Russell said. "We're looking for the quickest way to bring segregation to an end. Period. Some want to picket. Some want to organize a boycott like they did down in Montgomery. One college guy even said that we should burn everything down. Nobody paid him any mind, but it's hard keeping a group like that together. When we started meeting in September, a lot of kids showed up, but we could never agree on anything and eventually people started dropping out. Now we're down to a few—oh, I don't know, no more than a handful—that are still committed to doing something. Most kids still don't want to get involved at all. They're scared they'll get into trouble, like they would for skipping school." Russell seemed so serious. "That's why I said we could use you." He sighed and finished his iced tea.

I realized I had missed a lot. While I was up North trying to make the honor roll, all I had been doing was thinking about myself, while Russell had been spending his time on things that were really important. He was more mature than I was.

"So where do you hold your meetings?" I said.

"You know that little rundown church in Parkside near school, Mount Calvary Baptist? The pastor, Reverend Lassiter, is pretty old. You know him. He used to go to the NAACP meetings. The church only has a few members left, but when we told him why we wanted to use it, he just took the key right out of his pocket, put it in my hand, and said, 'Make sure you lock the door when you leave.' Maybe he thinks we'll join the congregation. He did come to our first meeting, but he fell asleep. He's a nice man, but he's getting old and he doesn't hear too well. When the meeting was over, he told us not to do nothin' to get him into any trouble. 'Clean up after yourselves before you leave, boys.'"

"Any other adults involved?" I said. "NAACP?" Russell shook his head.

"They think we're just fooling around. A few college kids have been coming," he said, "but it's mostly high school kids. The adults move too slow. They want to study everything and think about it and try to outsmart the white man. We think the situation is past that point. We're looking for action. If you were here, you'd be at every meeting. I know you would. We're having one right after Christmas."

"I'll be there," I said. "I wouldn't miss it for the world."

chaptereighteen

On Christmas Eve, I went downtown to Pritchard's Department Store to shop for gifts for my parents. I picked out a tie and a box of linen handkerchiefs for my father and a silk scarf and a small bottle of Evening in Paris toilet water for my mother. Pritchard's was crowded and, as I stood at the counter to make my purchases, in chinos and a sport coat with a white oxford cloth shirt and tie, I had to wait, as usual, until all the white customers had been served. I noticed while I was standing there that the saleswoman kept glancing at me out of the corner of her eye. She was tall and thin, a middle-aged white woman with bleached blond hair and scarlet fingernails. Her long, pale face was creased by a frown as she waited on the white customers, and when it was my turn and I paid, it was apparent that she was furious about something. She slapped the receipt and the change down on the counter, and I put them in my pocket.

"I'd like to have these gift-wrapped, please," I said.

She looked as though I had insulted her. "What is the matter with you nigras anyway?" she said.

"Ma'am, I don't know what you're talking about," I said. "I just want to get my packages wrapped."

"Don't you sass me!" she said. "I'll call the floorwalker!" I tried to calm her.

"Look, ma'am," I said. "I don't want any trouble. I just want my presents wrapped." Her face turned purple. She balled her hands into fists, planted them on the countertop, and abruptly leaned across toward me, as though she was about to vault over the display case. The air around us was thick with the smell of her perfume. I felt nauseous.

"You people are trying to destroy everything we've got, aren't you?" she hissed. "You and the Communists! Don't you think your race has done pretty well by us? We've been like family, and now y'all want to pitch it away and destroy *everything*. You and the Communists!" I gathered my packages, figuring I'd be better off wrapping them myself. "But we're not gonna let y'all get away with it," she said. "Mark my words. We *know* how to *stop* you." And she marched off in a huff to wait on another customer. As I turned away from the counter, a florid, heavyset white man with a crewcut was quickly working his way toward me through the crowd of shoppers. I walked straight ahead, pretending not to notice, but near the door he caught up to me. He was dressed in a dark suit and white socks and I could see a bulge under his suit coat. He was carrying a pistol.

"Come here, boy. Lemme see what you got in those bags," he demanded. I handed him my shopping bags and he rummaged through them. "Ain't your Momma and Daddy gonna be surprised. You got a receipt for this stuff?" I found the receipt in my pocket and handed it to him. He glanced at it and handed it back. "All right," he said gruffly. "Go 'head."

I fled outside onto the busy sidewalk and started to make my way through the teeming crowd. Whites and Negroes clogged the sidewalks in the pink haze of the late afternoon, everyone avoiding each other's eyes, careful not to touch each other. I passed a Salvation Army lady in a stiff navy blue bonnet and cape ringing her bell as if she was sounding an alarm. I dropped some change into her pot and took a moment to catch my breath, now that I had escaped from the floorwalker's clutches. I was standing in front of Pritchard's big windows. A tinny version of "God Rest Ye Merry Gentlemen" was blaring from loudspeakers stuck over the windows, behind which several elaborate Christmas scenes had been arranged: Santa's Workshop, with mechanized elves assembling toys; a jolly Santa with rosy cheeks and a red suit, with a bag of toys over his shoulder, seated in a sleigh being pulled by reindeer in simulated flight on a moonlit night; and Santa sliding down a chimney, his face and beard covered with soot, his raccoon eyes and pink lips frozen in rings of mock surprise. Santa had become a minstrel. White parents were holding their children up against the glass or hoisting them on their shoulders to view the display and were laughing at the minstrel Santa. As soon as colored parents saw the minstrel Santa stuck in the chimney, however, they passed it up altogether. Aletha Watkins was there with her children dressed up in their Sunday clothes, and when she saw it, she covered their eyes and quickly led them away. It was almost closing time and the crowds were pouring out of Pritchard's; throngs of white folks were pushing me toward the minstrel Santa and I was unable to escape. Soon I was being pressed against the plate-glass window by the crowd, while on the other side, the minstrel Santa, with his soot-covered face and bug eyes, was mechanically rising and falling in a cardboard chimney under an artificial snowfall.

"Well, I never," said an old white woman, standing next to me and shaking her head with a grin. "What will they think of next?"

"Show me, Momma. I wanna see," said a little white girl in pigtails, straining on tiptoe to see the display until her mother picked her up in her arms. At first, the child was unable to detect what all the excitement was about. "Well, what is it, Momma? What's everybody looking at?"

"Look over there at Santa Claus, Patsy," said her mother, pointing out the minstrel Santa on the other side of the window. "What do you see?"

"His face is dirty. Santa Claus has a dirty face," said the child excitedly.

"And what does he look like?" said the mother, waiting patiently for her daughter's response. With one finger in her mouth, the daughter studied the figure in the window thoughtfully.

"A nigger!" she exclaimed.

"That's right!" crowed her mother, giving her a hug.

I returned home just before dark, and Dad was standing in the living room with a Christmas tree.

"You want to give me a hand with this, son?" he said. After we had secured the base of the tree, Mom brought out boxes of Christmas-tree decorations we had been using since I was a child, and the three of us trimmed the tree with lights and bulbs. When we finished trimming, we had dinner and I went off to my room to be alone for a while. I sat down on the side of my bed. I was still upset about what had happened at Pritchard's. I hadn't said anything to my parents about the run-in with the saleslady or the scene in the store window, but the incidents served to confirm, once again, my resolve to leave the South for good. And even if I did tell them, there was nothing my parents could do. Or would do. The doorbell rang.

"Rob!" called my mother. "Come on out here and say hello to Miss Bernice Gibson!" I got up from my bed and headed for the living room. Miss Bernice was an old friend of my mother's from their college days. Her husband, Mr. Leroy Gibson, was a little brown-skinned man, shorter than his wife and very thin. A chain smoker with a chronic cough, he sold insurance policies door-to-door. Mr. Gibson had started college but had never finished, and he was often cited by my parents, in private, as an example of the fate that awaited me if I failed to graduate. Like a lot of my parents' friends, Miss Bernice and Mr. Gibson had only one child, a girl named Charlene, who was just my age. I had always suspected that Miss Bernice was plotting to arrange for me to become Charlene's future husband. When our families visited, she would always comment on how well Charlene and I played together and how much we were alike. When I was seven, she even tried to persuade my mother to put me in a children's fashion show at her church. Charlene was going to be dressed up as the bride, and I was to be the groom.

I took my time going out to the living room.

"Well, will you looka here!" said Miss Bernice as I walked into the room. "Come here, boy, and gimme some sugar!" She was standing on the other side of the room in a floral print dress that covered her big, heavyset frame like a tent. Her fleshy, yellow arms opened wide, and reluctantly, I walked over to be enveloped in them. "Don't he look fine, Charlene?" said Miss Bernice, looking over my shoulder at her daughter while locking me in her embrace. I hadn't even noticed Charlene, standing demurely behind me in a corner. She was wearing her overcoat. Charlene was perpetually in her mother's shadow, dragged along everywhere to be displayed like a sample from a drummer's suitcase. When she was younger, everyone thought of her as spoiled. She had more dolls and more clothes than any girl I knew, and as she got older, Miss Bernice would take her to the hairdresser when other girls her age were still wearing braids, but I didn't think she was spoiled. To me she seemed unhappy, and I always felt sorry for her. "How long you here for, Rob?" said Miss Bernice.

"Just a few days," I said. "I have to go back to school right after New Year's."

"Well, I certainly hope we get to see some more of you before you leave. Charlene was saying just the other day how much she missed seeing you at school." Charlene rolled her eyes, covered her mouth, and looked away. "Maybe we can get y'all over for dinner one day before you leave," said Miss Bernice.

"Well, maybe so," said my mother, stepping in. "Why don't we talk about it sometime," said Mom. "Now, Bernice, if you'll excuse me, I've got to start getting my Christmas dinner ready. How are you coming on that reading assignment, son?" She was tossing me a life preserver, which I gladly accepted.

"I still have quite a few pages left," I said.

"Well, you better go read 'em," said Mom. "We don't want you slippin' off that honor roll while you're down here." Miss Bernice's eyes got big as saucers.

"Say what? *The honor roll?* Did you hear that, Charlene? Robby is up there on the *honor roll.* Well, I do declare. That boy is gonna make some woman mighty happy one of these days." She grinned at me and batted her eyelashes. "Come on, Charlene, we don't want to keep this boy away from his schoolwork." Charlene headed for the front door. She still hadn't bothered to take off her coat. Halfheartedly, she waved at us and rushed out the door without speaking. "That child is gonna be the death of me," moaned Miss Bernice, shaking her head. "I try to give her some home training, but it just goes in one ear and out the other," and she followed Charlene out the door. I stood in the living room looking out the picture window, and I watched her catch up with Charlene on the sidewalk.

We had a quiet Christmas at home, which suited me just fine. My mother wanted to have a party and invite a lot of people, but I didn't feel like celebrating, and Dad was on my side. "We don't need to have a party, Clarissa. You know some people are gonna be stopping by anyway. Just leave it at that." Mom didn't resist, and the three of us sat down to dinner on Christmas afternoon. Mom had made a roast turkey with all the trimmings and a corn pudding with nutmeg sprinkled on top. After a dessert of ice cream and fruitcake, we sat in the living room and exchanged gifts. My parents gave me a fancy pen-and-pencil set from England and some ties and dress shirts.

Finally, my father settled into his armchair for his annual holiday talk. Dad always opened up on Thanksgiving or Christmas in the privacy of his home. He started with bromides, but he would also impart the wisdom of a lifetime, recalling what it had been like to overcome the doubts of others again and again, explaining to me, in his own way, how he had managed to survive. And now that he and Mom had sent me off to boarding school, there were things he wanted to say, things he wanted me to know. "We got so much to be thankful for, son. Lots of rich folks don't have half what we've got. No matter what *they* say up there at that school or anywhere, money can't buy what's most important in life. Can't buy love. Can't buy peace of mind. Can't buy character. Never could." He paused for a moment and sighed. "But most people don't realize that until it's too late." Seated in his favorite chair with his arms extended on the armrests and his legs stretched out, he looked immense. "When I was growing up," he said, "nobody thought I would amount to anything. That's how it was in those days. People took a look at you and your nappy hair, your thick lips, your flat nose, and where you came from, and they thought they could tell your future. I'm talking about Negroes as well as whites. My momma did day's work and I didn't have a daddy around, so they thought, well, this little nigger's just gonna end up shining shoes somewhere, and they wrote me off. But I worked hard in school and then I got the scholarship to college. I lived at home to save money and Momma took in laundry and cleaned white folks' houses seven days a week to help me out. She always believed in me. That was the most important thing of all." There were tears in his eyes when he said it. "When I finished dental school, I met your mother. You can imagine how popular I was around here, a colored dentist just starting out. The women wouldn't leave me alone. Sometimes they would even call me at my office, trying to get me to meet them somewhere. All they were looking for was my money. All of 'em except your mother. She used to say all she was looking for was a man she could trust. She believed in me too." I had heard most of this before and it still moved me, but it also seemed to be rooted in the values of patience and individual perseverance that had become the hallmark of black professionals. On the other hand, once they had achieved professional status, some of them seemed to tolerate racial indignities to an alarming extent, not only inflicted on their patients and clients and customers, but on themselves, without even bothering to put up a fight.

"Dad, did you ever do anything to challenge segregation?" I asked.

"What do you mean?" he said, looking at me from the soft recesses of his armchair. "You mean walk a picket line or something like that?" He regarded me with patronizing skepticism, as though I was broaching a subject that I didn't know anything about.

"Exactly," I said. "Did you ever do *anything* like that?"

"Never had time," he said, shaking his head firmly. "When I wasn't working, I was in class, and after I finished school I had to set up my practice. Get a loan from the bank. Buy my equipment. Rent an office. Nobody ever gave me anything. I had to work for everything I have." He looked at me sternly. "And everything *you* have."

"I know, Dad," I said. "But nothing's going to change around here unless everybody gets involved in the struggle."

"I do my part," he said testily. "I give money to the NAACP every year."

"I'm talking about more than that," I said. "I'm talking about standing up to the system." He sat brooding in the armchair for several minutes, without looking at me. Then he sighed and looked me straight in the eye.

"Boy, let me tell you something. You aren't going to that school up there for free. And nobody's giving us clothes to wear or putting this roof over our heads. If I spend my time standing up to the system, when am I going to earn a living? If I don't work, we don't eat. It's as simple as that." He was in a huff, insulted by my questions, and I decided there was no point in pursuing the subject on Christmas, but I knew it was something I would discuss with him again.

The doorbell rang several times that evening, with friends and family dropping by for a cup of eggnog and some fruitcake, and a glimpse of me, of course, the hometown boy who had gone away to a New England boarding school and had returned to tell about it. Mother ushered the guests into the living room and I sat politely answering all the perfunctory questions. "How you getting along up there?" "Must be cold up there this time of year?" "Any snow yet?" No one asked me about courses or books or what my days were like. If I was breathing, I must be doing all right. And so I sat there on the sofa like a celebrity, until the last guest, Mozelle Thomas, my mother's cousin on her father's side, had finished her fruitcake and stood up to leave. She was getting along in years and walked slowly, so I got up to help her. I always liked her. When I was younger, she took a special interest in me, since my mother's people were not around.

"Sure is nice to see you, Rob," she said, thrusting her wrinkled brown cheek toward me for a peck, which I gladly supplied. "You certainly are becoming a fine young man. Now don't let those folks up North change you any. You make sure you come back home when you finish up." I didn't say anything. I helped Cousin Mozelle to the front door and opened it for her, and even though the houses on the street were bristling with Christmas lights and decorations, the true spectacle was overhead in the night sky filled with stars, the same stars I had seen at Draper and in Harlem.

"So beautiful," I sighed as I looked up.

"They sure are pretty, aren't they," said Cousin Mozelle as I helped her down the front walk to her car. "But you should see the decorations on my block. We got Santa Claus, reindeer, angels, we even got a baby Jesus lying in a manger, everything all lit up, sitting right there on the front lawn so you can't miss it." She chuckled and shook her head. "Big as life," she said. "Big as life."

I helped her into her car and headed back up the walk to our house, stopping again to look at the flood of stars overhead, wondering if I would ever find my place in the universe.

chapter nineteen

Two days after Christmas, Russell picked me up in his father's car, a new Ford coupe, two-toned in yellow and black, to take me to the meeting. I was impressed and I was jealous. "When did you get your driver's license?" I asked.

"Couple of months ago," he said.

It was a balmy afternoon and people were walking around outdoors in shirtsleeves. Russell drove slowly through town, carefully working his way in and out of the traffic. We passed the high school and eventually entered Parkside, a little neighborhood of tarpaper shacks with abandoned cars on the streets. Parkside had a tough reputation, and a lot of the kids who lived there never finished school. Russell pulled up in front of a small, shabby building covered with asbestos shingles. It looked like an old garage. There were weeds growing around the foundation and loose shingles lying on the ground. "This is it," said Russell, as he parked the car in front of the church.

"Place is in pretty rough shape," I said, looking it over as we got out of the car.

"Just pray it don't rain," said Russell.

"How come?"

"Roof leaks."

We walked up to the front door, which was painted bright red. On one side of the door was a hand-lettered sign that said

MT. CALVARY BAPTIST CHURCH

REV. ISAIAH LASSITER, PASTOR

On the other side was a cross, painted white, with the words JESUS SAVES. Russell took a key from his pocket, unlocked the door, and kicked it open. There was enough light in the shadowy room to see the simple wooden pews and, in the front, a little altar and an upright piano. In the darkness, I thought of one Saturday afternoon when Russell and I were sitting in the Hippodrome eating popcorn and waiting for the feature to begin, and suddenly, the newsreel came on and there was Willie Mays racing toward the center-field wall and making this *unbelievable* catch, his back to the ball as it was coming down. "Did you see that?" I had shouted. Russell's mouth was filled with popcorn but he nodded vigorously, and others in the theater were shouting, "Show 'em how to do it, Willie!" "Do your stuff!" After the feature, Russell and I had decided to wait around to watch Willie Mays in the newsreel again. The opening frames of the newsreel, however, showed President Eisenhower teeing off at Augusta. With the memory of Mays's phenomenally graceful catch still fresh in our minds, we laughed at the sight of this baldheaded old white man in high-water pants swatting at a little ball.

Russell led the way downstairs to the basement and turned on the lights to a simple room that ran the length of the building. Photographs of famous Negroes were tacked to the walls: Lena Horne, Jackie Robinson, Ethel Waters, Canada Lee, Marian Anderson, Paul Robeson. Everyone was there except Joe Louis. I was sorry that he was missing. A long table stood on the cement floor with folding chairs scattered around. At the front of the room, a battered wooden lectern stood in front of a framed picture of Jesus of Nazareth, the color-tinted one of him with a beard and flowing locks in long robes, looking off into the distance. I walked over and took a closer look at the black-and-white photographs of famous Negroes, stiffly posed subjects, mostly entertainers, pictures clipped out of a magazine. How many of these people had really been able to escape the white man's world, I wondered. And then I heard voices and footsteps coming down to the basement.

"Well, I'll be damned!" I heard a familiar voice. "Rob Garrett! What are you doing here? Come back to see how the home folks are doing?" It was Roosevelt Tinsley, an old friend from junior high school. We had been in the same gym class, and our parents knew each other socially. Roosevelt's father had a dry-cleaning business. "How they treating you up there, man? Made your first million yet?" Roosevelt liked to kid around, but he could also needle.

"I'm doing all right," I said. "Working my tail off."

A nice-looking girl whom I didn't recognize had come in with Roosevelt. She was lingering by the stairs, and Roosevelt noticed me looking at her. "That's my cousin Paulette. She just started high school. *Fine,* ain't she?" Roosevelt smiled at me and I smiled and nodded in agreement. She certainly was fine. I studied her from a distance. Willowy but not too tall, with honey-colored skin, dark brown eyes, and long thin fingers that I could easily imagine playing the piano. When she looked at you, her right eye would sometimes wander slightly, but I thought she was pretty just the same. She was wearing her hair back in a ponytail and was dressed in a pink short-sleeve sweater, a gray skirt with a crinoline, and saddle shoes and bobby socks. Except for her color, she could have been on *American Bandstand.* I wanted to get to know her.

There were more voices, and more footsteps coming downstairs. Sylvia Newsome arrived. Her father, the Reverend Viceroy Newsome, was pastor at Greater Ebenezer Baptist Church, which our family attended. Greater Ebenezer was the largest and oldest colored church in the city, and I wondered if her father knew where his daughter was at that moment. I had always wanted to ask her out when we were in school together, but she was a year ahead of me and so popular that I had never been able to bring myself to do it. She was an excellent student, president of the math club, short and dark, like her father, with alert brown eyes. As soon as she arrived downstairs, we exchanged glances. Behind her were two fellows who looked a little older than the rest of us. I didn't recognize them at all. I hadn't known Sylvia very well before I left for Draper, so I decided to introduce myself. "I'm Rob Garrett," I said. "I don't know if you remember me, but I was in high school with you last year. I was a year behind you."

"Sure, I remember you," she said with a big smile. "You went away to a school up North, didn't you?" For a moment I felt as famous as the people in the pictures on the wall.

"Yeah, that's right," I said casually.

"How's it going up there?"

"It's all right, so far. It's a lot different from here."

"I can believe that," she said with a laugh, and then she became serious. "How come you're here?"

"Well, Russell was telling me about what you all were trying to do," I said, "and I was interested."

"Why don't we get started," said Russell. He was sitting at the head of the long table, and the rest of us took seats across from one another. "Everybody know each other?" I still hadn't met Roosevelt's cousin or the two fellows who had come in with Sylvia, so I introduced myself.

"I'm Rob Garrett," I said. "I grew up here and went to school here until last year. Right now I'm going to school up North, but I'm still interested in what's going on around here." Russell looked at Roosevelt's cousin.

"My name is Paulette Gentry," she said. She spoke confidently, but she held her head down in a way that made her seem shy. "I'm a freshman in the high school and Roosevelt is my cousin." She looked at Roosevelt and smiled.

"What about you fellows?" said Russell, nodding at the other two boys.

"Joseph Rivers," said the smaller of the two. "I'm a freshman at Virginia Baptist College. I'm from Montgomery, Alabama."

"Albert Jarvis is my name," said the other boy, in a deep voice. "I'm also a freshman at Virginia Baptist and I'm from Atlanta, Georgia." He was dark-skinned and muscular, with a thick neck and a shaved head. He looked like a football player or maybe one of Minister Malcolm's men.

"All right," said Russell, "this is the meeting where we're finally going to decide what we're going to do. With the right kind of pressure, we can force an end to segregation in the city a lot sooner than the courts will. The suits filed in the courts are so tied up in knots, we could be stuck living with life the way it is now for years. We been meeting down here for months trying to agree on some action we can take that will speed things up, but all we done is talk." Russell looked impatiently at each of us. "We got to make up our minds whether we gonna do something. And if we're not, we should admit it and go home."

"Well, I feel we should pick out a business downtown that practices segregation, like White Tower, and start picketing," said Sylvia. "They make a lot of money off our kids buying those hamburgers. We can make signs, and I know a lot of kids who would want to help."

"When you gonna do it?" said Roosevelt, sounding skeptical. "On the weekends? Most kids are in school during the day, and the ones that aren't in school, you don't want to have on a picket line. And by the way, Sylvia, if your daddy finds out you're skipping school to walk on a picket line, he'll whip you so bad you won't be able to sit down for a week." Roosevelt snickered at Sylvia from across the table.

"So what do *you* want to do, Roosevelt?" said Sylvia, clearly irritated at Roosevelt's foolishness.

"Why don't we start by passing out leaflets after school? We could divide up the leaflets and pass them out in front of stores that we know discriminate," said Roosevelt.

"In other words, all of 'em," said Russell with a smile. "What would you put on the leaflet?" Russell seemed mildly interested in what Roosevelt had to say.

"'A Call to Action! This store discriminates against Negroes. Don't give them your business,'" said Roosevelt, writing out the words in the air with his index finger. "Something like that."

"Y'all talking about a *boycott*," said Joseph, the college student from Alabama. "That's what they did in Montgomery with the buses. Finally won too, but it took a long time. Over a year, three hundred eighty-one days, *and* we had the whole Negro community behind us. Let me tell you, a boycott is hard to keep up. People get discouraged. They lose interest. If you start one, just make sure you can finish it, because if you can't, the whites will finish it for you."

"What do you mean?" I said. Joseph looked at me with surprise.

"We talking about changing *their* whole way of life, as well as our own. For years, they've been used to treating us any old kind of way, without any back talk. Well, a boycott is back talk, and a lot of white people won't tolerate it. They will strike back. In Montgomery," said Joseph, "they tried to kill Dr. King. Bombed his house. One time I was on my way home with a group of my friends after a rally for the boycott. We were walking down the street on the sidewalk and a pickup truck jumped the curb and followed us right onto somebody's lawn, trying to run us down. I saw the guy behind the wheel. He was an old white guy with a red face. And you know what? The guy was smiling, with both hands on the wheel, smiling like crazy. We ran up on the nearest porch and rang the bell, and a colored guy came to the door and let us in, but I was shaking so hard I could barely talk."

There was a long silence after Joseph spoke, and I thought of Tyrone and how he had come after me on Seventh Avenue for my back talk. I thought of Tyrone's smile and what was behind it, and how I was shaking when I got back to Cousin Gwen's apartment that night, and the danger that lurked in being different, especially when you start standing up for yourself. And I recalled Cousin Gwen in the kitchen after Thanksgiving dinner, telling my mother how it was important for me to stand on my own two feet. I thought she would be pleased that I was at this meeting. I looked around the basement, at the picture of Jesus hanging on the wall in the front of the room and the photographs of famous Negroes. I felt like I was in Sunday school. Threadbare hymnals were piled on a table, together with a box of old crayons and a few dog-eared religious coloring books. Despite the grim turn in the discussion, I was thrilled to be there, sitting at a table with other kids just like me, all of us wanting to bring segregation to a halt. I knew I would never have a discussion like this in a class at Draper.

Finally Roosevelt broke the silence. "What's your idea?" he said, looking across the table at Joseph.

"Direct action," Joseph quickly replied. "You got to be willing to put yourself on the line and take the consequences." He was a small, wiry fellow, with reddish brown skin and intense, dark brown eyes. When he spoke, his arms were extended across the table with his hands clasped, as though he was pleading. "A couple of us at the college have been talking about starting a sit-in." Except for Albert, the other college student, who seemed impassive, the others around the table, including me, looked at Joseph with curiosity. It was obvious that he knew a lot more about this stuff than any of us.

"What do you mean?" said Russell.

"I mean directly confronting the system, throwing yourself in front of the train, man, putting yourself in the gears of the white man's machine and bringing that sucker to a halt!" said Joseph. Like a preacher, he was feeling the spirit of his message and transmitting it to those around him. "We're talking about picking out a store downtown like Woolworth's. A group of us will go in there and sit down in the white section of the lunch counter and wait to be served, and we won't be looking at no clock to see if the bell has rung for class."

"But suppose they don't serve you?" said Sylvia.

"We wait until they do," said Joseph. "We wait and wait and wait some more."

"Yeah, but they could make you wait forever," Roosevelt said.

"That's right," Joseph said. "But as long as we sit, they can't do any business at our seats. Sooner or later, something's got to give." He seemed to have an answer for everything. It was a simple idea and I could tell that it was catching on with the group, but I could also imagine how something like this could get out of hand.

"What are you going to do when somebody calls the cops?" I said.

"Nothing," said Joseph.

"*Nothing?*" said Roosevelt, leaning back in his chair in disbelief.

"That's right, nothing," said Joseph evenly. "If you agree to go through with this, you have to be prepared to be arrested and take the consequences."

"You mean go to jail?" said Russell.

"That's right," said Joseph, "if it comes to that." Again a hush fell over the room as Joseph's words began to sink in. Then Albert spoke, and it seemed as if the walls were shaking.

"We think if the first group gets arrested, there will be others to take its place."

"Yeah," said Roosevelt. "But when does it end? They can keep arresting y'all and putting y'all in jail, as long as they want." He seemed to be having doubts.

"We wouldn't ask the high school kids to get arrested," said Joseph. "But we would like to have your help in passing out leaflets outside the store, explaining to customers what's going on inside and asking them not to patronize the store until the lunch counters are integrated."

"So we're gonna pass out leaflets and have a boycott after all," crowed Roosevelt. "What did I tell you?"

"When are you planning on doing this?" Russell said.

"Sometime in the spring," said Joseph. "We'll let you know."

When the meeting ended, the basement of the church was buzzing with excitement. Everyone walked out of the church together and stood on the sidewalk waiting for Russell to lock up. The sun was setting and the crickets were starting to sing, and you could feel the night approaching. Roosevelt's cousin, Paulette, was standing near him, but in the dusk, I could barely see her features. She hadn't said a word during the meeting. Probably scared, I thought. After all, she was just a kid. Russell put the key in his pocket and came over. "All right, Joseph, you gonna let me know when you're ready to do it," he said. "But give me a couple of weeks to get my side ready. I gotta line up enough kids to keep leafleting as long as you're in there."

"That means we'll need paper for the leaflets and a mimeograph machine to run them off," I said. "We can take up a collection to buy the paper, but I can't help you with the mimeograph machine."

"There's one in the office at Daddy's church," said Sylvia. "And it's brand new. Now I just have to figure out how to sneak in there and run them off without getting caught. How many you think we'll need anyway?" she asked Joseph.

"Four, five thousand to start with," said Joseph. "Maybe more. You can pass out a lotta leaflets in one day alone."

"Oh, Lord," said Sylvia. "I could be in there with that mimeograph machine all night. I'm gonna have to think about this." Everybody said goodbye, and Russell and I rode back to my house together.

"We have to keep this quiet," said Russell. "If anyone finds out, our parents will do whatever they can to stop us."

"Well, you don't have to worry about me," I said. "It's easy for me to keep things to myself." We both laughed. Russell dropped me off in front of my house. The lights were on inside and I knew Mom was inside getting dinner ready. I'm going back to school right after New Year's Day, I thought, and then it hit me. If the sit-in was in the spring and I was in Connecticut, I could miss the whole thing, unless it was still going on when I finished the school year. The school year ended early at Draper, sometime in May. With luck, the sit-in would still be going and I could participate. I didn't think about the danger. After all, I would be away at school most of the time. There would be plenty of time to be scared, and, in a way, I was looking forward to it. I said goodbye to Russell, promised to send him a couple of bucks each week from my allowance to help pay for the leaflet paper, and went inside to wash up for dinner.

Before sitting down at the dinner table, my father had taken off his coat and loosened his tie. Now, strapped in his red suspenders, he sat carving a small roast of pork while my mother served boiled potatoes. I was still so excited from the meeting that I had lost my appetite, so I ate very little. Of course, my mother noticed.

"Aren't you hungry, son?" she said. "You always used to like roast pork." She sounded as though I had forsaken my connection to the family.

"It's okay, Mom," I said. "I've just been thinking about going back to school. My mind is elsewhere."

"Your mother said you were out with Russell this afternoon," Dad said.

"Yeah. We were driving all around," I said. "You know, Dad, Russell has his license. I want to get mine soon. Maybe the next time I come home?"

"That's fine, son," answered my father, "but I'd better teach you how to drive first."

chaptertwenty

On New Year's Eve, my parents and I went to a party at the home of Dr. and Mrs. Edgar Braxton. It was a big party, with lots of doctors, lawyers, businessmen, and teachers, many of whom had lived in town all their lives, earning a comfortable living serving the Negro community but making the necessary accommodations that segregation required. Teachers, of course, had to teach in a Jim Crow schoolhouse every day, and because they didn't make as much money as other professionals, they sometimes took side jobs. Mr. Eddie Gilliam, a science teacher at Booker T. Washington Junior High, lived two doors down from us. He drove a dark blue Lincoln Continental that he traded in every year for the latest model, and to pay for it, he also waited tables at the Jefferson Davis Club, an exclusive downtown men's club, or the Cavalier Country Club, also very swank but located outside the city. Sometimes I saw Mr. Gilliam leaving his house after school in the late afternoon dressed in his white waiter's coat, black pants, and a black bow tie, and as he climbed into the

Lincoln, I wondered what it was like for him to smile and bow and serve white men who were professionals like himself, with college degrees and positions of respect just as he had. What was it like for him to overhear their chatter about Bobby Jones and Ty Cobb and the heat and the niggers and how they were becoming more lazy and trifling every day, and, at the same time, more uppity.

Still, colored professionals were better off than most Negroes in town, and most were looked up to, even envied. But success, like everything else, often came at a price. W. K. Evans, the busiest undertaker in town, had a terrible drinking problem, so bad, people said, that you could smell liquor on his breath at the cemetery. And a lot of the doctors had family trouble. Keeping late hours and making house calls made it easier for them to chase women. I once overheard my parents talking about Dr. Walter King. His wife had recently learned that he had another whole family with two children living in secret on the other side of town. Mrs. King had called Mom in a daze, trying to figure out what to do. "I told her to put him out," said Mother. "Get all his clothes and put 'em in a box and leave it on the sidewalk in front of the house and change all the locks on all the doors."

The Braxtons lived in a new brick house on a corner lot with a two-car garage that housed a new Cadillac on each side. We found a parking space on the street and rang the doorbell, and Mrs. Braxton, a woman in late middle age with smooth olive skin, answered. Her hair, piled on her head in a bouffant style, had a piece of mistletoe pinned on top, and she was wearing a low-cut pale green evening gown, with a long pearl necklace wound several times around her neck but with enough slack left to disappear into her ample bosom.

"Well, if it isn't the Garrett family! Happy New Year! And who's that handsome young man you brought along?" said Mrs. Braxton, batting her eyes at me. It was rumored that, years before she landed Dr. Braxton, she had been a showgirl in the entertainment world. Judging from her false eyelashes and heavily applied make up, I could believe it.

"How are you getting along up there at that school in Connecticut?" she said. "Have you met any nice young ladies since you've been there?" Her eyelashes fluttered like a butterfly's wings and when she grinned, her frosted pink lipstick glowed in the darkened doorway.

"No, ma'm," I said. "We don't see too many girls."

"Well, I think we should do something about that right now," said Mrs. Braxton. Without hesitating, she plunged into the crowd with me in tow. We only managed to get a few feet before she was intercepted by one of her guests, a light-skinned woman in a slinky black dress. "*Latrice!* Where have you *been,* child? I haven't seen you in a world of time. I have to come out to your parties just to make sure you are *alive.* And who is that *gorgeous* young man you're holding hands with?" she said, looking me up and down before giving Mrs. Braxton a sly smile. "Latrice, have you been holding out on me?"

Mrs. Braxton barely acknowledged her. "I can't talk right

now, Dorothy," she said. "I got some business to attend to," and she yanked me deeper into the crowd. With Mrs. Braxton in the lead, we wound our way through the crowd to the other side of the living room, fending off additional attempts by guests to engage her in conversation until we reached the dimly lit sun porch. It had apparently been reserved for young people who had accompanied their parents to the party. Standing around on the porch was a group of teenagers, mostly younger kids I didn't know, listening to Lloyd Price singing "Lawdy Miss Clawdy" on a little forty-five record player.

"Hey, Rob!" said a voice I recognized, "what're you doing here? I thought you'd left!" It was Roosevelt, rocking back and forth on an aluminum lawn chair with a bottle of Royal Crown Cola in his hand. I had a feeling it was spiked.

"I'm going back day after tomorrow," I said.

"You know, Rob," said Roosevelt, "you been talking kinda different since you got back from that school you attending with those white boys. You starting to sound like you from *up there.*" He covered his mouth and laughed.

"Well, I'm glad to see you know someone here," said Mrs. Braxton, ignoring him. "But there is one young lady in particular I wanted to introduce you to. Now, let me see. Where is she?" and she peered around the shadowy porch, searching for the right face until she caught a glimpse of the young woman she was looking for. "Come over here, darlin'," she said, motioning to a slender girl who was standing by herself with her back to us. When she turned toward us, the first thing I noticed was her glasses. They were black, with those cat's-eye frames, and it took me a moment to realize that it was Paulette who was wearing them. When I did, though, I smiled. She had on a red plaid dress with gold buttons and a white lace collar and a crinoline underneath, and she looked festive and bright. When she saw us, she quickly took off her glasses, folded them, put them in the pocket of her dress, and came over. She was smiling, and I could tell by her expression that she remembered me. Latrice Braxton took her hand and stood between us, holding my hand as well. By now the other kids on the porch sensed that something unusual was going on. The Christmas tree lights gleamed in their eyes, and they covered their mouths to hide their amusement.

"Now, Paulette Gentry," said Mrs. Braxton. "I want to introduce you to Rob Garrett. You both come from fine families. I know each of your parents well and I know they will be very happy to learn that you have made each other's acquaintance." She gave both of us a squeeze of the hand and a flutter of the eyelashes, smiling and swiveling her powdered face back and forth, and then she turned and disappeared into the crowd in the living room. As soon as she left the porch, the kids broke out in laughter.

"What y'all gonna do now?" said Roosevelt. "Get married?" and everyone hooted. Paulette blushed. Her right eye was slightly awry, drifting just a bit as it had at the meeting, but her face was so lovely.

"You want to get some punch?" I said. It was the only thing I could think of to get us out of there. Paulette nodded quickly and looked at me and, sure enough, her eyes were now as aligned as the planets. We made our way into the dining room, crowded with adults, all of whom seemed to be staring at us. I squeezed in between several of them who were standing near the punch bowl and carefully ladled out two cups of eggnog.

"I don't know what these crackers expect," I overheard someone say, an older man with mixed gray hair and a red and green bow tie. "Are we supposed to lie down and take this stuff *forever?*"

"Yeah, but you don't want to get 'em too riled up, Fred. You know they can be hell on wheels."

"Well, I don't give a damn!" said Fred. "I'm tired of their crap. *Nigger* this. *Nigger* that. They tell you to make something of yourself, and when you do, they *still* treat you like a *nigger.*" His eyes were blazing and he glared at his companion as though he would take a poke at him if he said the wrong thing. I handed Paulette an eggnog and looked around for a quiet place to talk, but it seemed that every available space in the living room and dining room was occupied. Suddenly, the kitchen door swung open and a heavyset, dark-skinned woman in a wrinkled white uniform entered the dining room with another heaping platter laden with hors d'oeuvres, deviled eggs, little Smithfield ham sandwiches, and cheese puffs which she put on the dining room table, and when she backed her way through the kitchen door, I could see that the room was empty.

"Follow me," I said to Paulette. We slipped into the kitchen, where we found the back stairway and sat down next to each other on a lower step. In addition to the woman who had come into the dining room, there was another woman in the kitchen, also dark-skinned but older than the first, with the same build and dressed in the same manner. They were both busily working at the sink, and it seemed they barely noticed us when we came in.

"So what's it like up there at that school?" said Paulette. It was a question that everybody had asked me since I had been home, but, except for my talk with Russell, this was the only time I felt I could be candid.

"It's like being in a foreign country," I said, "where you know a lot of stuff is going on, but you can't really be sure where you fit in because you don't speak the language and you don't know the people. I've been there since September and I've only made two friends, and one of them had to move out of the dorm because the other kids treated him so badly. All I do is work and try to stay on the honor roll. I figure that's the one language they can understand." I looked at Paulette. Her elbows were resting on her lap and her palms were under her chin, and her eyes were concentrating intensely on mine. "Do you know what I mean?" She nodded.

"Sounds pretty bad," she said. "I used to live in a foreign country." At first, I thought she might be kidding.

"Which one?" I said.

"Germany," she said. "My father was stationed there in the army. He was a surgeon with the medical corps. Our family lived there for three years. I can still speak some German, but I've lost most of it."

"What was that like?" I said.

"Lonely. I didn't really get to know any German kids, and they didn't seem to want to get to know us either. I guess they could still remember the war. And so could we. We lived in an apartment. We didn't live on the base, so we didn't see too many Americans either. I was glad I was there with my family, but even then it got lonely."

"I keep thinking I should leave. I'm the only colored student in the whole school. They never had one of us before."

"But if you leave, won't that make it harder for another one of us to get in?" I had never thought about it like that. Of course, I thought, that's the whole idea of being the first. It's so there will be a second and a third. Paulette's chin was still in the cup of her palms, but her right eye had strayed.

"I guess you're right," I said. "But if something comes of that sit-in we were talking about, I want to be a part of it and I can't if I'm at Draper."

Paulette sat up straight and looked surprised. "You think it would be worth it to leave school over *that?*"

"Why wouldn't it?" I said. "If it would help to end segregation."

"But you have an opportunity to get the kind of education that most of us dream about," she said. "Look, something may come of that sit-in, but suppose, just suppose it doesn't. Where does that leave you? Think about what you'll be giving up."

"Don't you understand?" I said. "It's not the education, it's the *life* of the place. I'm afraid I won't recognize myself by the time I graduate."

"I'll recognize you," she said, placing my hand in hers. I

wanted to kiss her when she said it, but I wasn't sure she wanted me to.

The cooks were hard at work carving the turkey and the ham and arranging the slices on a platter. The older woman had taken one of the pots from the stove and was draining it into the sink. When she had finished, she poured a steaming mound of black-eyed peas and ham hocks into a big serving dish. Then she drained the second pot and filled a large bowl with steaming gray pigs' feet. When all the dishes were assembled, the cooks took them into the dining room and placed them on the table. We could hear the guests on the other side of the kitchen door murmuring over the display of food. Despite the smells circulating in the kitchen, I wasn't hungry, but I thought Paulette might be. "Do you want to get something to eat?" I said.

"Not right now," said Paulette. "I may have something later. Do you want something?"

"I'm fine," I said. "Just fine," and I gave her hand a squeeze. The voices outside the kitchen were rising, some people even shouting. "It's almost time!" "It's almost here!" "Wheeee! This is it!" and then everyone started to count down in unison. "Five! Four! Three! Two! One!" and there were shouts of "Happy New Year!" The crowd started to sing "Auld Lang Syne," blow whistles, and crank noisemakers. In the kitchen, the cooks were dancing the jitterbug in the middle of the floor and hugging each other, and suddenly, the older one stopped dancing and turned to us. "Y'all sweethearts so quiet over there, like you talkin' about somethin' mighty important," she said. "Don't y'all want a plate with somethin' to eat?" We both shook our heads. "Maybe later," I said. "But thanks anyway."

By now the crowd was roaring through another round of "Auld Lang Syne" and fireworks were crackling outside. The cooks had resumed jitterbugging, holding each other's hand and leaning back and twirling dishtowels in the air to celebrate the arrival of another year. I looked at Paulette and she looked at me, and I thought she was waiting for me to kiss her. She lowered her eyes in the shy way she had, and then she leaned toward me and so I did, I kissed her. I closed my eyes and I kissed her.

New Year's Day was my last day at home, and I spent the morning on the telephone. I called Paulette twice and she called me three times. Each time she called, my mother came to the door of my room. "There's a young lady on the telephone asking for you," she said, with a suppressed smile and batting her eyes. Toward the end of the day, I told Mom I was going out for a walk. She must have known I was going calling because I had on a jacket and tie, but she never let on. I caught a bus that let me off near Paulette's house. It was a large house, a two-story brick with a big magnolia tree in the front yard. I rang the bell and a slightly stooped old lady answered the door and looked me over carefully through the inner screen door.

"Yes?" she said, as though I should explain my presence. She checked the screen door to make sure it was locked.

"Good evening, ma'am," I said. "I'm Rob Garrett. Is Paulette at home?" She was still looking me over.

"Paulette!" she called out. "You got company." Paulette came quickly down the stairs and rushed to the door.

"It's all right, Grandma," she said, "I've got it." She opened the door to let me in as her grandmother hobbled into the kitchen looking mildly suspicious. Paulette and I walked into the living room and sat down on the sofa next to each other. It was the end of the day and the sun filtered into the room through the huge magnolia tree, covering us with soft orange light. As we looked at each other, I felt as if I would die if I had to leave her.

"I have to go back tomorrow," I said. I reached toward her and she gave me her hand.

"What time does your train leave?" she said.

"Seven in the morning," I said.

"I'll just be getting ready for school," she said with a light laugh, followed by a sigh.

"Will you write to me?" I said.

"Of course I'll write to you," she said. She took my hand in both of hers and held it against the side of her cheek.

"Will you wait for me?" I said. "Until I come back?" She looked at me with an expression of great seriousness, as though nothing else mattered in the world at that moment. She nodded her assent and threw her arms around my neck.

"I'll wait for you," she whispered in my ear. "Of course I will." We started to kiss, but there were footsteps approaching.

"Paulette, I need you in the kitchen to chop some celery," said a woman in a husky and commanding voice from the hallway. An attractive brown-skinned woman appeared at the entrance to the living room. She was wearing an apron and had a dishtowel in her hand. I stood up and so did Paulette, still holding my hand in hers. I was embarrassed, but Paulette spoke right up.

"Mama, this is Rob Garrett," she said. "He's a friend of Roosevelt's. He goes to a school in Connecticut and he's going back tomorrow."

"Pleased to meet you, young man," said Mrs. Gentry. "I saw you at the Braxtons' New Year's Eve party. Latrice told me she had introduced you two." She nodded at Paulette holding my hand. "I guess things must have moved along pretty quickly after that," she said in a good-natured but serious way. There was the slightest hint of a smile at the corners of her mouth. "Well, I hate to interrupt you two, but I need Paulette to help me out in the kitchen."

"I'll be there in just a minute, Mama," said Paulette, looking at her mother with an expression of polite exasperation.

"Nice meeting you," said Mrs. Gentry, and she turned and went back into the kitchen. Paulette and I walked outside onto the front porch, still holding hands. It was almost nighttime. Scraps of sunset could be seen through the dark green leaves of the magnolia tree, providing us with enough light to see each other's eyes, each other's mouth, and so we kissed and kissed and kissed some more, clinging to each other until, finally, we parted, waving to each other until we had both disappeared into the darkness. I raced back to the bus stop feeling on top of the world. Though I was sure my parents would be wondering where I was, I didn't care. When the bus arrived I paid my fare, took a seat, and started to think about Paulette and what she had said about me staying at Draper. I could see her point, but I couldn't imagine being away from her. Suddenly, I noticed the other passengers on the bus. There were only a few. All of them were colored and all of them were seated behind me in the back. I was the only one not sitting among them, and for a moment, I thought of trying to talk them into coming up to the front with me in the white section to start a protest like Miss Rosa did in Montgomery, but before I could do anything, the bus arrived at my stop. I got off and ran all the way home. I had a girl-friend. A real girlfriend. For the rest of the evening, every time I closed my eyes, I could see Paulette's face, with her wonder-ful crooked eye.

At 6:30 the next morning, I was standing on the platform at the railroad station with my bag packed, about to climb onto a train that would take me back to school. I kissed my parents goodbye and climbed aboard the last coach, where, as usual, I had to re-main until we reached Washington. I found a seat next to a win-dow so that I could wave to my parents as the train pulled away. I was still thinking about Paulette, about kissing her on her front porch and remembering what she had said about my returning to Draper. I also thought about the meeting in the basement at Mt. Calvary and how that college fellow Joseph seemed to have an answer for everything. I had felt uncomfortable when I listened to him, the same discomfort I had felt with Michaux. I had to admit, though, that Joseph had thought things through. If he was right, we could do something that Negroes in town had wanted to do for almost a hundred years, maybe even longer. We could make history, which would be a lot better than the history I was making as a student at Draper. The coach lurched, the wheels squealed. Slowly, the train began to move forward, and I looked out the window to wave to my parents, watching them disappear from view. All the while I was thinking about what would happen if I didn't go back to Draper next year. I would be near Paulette, of course, but how would my parents take it? Would I be a failure in their eyes? Would they get over it if I left?

chapter twenty-one

It was snowing lightly when I got back to Draper. Before I went to bed, I could still see individual snowflakes floating outside my window, but when I awakened, the campus and the distant hills were barely visible through a thick curtain of falling snow. It rarely snowed at home, and when it did, it was usually a surprise and a cause for celebration. School would be called off for the day and everyone would try to build a snowman before it got warmer and the snow began to melt. At Draper, however, snow was considered a force of nature, like the summer heat at home, to be endured until the change of season. Every day we trudged back and forth through the ice and slush, from our dormitories to our classrooms, ignoring it, unless a snowball came sailing our way.

Having made the honor roll for the fall marking period, I felt a certain pressure to repeat my success. I had always been on the honor roll at home, but at Draper it seemed like a much bigger challenge. I thought the bleakness of the winter days would eliminate distractions and help me concentrate even more on my schoolwork. After making the honor roll, I had begun to feel confident in my classes. My teachers, especially Mr. McGregor and Mr. Althorp, my English teacher, were calling on me more often. But there was also more to think about in my life than ever before, and after dinner, I would sometimes return to my room with my books and assignments piled on my desk and collapse on my bed, imagining I was sitting next to Paulette on the front steps of her house in the shade of the big magnolia tree with my arm around her waist and her head resting on my shoulder. Or I'd recall the meeting in the basement at Mt. Calvary and my excitement at planning for the sit-in. Even though I wasn't going to get arrested, I would still be able to say I was a part of things, the way Russell and I had been a part of things at the Majestic. And sometimes I'd think of Vinnie, alone in the infirmary, and I'd remind myself to stop by for a visit. Eventually I would struggle to get up from the bed, and would make my way over to the desk to start reading for the next day's assignment. I would get up and raise the window to feel the freezing air in my face before returning to my desk to study, until I couldn't see the words on the page or hold the pencil in my hand and I would fall asleep on the bed without bothering to undress.

"Garrett, I'd like to see you after class," said McGregor one morning as I entered his classroom. "I want to have a word with you." He sounded so distant, as chilly as the weather, and as the class began, I looked out the classroom window at the surface of the snow, smooth and white, trying to imagine why he would use such a tone with me, what he wanted to see me about. Maybe I had been slacking off a little bit, but not enough to justify a warning, if that was what he was going to give me. As McGregor began the class, his voice sounded warm again. I felt better and, reassured by his tone, I continued to gaze out the window at the snow-covered ground and the leafless skeletons of the trees rising through the snow. Several thin upper branches were trembling under the weight of a flock of sparrows arriving and departing in their midst. "Garrett," said McGregor. I knew he was calling on me to answer a question, but I had no idea what the question was. The sparrows were flitting through the branches, spilling powdered snow onto the ground, when suddenly something startled them and they took off like a swarm of bees in the summertime, taking cover in the shadowy depths of a massive evergreen. "Garrett?" McGregor repeated in an intimidating voice. "Do you wish to be excused, Garrett?" He had never spoken to *me* that way before, and his tone brought me abruptly back into the classroom. The other students were staring at me with curiosity. A couple of them were smiling.

"No, sir," I said.

"Then tell us, if you will, what were the factors that brought about the Civil War." He was standing in the front of the classroom, looking out the window with his arms folded.

"The inability of the northern states and the southern states to compromise on the issue of slavery was one," I said. "The fact that the economy of the South was heavily agricultural and the North's was more diverse and becoming more industrial was another, and the other was the fact that the South could not accept being a part of the Union."

"Why couldn't the South accept being in the Union?" said McGregor. He was still looking out the window as though he was the master of all he surveyed. Out of the corner of my eye, I could see the sparrows dancing in the air. I would have loved to have been among them.

"Because they knew the North was stronger," I said, with a faltering voice.

"What evidence do you have to support that statement?" said McGregor, his right eyebrow arching on his otherwise impassive profile. I could feel him closing in on me.

"Well, the North *was* stronger," I said. "More people, more wealth. They must have known it."

"Yes, yes," McGregor said impatiently, cutting me off. "But what leads you to say that this was the cause of the South's resistance to being a part of the Union? " I knew he had a specific answer in mind, a point that he wanted me to make on his behalf for the class, but I didn't have any idea what it was. In the past, he had often called on me to supply just such an answer, but this time I couldn't help him. Instead I sat mute, for what seemed to be an eternity.

"Did you read the assignment, Garrett?" he said in a cold, sharp voice.

"Yes, sir," I said. "I did." I was lying.

"Then why are you unable to answer my question?" he said.

"I don't know, sir," I said.

"Bingham?" said McGregor. Marty Bingham was overweight and wore thick horn-rim glasses. His beard was so heavy he had to shave twice a day. He sat in the front row of all his classes and always had the answer to every question on the tip of his tongue.

"The South wouldn't accept being a part of the Union because the Southern people found it politically unacceptable, sir," said Bingham. McGregor turned away from the window with a tight smile and went on with the class discussion, mercifully not calling on me again. When the class was over, I stayed behind until the other students had left the room.

"Sit down, Garrett," said McGregor. I took a seat in the front row. He sat on the edge of the desk with his arms folded. "Garrett, I don't know if you realize it, but you have been the subject of considerable discussion recently among the faculty." I was trying to guess what he was driving at. I couldn't think of any rules I had broken.

"How's that, sir?" I said.

"Well, as you know, you're the first colored student we've had at Draper, and there is a great deal of interest among the faculty in having you succeed." This was the first time I had heard anyone mention the faculty's interest in me. In fact, this was the first time anyone at Draper had brought up the subject of my being the first colored student or what was expected of me, except, of course, in a general sense when Spencer gave his talk to new boys at the beginning of the year. At Draper, there seemed to be an understanding, among the students as well as the faculty, that everyone here was on his own, to sink or swim as best he could. If you had a sound character, you would swim; if you didn't, you would sink. Life was as simple as that.

"I do my best, sir," I said, looking up at him.

"You certainly have," he said, and he cleared his throat. "That is, until recently." He paused, and then continued. "Since you returned from Christmas vacation, you've appeared distracted. I've noticed it and your other teachers have as well. Your papers have been satisfactory, but they are not what we are used to seeing from you. And when you're in the classroom, much of the time you're looking out the window as though your mind is a million miles away. If this keeps up, Garrett, you'll have trouble making the honor roll again." There was another pause. "Is something wrong? Is everything all right at home? If there is something your teachers can do, something we should know about, I assure you, we stand ready to assist you in any way we can."

I didn't know how to respond. Of all my teachers, I liked McGregor the best. I knew that I hadn't been working as hard as before, but I thought I had been doing my best to keep up, and I was turning my papers in on time. I wasn't about to tell him everything that was on my mind. There was a long, uncomfortable silence, and for some reason I thought of my mother, when she had hugged me in the kitchen.

"Is there anything else, sir?" I finally said.

"There is one more thing. You have an exam coming up at the end of next week. Judging from your performance so far this marking period, you'll have to do very well on it to receive an honors-level grade in this course." He gave me a long, somber look with his gray eyes until his face eventually broke into a little half-smile. "Your work's cut out for you," he said, sounding almost apologetic.

As I walked back to the dormitory, I kept thinking about what McGregor had said. It was as though he knew something about me, some secret that he was keeping to himself. I also contemplated the reality that once anyone made the honor roll, there was always the danger of falling off. But if you were colored and trying to succeed, the fall could be terrifying, a long, long way down. Even for professionals like my parents and their friends, or famous Negroes whose pictures were in magazines and hanging on the walls of church basements, or colored entertainers who appeared on television sometimes, or even if you were a Negro whom nobody had ever heard of but who had managed to survive, there was always the risk of falling.

McGregor had put the challenge squarely before me, and it was up to me to respond. But the more I thought about it, the more his challenge bothered me. Hadn't I committed myself to the struggle to end segregation? If I wasn't thinking about my courses all the time, it was because I was often thinking about something more important. I wasn't just whiling away the time in the television room, like some students. Of course, McGregor couldn't know about my involvement with Russell and Joseph, but he could certainly look at me and see that I was different from the others. He had said as much himself. I decided that for the time being, at least, I wasn't going to change a thing. I would still do my schoolwork, but I would also continue to spend time thinking about the future and what it held for me.

On the night before the big exam, I got my homework for my other courses out of the way, and then took a break to read the newspapers. Before I realized it, it was almost midnight. I decided I would have to pull an all-nighter if I was going to study for the exam. I considered not studying at all, just going into class the next morning and taking it cold, but that seemed too much like throwing myself over the edge of the precipice, so I opened my notebook and my classroom texts at 12:10 A.M. and began to study. By 3:00 A.M. I could barely keep my eyes open. My head was leaning to one side, and several times I almost fell off my chair. I stumbled downstairs to get a cup of coffee from the vending machine in the dormitory basement. It tasted awful, scalding and burnt, but I drank it anyway, right there in the basement, and it brought me back to life like an elixir. The dorm was silent as a tomb. I trudged back upstairs to my room with only the echo of my own footsteps to accompany me. I resumed studying, but by five o'clock, I was falling asleep again in my chair. I knew I had to get a few hours of sleep before the exam or I wouldn't be able to get through it. I set my alarm clock for 8:30 and fell onto the bed. The exam was scheduled for 9:00 A.M. At 8:30 the alarm went off. I reached over and shut it off and lay on my back, trying to clear the cobwebs from my brain, but my fatigue was too great and I slowly drifted back to sleep. I have no idea what awakened me. Perhaps it was the instinct for survival, but at 9:05, I opened my eyes and looked at the clock and realized that I was already late. I grabbed my notebook, put on my jacket, and raced down the stairs and out of the dormitory to McGregor's classroom. When I entered, the other students in the class were already writing in their exam books. McGregor was seated at his desk in the front of the class and looked annoyed when he saw me. He nodded at me and pointed at the edge of his desk to the test questions and the exam books, and I walked over and took them and found a seat. As soon as I read the questions, I knew that I would do well on the exam, if I could stay awake. I was yawning for the entire hour, which drew several angry looks from classmates who were seated nearby. I held my head in my hand the entire time, but I wrote and wrote and wrote. Somehow the answers came to me, and by the end of the class, I was sure I had done well. I was giddy with fatigue and relief when I handed in my exam book. I stumbled to my next class, took a seat in the back of the room, and slept through it with my eyes open.

chapter twenty-two

A few days after I returned from Christmas vacation, I stopped by the mailroom to check my mailbox. The mail usually arrived in the late morning but it had to be sorted, so it wasn't in the mailboxes until after lunch. I had a free period before lunch and I was hanging around the Dutch door to the mailroom, the top half of which was always open, watching Connie sorting. Connie was in charge of the mailroom. He was a crusty old man, so badly stooped from arthritis he had to lean his head to one side to look you in the eye. Connie knew every boy in the school. Finally he took the stub of a cigar out of his mouth, stopped sorting for a moment, and leaned his head to one side to look at me standing in the doorway. "Where does she live?" he said.

"Virginia," I said, surprised that he knew I was expecting to hear from a girl. "Connie, how did you know I was expecting a letter from my girl?"

"Happens all the time after vacations," he muttered. "Won't be hearing from Virginia for at least another three, four days though. They're slow as hell down there." I was stunned. My parents had written to me, but I'd never paid attention to how long it took their letters to arrive. I didn't know if I could last that long. I was certain Paulette had already mailed a letter, and the thought of having to wait another three or four days to read it was agonizing. "If it gets too bad, you can always call her," said Connie, and he put the cigar butt back in his mouth and resumed sorting.

Since I was saving my money to send to Russell, I decided to hold off on calling, and, by some miracle, Paulette's letter arrived the next day. I whooped and showed the envelope to Connie. "Must have mailed it early in the morning," snorted Connie. On her way to school the morning that I left, I thought, looking at the postmark. I tore open the envelope and walked over to a hallway window to read the letter.

Dear Rob,

I just can't believe you have left. I miss you so much already. When are you coming back?

After you left last night, my grandmother kept asking me about you. She wanted to know what you are studying in school and whether you are going to be a doctor like my dad. I told her I didn't know and it didn't make any difference to me, anyway. She said I would be better off to know something like that now, rather than later. I wanted to tell her to mind her own business, but I knew if I did, my mother would have a fit. Old people think they can say whatever they want.

When I went to sleep last night, I dreamed that we were climbing a mountain together. We were climbing through these woods and every time we got close to the top, the mountain got higher, and when the sun started to go down, we could see it set through the trees and the sky turned black and it was so dark I was afraid we wouldn't be able to find our way back, and I was holding your hand like I did in the living room yesterday afternoon, but when we looked up, the sky was covered with stars and the moon was glowing like a big silver lantern, and the woods were as bright as day, and we walked all the way back down the mountain holding hands until we reached the bottom, and when I woke up this morning, I felt like I was still holding your hand, and I still do.

Please write me a letter as soon as you can.

Love,
Paulette

For the next month, I heard from Paulette two or three times a week. I tried to keep up with her, but I was also trying to stay on the honor roll. When I sat down to write her, she was all I could think about for the rest of the day. So I wrote her once a week, on Sunday afternoons when I had finished studying. My letters would go on for five or six pages, describing what life at Draper was like and how much I missed her. I always made sure I asked her about Russell and what was happening with the plans for the sit-in, and she always wrote back to me with the latest news. "Russell says there is nothing new to report." "Russell talked to Joseph and they want to start it in April, but some students at the college are backing out because they don't want to be in jail during exam time (beginning of May)." "Russell says thanks for the money. Sylvia bought paper for the leaflets and she taught herself how to run the mimeograph machine without her daddy finding out." But at the beginning of February, Paulette wrote to say that something had come up and there might be a problem with the plans for the sit-in. She said she couldn't go into it then, but she would write to let me know as soon as she could find out more.

A week went by and I still hadn't heard from her, and I was becoming anxious. I was able to keep up with my schoolwork, but I knew it was going to become harder and harder for me to concentrate if I didn't hear something soon. I finally decided one morning that if I didn't get a letter by the end of the day, I'd follow Connie's advice and give her a call. Just before lunch, I stopped by the mailroom to check my mailbox. Connie was still sorting, but I thought I'd ask anyway. "Anything for me, Connie?" I said.

"Dunno," he muttered, without looking up. "Come back after lunch."

Lots of Draper students subscribed to their hometown newspaper, but the most popular, by far, were the *New York Times* and the *New York Herald Tribune.* Newspapers were usually picked up from the mailroom in the morning, glanced at to see if there was anything interesting on the front page or the sports page, and then either discarded or tucked under the arm to take back to the dormitory. I was on my way to the dining room for lunch when I noticed the headline "Negro Students Stage Sit-In" on the front page of a discarded copy of the *New York Times.* The paper was lying on the floor in a hallway and I picked it up to read the article. It was about four students from North Carolina A&T who had started a sit-in at a lunch counter at Woolworth's in Greensboro, North Carolina. There was even a picture of them sitting alone at the counter, with a handful of white people looking on warily, as though they weren't sure what to do next. And then I read a passage in the article that shocked me. "A Negro woman kitchen helper walked up, according to the students, and told them, 'You know you're not supposed to be in here.' She later called them 'ignorant' and a 'disgrace to their race.'" So this is what it's going to be like, I thought. My heart was pounding with every sentence I read, but when I finished the article, I felt a strange sense of calm. The Greensboro sit-in simply confirmed the importance of what we wanted to do. Now it was up to us to make sure that everything fell into place at home. I folded the newspaper, tucked it under my arm, and walked into the dining room.

At lunch, I had to sit through an explanation of the different kinds of igneous rock provided by Mr. Bellard, the geology instructor, to whose table I was assigned. It was so boring. I don't think anyone at the table listened to a word of it, although we all pretended to be on the edge of our chairs. All through the meal, I was thinking of the article in the *New York Times* and wondering if the Greensboro sit-in had anything to do with why I hadn't heard from Paulette.

As soon as lunch was over, I went back to the mailroom, and sure enough, there was a letter from Paulette in my mailbox. I opened it and read it. I felt like a spy who had just received a secret message. "The sit-in is set to start on Friday, March 19, at the big Woolworth's downtown on Main Street. Joseph and Albert are going to lead a small group of students from the college inside the store to sit down at the lunch counter when it opens, but there are some problems. If the first group gets arrested, right now there are only a few students at the college who are willing to show up and take their place, and if there are no replacements, the sit-in will be over. The other problem is that the parents of some of the high school kids found out that we are planning to be at the store to support the sit-in, and they are trying to stop us. Roosevelt's daddy told him if he went out there he was going to get a whipping he would remember for the rest of his life, and Reverend Newsome told Sylvia if she went, she would have to stay in the house for three months. My mother hasn't said anything to me about it so far, but I'm sure she will. Right now, we're trying to keep it quiet so the people at Woolworth's don't find out and try to stop it before it starts. Russell has been telling everybody 'Don't talk about it anymore,' but a lot of kids in school know about it already and they say they want to help. Did you hear about Greensboro? Their sit-in has made everyone around here even more excited. I hope you are able to come down on March 19. I miss you so much." I started to read through the letter again, to make sure I hadn't missed anything. When I came to the part about Roosevelt, I wrinkled my nose, since Roosevelt was a half a foot taller than his daddy, and I began to wonder if some kids had other reasons for backing out.

"Must be pretty important," said a familiar voice over my shoulder. "Anyone I know?" It was Gordie. I hadn't seen much of him recently, and it seemed like ages since the night we had gone out on the town in Harlem. He had told me that after Christmas, he had gone back to Jinxie's to try to find the waitress for me, but it turned out that she no longer worked there. He was still my only real friend in the school, but I also felt my life was speeding past him, just as it was speeding past Draper.

"It's from someone back home," I said. "A girl I met over the Christmas holidays."

"How'd you meet her?" said Gordie.

"At a party," I said with a quick smile, thinking of how Mrs. Braxton had led me through her living room and straight to Paulette. "Hey, I haven't seen you in a while. How's it going?"

"Same old story," said Gordie with a sigh. He sounded bored. "Still in the rat race and the rats are winning. I'm hoping to make the honor roll again this marking period, but it's going to be close. Greek Two is a killer and physics is worse. What about you?"

"Same boat," I said. "When I got back from Christmas vacation, I had so much on my mind that I guess I kind of let things slide. I was in sort of a daze. McGregor even kept me after class to talk to me about it."

"Oh, yeah?" said Gordie. "What did he say?"

"That I was in trouble," I said. "That my work hadn't been up to honor roll standards and I was in danger of falling off." I felt an awkward silence that I was reluctant to fill. I wasn't sure if I should mention what McGregor had said about the faculty, but then I decided that since I was talking to Gordie, it was okay. "Oh, yeah, he said that the faculty had been talking about me being the first Negro student here and they were hoping I would succeed. I'd never heard that one before."

"Sounds like he was doing you a favor," said Gordie.

"Yeah, I guess he was. But it was still hard for me to really bear down again. I managed to do it, but I'm just hoping I did it in time to stay on the honor roll." I hesitated to say anything more, and then I did anyway. "I've just had a lot on my mind."

"Like what?" Gordie looked curious as well as sympathetic, but we were standing in the mailroom and lunch must have been over, because students were coming in and out all the time.

"Let's go for a walk," I said, and we went outside and drifted across the campus into a stiff March wind that billowed our clothes.

"This girl I met at home over Christmas vacation," I said. "I really like her."

Gordie was listening closely. "Wait a minute," he interrupted. "You didn't do it with her, did you? She's not pregnant, is she?"

"No, no, no," I said, laughing. "It's not like that at all. It's just hard to be away from her. And I also got involved with this group of kids at home that's planning a sit-in to protest segregation at the Woolworth's in town."

"Did you see the *New York Times* this morning?"

"I sure did. We're planning the same kind of thing."

"Why Woolworth's?"

"Because they won't allow Negroes to sit at the lunch counters at their stores in the South. You can buy a notebook or a box of pencils, but you can't sit down and have a cup of coffee."

"But you can sit at a lunch counter at the Woolworth's in New York. I've seen colored people at the lunch counter in the store on Forty-second Street many times."

"That's the point. Woolworth's is being hypocritical. It has one policy for stores in the North and another for stores in the South."

"What are you going to do?" said Gordie. We had veered away from the footpath and were walking on the stiff brown grass. The earth felt as hard as stone.

"We're going to try to break the back of segregation at home by making an example of Woolworth's," I said. "We're going to start on March 19 with one group of college students who'll sit down at a lunch counter until they are either served or arrested, and if they are taken away, another group will be standing by to take their seats, and we'll fill up the jails with as many people as we can." Gordie and I were walking toward the golf course, directly into the sun, and I was squinting and my eyes were starting to water, and I felt far, far from home. I realized that I was describing a world to Gordie that he knew nothing about.

"And where do *you* fit into all of this?" he said. "I hope you're not planning to go down there and get arrested yourself?" He looked very concerned, but he sounded patronizing.

"They aren't asking the high school students to get arrested. They just want us to pass out information leaflets in front of the store," I said. "But now my girl says in her letter that the parents are putting pressure on the high school kids to stay away altogether." The wind was brisk and I was shivering, but it felt good to finally talk to someone about everything that had been on my mind.

"You haven't answered my question," said Gordie, in a schoolmaster's voice, and I thought he was acting pretty cocky, though I was relieved that I had taken him into my confidence.

"I want to be there when it happens," I said. "I want to be *there*, not up here in this no man's land—or this no colored man's land, anyway—but I don't know how to pull it off. I can't be in two places at one time."

Gordie seemed to be lost in thought for a moment. "It may not be that difficult," he said, and at last I felt that he was on my side.

"What do you mean?" I said.

"Just apply for a weekend furlough," he said. "March 19 is a Friday. You can leave Thursday afternoon after classes and take the night train to Virginia. You'll be home early Friday morning. I'll lend you the money for the train if you need it." It sounded so simple. Tears rolled down my cheeks as I smiled into the face of the sun. "How much do your parents know about this?" Gordie asked.

"I don't know. I haven't really talked to them about it, but I'm sure they've been talking to other parents at home."

"What are they going to say when you tell them you want to come home to be a part of a protest?"

"They probably won't be too happy about it," I said. "I know I've got to talk to them."

"Just pray that you make the honor roll again," said Gordie, "because if you don't, you won't need to talk to your parents. Your request for a furlough will be denied."

chapter twenty-three

I wrote a letter to Mr. Spencer right away applying for a furlough for the weekend of March 19. While I was waiting for his reply, I studied as I had never studied before, staying up until three or four every morning, until I couldn't keep my eyes open any longer. I still had a chance for the honor roll—I was coming up with the right answers again in classes when my teachers were calling on me, and the teachers' comments on my papers and quizzes were once again positive. But I was exhausted.

In Mr. McGregor's American history class, we were studying the Reconstruction period, the decade or so following the Civil War when the government was faced with providing for the citizenship and well-being of emancipated slaves and, at the same time, rebuilding the defeated South. For the last grade of the marking period, Mr. McGregor asked everyone to write a big paper comparing contemporary conditions in the country to those of the Reconstruction period. I was looking forward to working on that one. Segregation had begun in the South in response to

Reconstruction. Our textbook said that there was actually a gentlemen's agreement between northern and southern politicians that the North wouldn't interfere with segregation in the South if the South would only support the Union. Over the years, the rights of Negroes became more and more restricted by segregation, and the Ku Klux Klan and other white groups used violence to keep Negroes from challenging the restrictions intended, as we said at home, "to keep us in our place." I could see lots of similarities between life after Reconstruction and life in the South today.

I worked hard on the paper. The more I wrote, the more I found myself pouring my heart out about the aftermath of Reconstruction—how Negroes had been taken advantage of by whites, losing their land, losing the right to vote, and how southern whites used lynching to keep Negroes in their place. Even though the government had promised to protect us, when all was said and done, we had been abandoned. "Since Reconstruction ended," I wrote in my conclusion, "things haven't changed much in the South. Segregation has become the accepted way of life, but lately, among Negroes, there is a feeling of change in the air."

Mr. McGregor held on to the papers for almost two weeks, and then on the last day of the marking period, he passed them out at the end of class. When he handed me my paper, I noticed that there was no grade on the front page. Instead, there was a note at the top that said, "See me," so I hung around the classroom until the other students had left.

"Have a seat, Garrett," said Mr. McGregor, in his warmest

voice. I sat down wondering if this was his way of telling me that I wasn't going to make the honor roll after all. "Your paper on Reconstruction, Garrett. Excellent, an excellent piece of work."

"Thank you, sir," I said. I wasn't sure if I should ask him about the grade, but I went ahead. "I didn't see the grade, sir."

"Didn't see it?" he said. "Look on the last page." I turned to it. In the margin, in McGregor's untidy script, was written "A+— This is the finest paper I've received from a student in the last ten years. You've obviously thought very deeply about these issues, but you have also documented your sources and maintained your scholarly objectivity to an impressive degree."

"I've decided to recommend your paper for the school's American History prize," Mr. McGregor said. "I can't say whether you'll win it. You'll be up against some upperclassmen who are pretty sharp, but I'm sure you've got a fighting chance."

I was shocked. I didn't even know about the American History prize. "When do they announce the winner, sir?" I asked.

"Not until the end of the year, on Prize Day," said McGregor. "By the way, Garrett, there was something about your paper that I found particularly interesting. You document a number of factors that could contribute to major changes taking place in the South, and you make a convincing argument that the days of segregation are coming to a close. If you're right, what do you think will be the most important factor in bringing about its end? The courts? The politicians in Washington? Or northern companies that do business in the South? As you point out in your paper, they all have a stake in the outcome. What do *you* think?"

"I think it will come from the young people in the South," I said, without hesitating. "Young Negroes, and maybe a few young whites, who decide they don't want to live like that anymore. Did you hear about what happened in Greensboro, North Carolina, last month? That's the kind of thing I'm talking about." I was tempted to mention our sit-in, but I thought better of it.

"But how will they do it?" Mr. McGregor asked. "They'll be up against an entire region of the country that has already succeeded in slowing the courts down to a crawl. How can a group of youngsters speed things up?"

"They'll have to stand up for what they believe in, and be prepared to accept the consequences," I said. Mr. McGregor shook his head doubtfully, but I could tell he was sympathetic.

"And resistance?" he said. "There's going to be a lot of resistance to something like this. Resistance in the South can be fierce. As you know from our readings, the South put up a hell of a fight in the Civil War, and I'm sure they won't walk away quietly from this battle."

"That's true," I said, "but young Negroes in the South have an advantage. Unlike our parents, we don't yet have anything to lose. And we haven't lived under segregation for so long that we can't imagine what it's like to live without it. When we read a magazine or watch television or go to the movies and see how people are living in other parts of the country, we *know* something is wrong at home. I think we are ready to try to change things."

chapter twenty-four

"Winter term grades are up," said Willoughby, sticking his curly blond head into my room. Willoughby lived next door and rarely left his room, except for classes and meals. He was considered a grind by the other students, but innocuous enough to be left alone, and he'd been on the honor roll for every marking period since he was a freshman.

"How'd you do?" I said.

"B-plus in Greek," said Willoughby. "But an A in everything else."

"Not bad," I said. "Congratulations."

"I've gotta get back to work," he said, and he disappeared from the doorway.

I left my dorm and walked across the campus to the mailroom. With an hour to go until dinner, shadows were beginning to form across the campus, but the sky was still pale blue and cloudless. At Draper, grades were posted on a bulletin board inside the mailroom for everyone to see. While you may have been able to keep others from knowing about trouble in your family or your social life, there were no secrets about where you stood academically. If you were failing French, everybody knew. My heart was thumping as I went through the grade sheets. When I saw my last grade, an unexpected B in Latin, I breathed a huge sigh of relief. I had done it. I had made the Draper honor roll again.

When I got back to my dorm, I went straight downstairs to the two phone booths in the basement to call home. On the weekend, the phones were in constant use, but now they both were free. I sat down in a booth, closed the door, put a dime in the slot, and dialed the operator. When she came on, I placed a collect call to my parents and waited for someone to answer. After several rings my mother picked up the receiver and said, "Hello." She sounded out of breath, as though she had rushed from the kitchen, maybe wiping her hands on a dishtowel, to get to the telephone.

"I have a collect call for anyone from Rob," said the operator. "Will you accept?"

"Oh, my. Yes, of course," said my mother. "Rob? Are you there? Is everything all right?"

"Everything's fine, Mom." I said. "Guess what! I've got good news. I just found out that I made the honor roll again."

"Really?" she said. "That's wonderful! Your father will be so pleased. You've made us so proud, son."

"There's something else, Mom. Mr. McGregor, my history teacher, has nominated one of my papers for the school's history prize. He says it was the best paper he'd seen in the last *ten years.*" Mom was silent for a moment, and then she said over and over, "Oh, Robby. Oh, Robby. Just wait until I tell your father. He won't know what to say." I could tell she was on the verge of tears.

"There's one more thing, Mom," I said. "Since I made the honor roll again, I'm allowed a weekend furlough and, if it's okay with you and Dad, I thought I'd like to come home for the weekend of March 19."

"Oh, wouldn't that be grand!" said Mom. "But why do you want to come all the way down here? It's such a long trip. Why don't you just go down to New York and we'll drive up and we'll all stay at Gwen's, like we did at Thanksgiving."

"Well, there's someone I want to see at home. A girl."

"You mean that little girl who kept calling you up the day before you went back to school? You don't have to worry about her. She isn't going anywhere."

"I still want to see her, Mom," I insisted. "And there's another reason, too."

"What's that?" she said. It was as if we were playing some sort of guessing game, and we had arrived at the turning point and I could tell from her voice that she knew what was coming next.

"You know Russell's group has been planning a protest with some of the college kids for March 19 at the Woolworth's on Main Street. We started talking about it at that meeting that I went to during Christmas vacation. Some college kids are gonna sit down at the lunch counter and wait to be served, while the high school kids leaflet outside. Since I've been in on the planning and thinking about it all winter, I just have to be there. Will you send me the train fare so I can get a ticket for that weekend?" There was a long silence.

"I don't know, son," she said. "I need to talk to your father. Of course we'd love to have you, but Robby, it sounds like there might be trouble. Don't you think there could be trouble?"

"I don't think so, Mom," I said. "Everything's going to be right out in the open."

"I know," said Mom. "But that won't stop some of these white folks around here. They'd shoot you in broad daylight. Let me talk to your father. Call us back this weekend. It sure is nice to hear about the honor roll, though. And that paper! Make sure you save it and bring it home, so we can read it!" She hung up quickly, as though she wanted to forget what I had asked of her.

I returned to my room to prepare my assignments for the following day, but there was only a little time left before dinner and the sun was quickly dropping behind the hills. I stood in my window as the sun disappeared and darkness engulfed the campus like the tide. I didn't feel like working. Although I still hadn't heard from Mr. Spencer, I was closer than ever to making the trip home, to seeing Paulette and Russell. One way or the other, I was going to the protest and passing out leaflets while Joseph and Albert and the others sat at the lunch counter. It was going to be a great moment, and I was going to be there. I couldn't wait to talk to my parents this weekend. I was sure I could persuade them to send me the train fare, but if they wouldn't, I could always take Gordie up on his offer.

On Sunday afternoon, I called my parents when I knew they'd be back from church. Dad answered the telephone and accepted the charges. "Hello, son," he said. "Your mother says you made the honor roll again. Congratulations."

"Thanks, Dad," I said. "Did she tell you about the paper?"

"She sure did," he said. "That's quite a feather in your cap. I'm looking forward to reading it."

After my earlier conversation with Mom, I thought I stood a better chance with Dad than I did with her, but before I could bring up the sit-in, he said, "Your mother told me about your call, and we've been talking about it steadily for the past couple of days. I don't think you should come down here now, son. I know the kids are planning this protest and all, but there's no telling what's going to happen, and if it gets out of control, you could get hurt. If you want to take a weekend off, I'll send you money for a ticket to go down to New York, and you can stay at Gwen's and your mother and I will drive up to see you."

I felt the same way I did when I wanted to go to the Ruth Brown concert. I knew I had to convince him that this was the most important thing in the world to me or I'd never be able to go.

"Look, Dad," I said, "I'm sure Cousin Gwen would rather have me go to the protest than to visit her right now. I'm at the point that I have to decide for myself what's best for me. I've been thinking about this for months. I know there's a chance that something could go wrong. There's even a chance that someone could get hurt, but this could be the spark that changes everything at home, Dad, and I want to be part of it. I want to be able to look back and say I was there at the beginning."

There was a long silence. I could hear my father breathing through the receiver, and I knew he was struggling with the truth in my words, but I also thought he had to be proud of what I was asking to do, to stand up to the white folks without any regard for the consequences. And I thought he might have even envied me the opportunity I had to avenge the humiliation and rage that all of us had felt.

Finally he said, "Well, son, if that's how you feel about it, the money's on its way. But the minute you see there's going to be any trouble, I want you to promise you'll leave. Is that a promise?"

"Don't worry, Dad, I promise," I said, and I really meant it at the time.

"Now, tell me about this girl you're coming to see."

"Her name is Paulette Gentry. She's a freshman at the high school. Her father's a doctor."

"Oh, yes, I've met Dr. Gentry. He's a surgeon. Seems like a nice fellow. How long have you been sweet on her?"

"I met her at the Braxtons' New Year's Eve party," I said. "We've been writing to each other since then."

"Is she going to be at Woolworth's too?" said Dad.

"I think so," I said. "If her parents will let her go."

chapter twenty-five

On March 10, I received a letter from Mr. Spencer informing me that my request for a weekend furlough had been approved. I was so excited that I ran back to my room and wrote a quick note to Paulette. "Meet me in front of Woolworth's on March 19. I'll be there handing out leaflets."

The days leading up to my departure flew by in a blur. I did my best to keep up with my assignments, but I was so excited about taking part in the protest that it was hard to concentrate. I thought about famous Negroes like Marian Anderson and Reverend King, the ones who had to stand up before big audiences, and I wondered how they did it, how they maintained their composure on the stage while representing the race.

The night before I was scheduled to leave I called Russell. "Hey, man," he said. "I was wondering what happened to you. Are you coming down?"

"I wouldn't miss it," I said. "My bags are already packed. How do things look?"

"Lookin' real good so far," said Russell. "Since the news about Greensboro, a lot more people want to get involved. We got about two hundred kids signed up to do leafleting. Joseph said he's already got seventy-five from the college that's willing to sit down at the lunch counter, and he's sure he can get more. We're gonna do it, man. We've been trying to keep it quiet, but it seems like everybody around here knows about it. I just hope the white folks don't lock the doors to keep us out."

"Have you heard from Paulette?" I asked.

"Talked to her the other day," said Russell. "She's been passing your messages along to me. I think she's having some trouble with her parents about showing up on Friday." In her letters, Paulette had said her parents didn't want her to go, but they were leaving it up to her. At least, I thought, they hadn't threatened to punish her like other parents.

"Anything you want me to do?" I asked.

"Naw," said Russell. "Just get yourself down here."

On Thursday afternoon, I took a cab to the station to catch the train to New York. The driver was an old, overweight white guy in a plaid shirt and suspenders. He was wearing a faded red baseball cap and driving a beat-up tan station wagon. A pair of old hunting boots and a tool box lay on the floor in the back.

"Where you headed?" he said after we'd driven for a while. He glanced at me through the rear-view mirror.

"Virginia."

"Long trip."

"Fourteen hours," I said. "If I'm lucky."

He was driving quickly, steering with one hand. I was gazing out the window at the landscape, which was finally turning green after the long winter. "That Joe Louis is the greatest fighter that ever lived," he said abruptly. "Now they're saying he's on drugs." He took his cap off and scratched his head. "You never know what to believe anymore." I didn't know what to say. The remark about Joe Louis caught me by surprise. I knew he had lots of problems, but I had never heard anything linking him to drugs. I wondered if it was true. The cab driver certainly had a point. You never know what to believe anymore. Or who.

"People believe what they want to believe," I said. "Even if it isn't true."

"I know just what you mean," said the cab driver. "And it's a rotten shame." When we arrived at the station, I paid him and boarded the train. I put my suitcase in the luggage rack, took a seat, and leaned back to try to take a nap. It was going to be a long trip and I was already tired from weeks of studying late into the night. But I was finally on my way home.

The sun was starting to come up when the train arrived in town. I hadn't been able to get much sleep on the ride down, but I was so worked up that I didn't feel tired. My dad was waiting inside the station.

"How was the trip?" he said with a warm smile.

"Long," I said, yawning. "I wouldn't mind a cup of coffee."

"Your mother's making breakfast right now," he said. We started off for the parking lot. "All ready for the big day?" Despite his reservations, I could tell how pleased he was that I had come home.

"I sure am," I answered. "Did you hear about Greensboro?"

"Been all over the papers," he said. "Wouldn't surprise me if there's quite a crowd down there this morning." When we reached the Buick, I put my suitcase in the trunk and we climbed in front and headed home. "Russell called last night. He said he would stop by the house this morning at eight o'clock to pick you up. Woolworth's opens at nine, but he wants to get there early."

When we arrived home, Mom greeted us in the kitchen. She gave me a quick hug and a kiss and then went back to the stove. The rich, salty smell of bacon and eggs saturated the room. I took my seat at the table and waited hungrily as Mom filled my plate. I started eating right away.

"You want coffee?" she said, standing over me with the pot. My mouth was full but I nodded, and she poured me a steaming cup. I took a gulp, washing down the food with the hot liquid. When I finished that cup, she poured me another and sat down at the table across from me as I finished the bacon and eggs. Dad was in their bedroom getting ready to leave for his office. Mom seemed wistful. "I don't suppose we'll be seeing too much of you while you're here," she said. "Between going to that protest and seeing that young lady, you'll be mighty busy."

"It's just a weekend, Mom," I said, but I knew what she

meant. I felt the weight of her presence, but it seemed lighter, as though the anchor was slowly being raised before the boat sailed out of the harbor.

The doorbell rang and I went to get it. "Guess you made it," said Russell, standing in the doorway with a grin. He was dressed, as I was, in a tie and jacket, so the white folks couldn't say we looked like troublemakers. "You ready?" It was almost eight o'clock.

"Come on in," I said. "I'll be ready in a minute. I just want to give Paulette a call." I went to the telephone in the hallway and dialed Paulette's number, and she answered.

"I was hoping it was you," she said. "I'm so glad you called. I want to see you so much. When are you going downtown?"

"Russell is here waiting for me," I said. "We're leaving in just a minute. Are you coming?"

"My parents won't let me. They say I'm too young." She sounded anguished. "I tried to convince them it was okay, but they keep saying if I go, I could get hurt." I wanted to talk to her more, but I couldn't keep Russell waiting.

"I wish you could come," I said. "I'll tell you all about it when I get back."

"I'll be waiting," said Paulette. "Please be careful."

I said goodbye to Mom and Dad, and they also told me to be careful.

"Remember what you promised me," said Dad. "At the first sign of trouble, you'll come home."

"I'll remember, Dad," I said.

Russell and I caught the bus downtown. The sidewalks were filled with people going to work. The stores along Main Street were starting to open, and a few whites were sweeping the sidewalks in front. The morning sun was full in the sky. "Now when we get down there," said Russell, "we're going to meet Joseph and Sylvia around the corner from Woolworth's. Sylvia's got the leaflets."

"Wait a minute," I said. "I thought Sylvia's father wasn't going to let her do anything."

"Changed his mind," said Russell with a wink. "She stood up to him. Quoted Scripture to him, from the Prophet Isaiah: 'They that wait upon the Lord shall renew their strength; they shall mount up with wings as eagles; they shall run, and not be weary, and they shall walk and not faint. They helped every one his neighbor; and everyone said to his brother, Be of good courage.' Nothing he could say after that one. He even let her use the mimeograph machine." Russell clapped his hands and we both laughed.

We got off the bus in front of Woolworth's and went around the corner to a side street where it seemed nothing was going on. There was a luncheonette and a barbershop, both of which were closed. The air was dry and sweet with the smell of tobacco curing in the warehouses nearby. We walked down the street and at the end of the block we found Joseph and Sylvia sitting in a car with cardboard boxes in the back seat. Behind their car were four more filled with young Negroes dressed like they were going to church. Joseph got out of the first car and came over to us.

"We got twenty people ready to go in as soon as they open," he said, "and there's more back at the campus just waiting for a call." He looked at his watch. "Five minutes left." He kept looking up and down the street. "Soon as we go in, Russell, y'all start passing out the leaflets. We can keep an eye on each other through the store window. If anything goes wrong inside, call lawyer George Cox. He's in the phone book. He works with the NAACP. I already talked to him and told him what we're doing. He said he had to file some papers in court today but he'd come down if he had to." Joseph looked at his watch again. "It's time," he said. Like a platoon leader in a war movie, Joseph motioned to the first two cars that were filled with students. "All right, I need the first ten," he said, and ten young men with various shades of brown skin climbed out. They were all wearing jackets and ties and their hair was cut so short you could see their scalps. Most were slender but a few were stocky, built like athletes. I recognized Albert in the group and waved to him, but I didn't know any of the others. Albert looked grim, like the others, and he nodded back but didn't wave. Everyone gathered around Joseph, who was smaller than the others, and dead serious. "All right," said Joseph. "As soon as they open the door, we're going to walk silently inside and take seats at the lunch counter. If someone comes over to tell you that you have to leave, you say, 'This is America and we have a right to be served like anybody else and we intend to sit here until we get served.' Everybody got that?" Joseph looked around at the group and everyone nodded. "One more thing," he said. "If anybody puts their hands on you, if they beat on you or kick you or hit you with something, *you cannot strike back*. We cannot stoop to their level. If you can't live with that, speak up now and we'll get somebody to replace you." Again Joseph looked at the group, but no one spoke up. They were somber, like young soldiers about to enter battle for the first time. Their eyes were bright, but their jaws were set and their skin was drawn against their faces. "Russell, y'all get those leaflets and follow us. We're going in," said Joseph, and he took off briskly up the street with the first ten protesters following him. A few were carrying schoolbooks but most were empty-handed. Sylvia and I each took a box of leaflets out of the car and quickly followed Russell up the street.

When we reached the front of Woolworth's, a few white shoppers were already entering through a revolving door, and Joseph and the others entered behind them, one by one, and walked straight over to the lunch counter. They took the first eleven seats in a long row of stainless-steel stools that were covered with maroon vinyl. Sylvia and I put our boxes down on the sidewalk and looked inside the store window with Russell to see what was going on. There were two waitresses behind the counter, blue-haired old white women in pink uniforms. As Joseph and the other students sat down, the waitresses moved immediately to the far end of the counter, watching the students from a distance and talking to each other with their arms folded. They seemed surprised, as though they didn't know what to do. Within seconds, a skinny white fellow dressed in a short-sleeve white shirt and a bow tie showed up. He went right behind the counter and took out several signs that said CLOSED and put them on the counter in front of Joseph and the others. Then he sent the waitresses away and stood behind the counter talking to Joseph and the other young men, waving his arms up and down. His hair was falling in front of his eyes and he looked nervous, but Joseph and the others paid him no mind and continued to sit. One student took out a book and started to read.

"We better get started," said Russell. We each took a handful of leaflets and started to pass them out to people on the street. Most of the white people refused to take them, walking by quickly without even looking at us. Others took one, balled it up, dropped it in the street, and walked away. On the other hand, colored people walking by reached for them and smiled when they finished reading. The leaflets said,

WOOLWORTH'S LUNCH COUNTER

PRACTICES RACIAL SEGREGATION

SUPPORT THE SIT-IN

WE ARE HOLDING INSIDE

DON'T BUY WHERE YOU CAN'T

GET SERVED

Some Negroes were curious about the sit-in after reading the leaflet. "Where is it at?" they asked. We pointed inside the store, and they went over to the store window and put their hands against the glass to shield their eyes and peer inside. When they had satisfied themselves that there really was a sit-in going on, they turned away from the window with a broad smile, and their eyes lit up as though they had seen something wondrous, like a sword swallower at the circus. Others were more adventurous, entering the store to witness the event in the flesh, pumping Joseph's hand and then the others' and patting the protestors on the back. But the Negroes we saw that morning seemed to be working people who happened to walk by. They were wearing simple clothing, uniforms or blue jeans and thick-soled shoes. Negro professionals like my parents, most of whom I would have recognized, were nowhere to be seen.

By the middle of the morning, a crowd had formed on the sidewalk outside Woolworth's. The word must have gotten out that the sit-in had begun, because more high school students were showing up to help pass out leaflets. College students wearing varsity sweaters and windbreakers with Greek letters were also arriving to show their support. I saw friends I hadn't seen since I left high school, and I even saw some students from Parkside in the crowd. The air was electric, charged with the presence of so many young colored people in one place. It felt as though it would be only a matter of time before Woolworth's would give in and the skinny white fellow would come outside and brush the hair away from his eyes and invite everyone in for a cup of coffee and a slice of pie. "Sit wherever you like," he would say. As the day wore on, however, it became clear that Woolworth's wasn't going to budge.

The lunch counter was deserted except for Joseph and the other students. The coffee urns had been drained. The pastries had been removed from the glass cases and the lights in the kitchen had been switched off. Closing time was approaching, and I realized that I didn't know what the plans were for tomorrow, so I looked for Russell and found him in the crowd.

"What are we going to do tomorrow?" I said.

"Meet back here," said Russell. "Same time, same station."

"How long do you think the store can hold out?" I said.

"Hard to say. Looks like they're losing money right now," he said.

"Have you noticed how we haven't seen many white people?" I said. Other than the whites who happened to walk by the store in the morning and a few white customers who had ventured inside, it seemed that white folks had decided to stay away from Woolworth's. Though the number of Negro students on the sidewalk swelled in the afternoon, whites could not be found anywhere outside. One white newspaper reporter did show up, a young blond fellow who talked briefly to a few of the students and then left. There were still only a few colored adults, none of whom I recognized, standing at the edge of the crowd, silently observing. A patrol car with two white police officers inside had been parked across the street all day, but they just sat there and watched us. It was clear that we were on our own.

"The whites are laying low," said Russell. "Just waiting to make their move. They aren't going to give up easily."

When the store closed at five o'clock, Joseph and the other students emerged through the revolving door onto the sidewalk and were greeted by a cheering throng of students. The sun was starting to go down and it was getting cool, and everyone was standing close together. The crowd covered the sidewalk for half a block, the traffic on Main Street had started to pick up, and someone started to sing the spiritual "I'm Gonna Sit at the Welcome Table." Pretty soon everyone in the crowd was singing along and clapping and laughing, especially when they got to the line "I'm gonna tell God how you treat me." People were holding hands and their bodies were swaying back and forth, as in church. There was a feeling of strength surging through the crowd that was new to all of us. We were no longer bound by the chains we had inherited from our parents and we were setting ourselves free, free to turn our back on the white man, if necessary, free to live the way we wanted. It was a feeling that I knew I'd never, ever forget.

"This is going be a long struggle," said Joseph after everyone had quieted down. His tie was loosened at the neck and he sounded tired, like he'd been through an ordeal. "We need everybody to come back tomorrow and every day after that, until we get to sit down at this lunch counter just like the white folks. If we stay together, we can do it." Everyone cheered as Joseph and the others made their way through the crowd and down the side street. Sylvia showed up and followed Joseph along with Russell and me. When we got to the first of the five cars, Joseph stopped to talk to us.

"Let's meet here tomorrow morning at eight and follow the same plan. It looks like we could be at this for a while," he said, shaking his head. "That store manager said they would *never* serve us. We gonna have to be *organized* to get through this." His voice was raspy, but he seemed determined. It was getting dark and the street was deserted, so we quickly said goodbye to each other. As the cars drove off, Russell and I walked up to Main Street and caught the bus back to our neighborhood. On the way, we sat silently in the back looking out the window at the shops along the street, which were closed. I kept thinking about returning to Draper on Sunday before the sit-in was over. I wanted to stay home to help Russell keep the protest organized. I realized that I had been naive about a lot of things. I had convinced myself that Woolworth's would give in right away and that Paulette and I would sit down at the lunch counter on Saturday afternoon and have a slice of chocolate cake and a glass of milk next to the white kids, and I could take the train back to Draper the next day feeling like a hero. But now I had to face the truth: the play was just beginning and the sit-in would probably go on for months. Maybe it would even be going on when I came home from Draper for the summer. And I realized that Joseph and Albert and the other students who had volunteered to put themselves on the line were true heroes. They were going to be showing up at Woolworth's every morning to sit at the lunch counter, day after day, missing their classes and their exams, unable, maybe, to even hold a summer job. Now I was longing to return home just as I had once been so desperate to leave, and somehow I knew then that I would always feel that way, yearning for home wherever I happened to be.

chapter twenty-six

"Did you have dinner?" said Mom when I walked in the back door. She was standing at the stove, and I could smell fish frying in the skillet.

"I had a peanut butter and jelly sandwich for lunch. We didn't want to buy anything to go from the restaurants downtown, since they won't serve us either, so we took up a collection and sent some volunteers out to a supermarket to buy peanut butter and jelly and bologna and cheese and some loaves of bread, and we made sandwiches for everybody. It was the best sandwich I've ever tasted." My mother gave me a long look. Dad came into the kitchen.

"Well, look who's here," he said. "How did things go today?" He had taken off his tie and his suit coat and unbuttoned the collar of his shirt, and he sat down at the kitchen table as though he was ready for a full account, so I described it all to him. Dad listened closely and didn't seem surprised. "Sounds like they are gonna try to wait you out," he said.

"By the end of the day, we were singing and clapping and everyone was volunteering to help, promising to come back tomorrow, and there was this feeling that we could do *anything*, that the sit-in at the lunch counter was just the beginning, and if we stayed together like this, we could end segregation all over town. But, you know Dad," I said, "there was just one thing that bothered me."

"What was that?" he said, looking at me standing nearby. Mom also glanced at me before returning her attention to the stove.

"No parents showed up," I said. "Not just you and Mom. Not a single parent, even though we were trying to do something to benefit the whole Negro community. It felt like the parents had washed their hands of the whole thing. I don't understand it. I guess they didn't take us seriously. I was really disappointed." Dad didn't respond, and neither did Mom. Dad was looking at the sugar bowl and the salt and pepper shakers on the kitchen table with his head bowed. I was upset. Without saying any more, I walked out of the kitchen and into the hallway and called Paulette. Her mother answered.

"Mrs. Gentry," I said. "This is Rob Garrett. May I please speak to Paulette?"

"Hello, Rob," said Mrs. Gentry. "You're back from school?"

"Yes, ma'am," I said. "I came down for the protest at Woolworth's."

"How did it go?" she said.

"Pretty good for the first day," I said. "Eleven college students sat in at the lunch counter and stayed there until Woolworth's closed. A lot of students came downtown from high school and college to show their support. There was a big crowd of students outside of Woolworth's by the end of the day."

"So I guess you didn't have any problems?" she said.

"None so far," I said. I was wishing she would get off the phone and call Paulette.

"Well, best of luck to you," she said, and she called Paulette to the phone.

"Rob?" said Paulette. She sounded breathless. "I've been waiting for your call. Did everything turn out okay?"

"It was sensational!" I said, and I told her everything that had happened during the day, and the feeling of strength that seemed to emerge from the sheer size of the group. "It was amazing!" I said. "I had never seen anything like it before."

"I feel awful that I wasn't there," said Paulette. "But I'm glad you got to go."

"Me too," I said. "I wish I could stay home longer. It's going to be important to keep everybody together. It's great to have so many kids show up on the first day, but they have to be organized so they will keep coming back. Russell's going to have that on his shoulders, but maybe you can help him."

"I'll do whatever I can," said Paulette. "Maybe we can get Roosevelt to help."

"Oh, yeah," I said. "I didn't see Roosevelt at all. I guess his father cracked down pretty hard on him."

"Yeah," said Paulette, "we were in the same boat. Defy your parents and take the consequences or accept the fact that you're living under their roof and do as you're told. I decided to do what they wanted this time, but it won't always be that way."

"Well, if you and Roosevelt can help Russell with the organizing, that will make a big difference," I said. I was hungry and tired, but I wanted to arrange to see Paulette, and then I heard my mother's voice calling me to the dinner table. "I've got to get off," I said. "My mother's calling me for dinner."

"Do you have to, right now?" said Paulette. "We just started talking."

"What was that you were just saying about doing what your parents want?" I said. "I'll come by after dinner."

We had a quiet dinner in the kitchen. My parents and I sat around the table silently picking the bones out of our fish. I had a feeling there was something that was going unsaid, but I didn't know what it was.

"You know, Rob, just because we didn't come over to the demonstration today doesn't mean we aren't behind what you're doing. I had appointments with patients scheduled all day today and your mother had to teach school." He still looked embarrassed, and so did Mom, but I guess he was trying to apologize.

"Look, Dad," I said. "If you really wanted to come, you and Mom had plenty of time to make arrangements. You've known about this for over a month! As I said, I don't think you took us seriously. You thought we were just a bunch of kids trying to show off and get a little attention." I was still annoyed, but I had said enough for the time being. "I'm going over to Paulette's for a little while after dinner," I announced. "I won't stay for long. I have to be back at Woolworth's at eight o'clock tomorrow morning." Dad nodded and looked at Mom, and they continued eating. I finished dinner and asked to be excused. I rinsed my plate and called Paulette to tell her I was coming over. As I rushed out the door, I said goodbye to my parents and they responded so softly I could barely hear them.

Paulette answered the door wearing a blue-and-red striped dress and the biggest smile. She looked prettier than ever. She took me by the hand and brought me into the living room and gave me a quick kiss and we sat down on the sofa, holding hands and cuddling. We were back together, gazing into each other's eyes, giggling as we recalled how Mrs. Braxton had introduced us, and how we spent New Year's Eve sitting on the steps in the kitchen with the cooks jitterbugging and the firecrackers popping outside. Even though her eye was crooked, it was now so much a part of her face, her beauty, that I couldn't imagine her without it. I put my arms around her and we kissed and it was as if I had never left. I wanted to stay with her on the couch, to hold her as I was doing, forever.

"What time does your train leave?" she said.

"Sunday morning, seven A.M. Same as before."

"Will I see you tomorrow?" she said.

"I'll do my best. My mother wants to spend a little time with me. I'm going to have to figure out when I can see you."

"How's school?" said Paulette. I told her about the honor roll and McGregor nominating my paper for the history prize. In the excitement of making the arrangements to come home for the weekend, I had forgotten to give her that news.

"Oh, Rob!" she exclaimed. "That's wonderful! What an honor!" and she clasped her hands together and closed her eyes. "I hope you win. It would be so great if you won it."

"Is everything all right in there?" said a voice from the hallway, and then a tall, light-skinned man appeared in the doorway. He was wearing a dark suit, a white shirt, and a striped tie. He had a carefully trimmed mustache and dark eyes, one of which wandered a bit like Paulette's.

"Daddy, come in," said Paulette. "I want you to meet Rob Garrett." I went over and shook Dr. Gentry's hand as he looked me over carefully.

"Why, yes," he said. "We've heard quite a lot about you." He was smiling, and he glanced at Paulette. "You're the fellow who goes to school up in Connecticut."

"Yes, sir," I said.

"I was just speaking with—that is, I've talked to your father fairly recently," he said. "He's a fine man, a man of real character. You're lucky to have a father like him."

"I know," I said.

"Well, I've got to get something to eat and get to bed. I have a full day tomorrow." He extended his hand toward me and we shook. "Don't stay up too late yourself, young man," he said. "I know you have a busy day tomorrow, too." He left us and I turned to Paulette again.

"He's right," I said, taking her hand. "I only napped on the train and I'm exhausted, and I've got to be at Woolworth's by eight thirty."

Paulette nodded slowly, but I could see she didn't want to let me go. I leaned over to kiss her and I didn't want to let her go either, but finally I pulled away. On the bus ride home, I thought about her father. He was so dashing, as a lot of the doctors were.

When I got home the house was dark but the back door was open, and I let myself in. My parents were asleep so I washed up quickly, changed into my pajamas, and climbed into bed. As I closed my eyes, I began to wonder why even the few white people who had ventured inside the store had deserted it by the end of the day and why the skinny white guy with the bow tie had also disappeared. Slowly the veil of sleep fell over me, and I was one with the darkness.

chapter twenty-seven

"Robby. Robby, wake up," said Mom. I opened one eye. She was standing over me in a housecoat with her hand on my shoulder, gently shaking me. The bedroom shades were still down, but the sun was out and my room was filled with filmy light. "It's a quarter past seven. Russell just called. He's gonna be here in fifteen minutes. Your breakfast is ready."

I jumped out of bed, quickly pulled on my clothes, and washed up. Mom served me pancakes and sausage. She poured me a cup of coffee without asking this time, and I drank it fast, while finishing my pancakes.

"Where's Dad?" I said. After the unpleasantness of our conversation at the dinner table the night before, I thought he might at least stay around to wish us well and say goodbye.

"He left early," Mom replied. "Something he had to do."

The doorbell rang.

"I'll get it," I said. "Must be Russell." I opened the door, and he was standing there.

"Let's go, man," he said. He was impatient to leave. "I want to get down there." I went into the kitchen to say goodbye to Mom. I gave her a kiss on the cheek and hugged her. "I know we haven't seen eye-to-eye this weekend, Mom, but I still love you." I looked at her and saw that her eyes were a little teary. She nodded and handed me a paper bag.

"Here's some fruit for you and the others while you're down there," she said. "Now you be careful, and I'll see you when you get back." I took the bag and thanked her and hugged her again, and then I left. Russell and I walked quickly to the bus stop. I could tell something was wrong.

"What's the matter?" I said.

"Trouble," he said, shaking his head. "Joseph called me this morning and said the president of Virginia State suspended forty students who attended the protest yesterday. Joseph already called the lawyer to see if there's something he can do."

"Damn," I said. "Were any of them a part of the sit-in?"

"Three," said Russell. "Joseph talked to them too. They're worried, but they're coming back this morning. But that's not all." We were almost at the bus stop, and Russell was looking up and down the street the way Joseph had the day before. "Joseph said he heard that the whites are gonna try to break it up today. The Klan may show up." The bus arrived and we climbed on. Even though we were wearing ties and jackets, the bus driver, who was an older white man with thinning hair, gave us a long look as we paid our fare and found seats in the back.

"What are we going to do?" I said after we sat down.

"Well, Sylvia made up some leaflets with instructions on how to protect yourself if you're attacked, how to cover up and so forth. We gotta make sure everyone gets a copy and reads it," said Russell.

"Now I know why there was only one police car yesterday," I whispered. "If it gets bad, the cops aren't going to do anything." Russell looked at me and nodded. When we arrived at the stop for Woolworth's, we got off the bus and hurried down the side street. The five cars were there again and everybody was standing on the sidewalk, gathered around Joseph.

"We have information that a group of whites are going to show up sometime today to disrupt the protest. If you're inside sitting at the lunch counter, remain seated at all times. If one of us is taking a heavy beating, you can try to cover him with your body, but just remember to cover up yourself. Otherwise, remain seated and be prepared to drop on the ground and go into a ball and cover your head and your face with your arms and hands, like this," and he dropped to the sidewalk like a cat, quickly drew his knees up to his face, and curled himself into a ball. He was lying on his side and his hands were clasped, covering the back of his head, with his arms shielding the side of his face and his knees under his chin. "Take a good look," he said as he lay on the sidewalk. "This is how you have to protect yourself." As we stood around him watching, I tried to imagine how I would keep my cool and follow his instructions if I was attacked. I knew that my instinct would be to run home as fast as I could. *"At the first sign of trouble,"* my father had said, *"I want you to promise me you will leave."* I had given him my word that I would. But how could I leave Russell and the others if there was violence?

At nine o'clock we were standing in front of Woolworth's waiting for it to open. The day was warm and sunny again. A group of students from the day before were already standing around in front of the store, and others were arriving. The manager appeared and unlocked the revolving door, and Joseph and his group solemnly walked by him and took their seats at the counter. The CLOSED signs were still sitting on the counter and the kitchen was dark. The manager stood by the door with a toothy smile, as though he was trying to be hospitable. After Joseph and the others took their seats, he disappeared.

For most of the morning, as the students continued to arrive, Russell, Sylvia, and I stood outside passing out the leaflets that explained how to protect yourself. We tried to talk with each person there to make sure he or she understood the instructions. Even though a lot of people were showing up, we managed to talk to everyone. I saw again a lot of friends I had grown up with and gone to school with, and they asked me about Draper and why I was back, and I told them this was something I didn't want to miss. I even ran into Charlene. I hardly recognized her without her mother around. She actually looked happy, and kind of pretty.

Occasionally a few white people appeared: young men driving by, hanging out the windows of their old cars, smart-aleck types with crewcuts, wearing T-shirts and waving Confederate flags and yelling "Nigger" and "Coon" and "Go back to Africa." The students on the sidewalk looked at them with curiosity, and a few even laughed, but we had to ask them to stop when we noticed, because, as Joseph had explained to us, "Laughter will set them off. They can't stand for you to laugh at them." Eventually the whites disappeared, and we started to take up a collection for lunch.

"Hey, what's coming down the street?" said someone in the crowd. People were straining to get a look up Main Street, where a long line of cars was approaching with their headlights on. At first I thought it might be the Klan, but there was a big black hearse in front. "It's just a funeral," someone said, and I resumed collecting contributions for lunch. As the hearse got closer, however, I could see the gray velvet drapes on the side window and the big silver letters W.K. EVANS. I saw several cars in the procession that looked familiar, including a Buick Roadmaster just like ours. The hearse turned the corner at Woolworth's and disappeared down the side street, and as the other cars in the procession followed, I looked into the Buick as it went by and saw my father behind the wheel. I was astonished and I rushed around the corner to follow. The procession stopped on the side street and cars were lined up at the curb for almost two blocks. The drivers got out of their cars, and they were all men I had known all my life, professional men like my father, all dressed up in suits and ties, colored men who had come up the hard way and had lived to tell about it. After they assembled on the sidewalk, W.K.

Evans himself, a somber little brown-skinned man in a dark suit, stepped out of a limousine. He held a folded white handkerchief up to his mouth while several of his assistants, also wearing dark suits and chauffeur's caps, stood behind him. The crowd had started to work its way around the corner to get a good look at what was going on. "Where you want to serve it, Garrett?" I heard W.K. call to my father.

"Why don't we serve them right here," my father replied. "We'll put the food on the hoods of the cars. That way, they can't arrest us for obstructing the sidewalk." W.K. motioned to his men and they started to remove platters of food from the hearse and from the limousine—fried chicken, corn bread, all kinds of sandwiches and potato salad—and blankets were produced to protect the hoods from scratches. My Brooklyn Dodgers bedspread covered the hood of the Buick. When the crowd realized what was taking place, they formed a line next to the cars, and W.K.'s men passed out paper plates and napkins and paper cups for lemonade that was dispensed from a cooler by a handsome, light-skinned man whom I recognized right away as Paulette's father, and they helped themselves to food. By now, the sidewalk was packed with students. I worked my way through the crowd until I reached my father standing alone near the hearse. I went up to him and we embraced, and I was as proud of him as I have ever been in my whole life.

"Dad, why didn't you tell me about this?" I said, putting my arm around his shoulder.

"Well, you got me thinking after you said at the dinner table that maybe it would be good for the adults to show their appreciation for what you young folks are trying to do. So after you went over to Paulette's, I got on the telephone and made a few calls." Dad was smiling proudly, and the students were talking and eating and drinking lemonade, and several of the professional men had taken off their suit coats and loosened their ties. It was really a sight, everyone talking with each other. The adults who were talking with the students had tipped back their hats and were even helping to serve the food. It was like a church picnic. I was just beginning to put some plates of food together to take to Joseph and the others inside the store when a piercing scream from the direction of Main Street froze me dead in my tracks. Everyone looked toward the corner where a colored woman was standing, motioning furiously for help. "Come quick! Please, somebody help!" she screamed, pointing to the entrance to Woolworth's. "They got jumped! Some white boys jumped 'em," she shouted. "They hurt 'em *bad.*" The crowd began to surge toward her, but the sidewalk was so congested that I knew I couldn't get through. I saw Russell cut between two cars and race up the street. I did the same thing and was right behind him when he went through the revolving door into the store. The first thing we saw was Albert, and then another student, seated on stools with their backs to us, lying face-down on the blood-spattered lunch counter. Then we saw the others, crumpled together on the floor, their shirts soaked with blood, their clothing ripped. A few were still curled up in balls with others lying on top of them for protection. At some point their attackers must have taken a bag of flour and scattered it over them like lime, the ghostlike faces of the students indistinguishable, eerie, like clowns at the circus, but at least they were stirring. Russell and I rushed to untangle the trembling limbs, and one boy shrieked in pain. Another boy was unconscious, with a wound freely bleeding at the base of his skull. We turned him over and saw it was Joseph. I held him in my arms to try to comfort him, even though he was unconscious. His eyes were rolled back in his head. I felt for his pulse and was relieved to find one. Sylvia rushed in and saw him. She gasped and began to sob, and I sent her back out for the doctors. "Tell them to come right away," I yelled. A few students who had entered the store were standing around crying, their backs against a locked display counter for small appliances, electric fans, hair dryers, and the like. Their hands covered their mouths in shock. The store saleswomen were huddled in a corner, clearly frightened. The doctors rushed in carrying their bags, first Dr. Gentry, then Dr. Braxton, followed by several others, including my father, and the first two started to work on Joseph. Dr. Gentry was shining a little flashlight into his eyes and holding a bandage against the back of his head and Dr. Braxton was taking his blood pressure, until Joseph came to, blinking his eyes and shaking his head, while the other doctors questioned each of the students carefully and consulted among themselves, cleaning the wounds and smearing them with salve, helping to their feet those who could stand.

My father examined the teeth of those who said they had been struck in the mouth, and he found a couple that were loose and one that was broken, and told the boys to call his office for an appointment. Dr. Braxton arranged with W.K., who had entered the store and who had seen such carnage before, to transport the most seriously injured to Northside Hospital. "Looks like World War Two in here," said W.K. when he first saw the blood and the students lying on the floor. Northside was a small colored hospital that had only five beds, but there was an x-ray machine and a small operating room and if you went there, at least you felt safe. W.K. told his men to bring the hearse and the limousine around right away. "And collect those blankets," he shouted, wiping his mouth with the handkerchief. "So's we can make pallets for 'em if we have to."

By now the store was full of students, and when they saw what had happened they were angry. "Let's go get those white motherfuckers!" someone shouted. By that time the saleswomen had slipped out and there was nobody white anywhere in sight. Russell went over to calm the angry students. When I looked outside, I saw a sea of brown faces pressed against the window as if they were looking at a display; other people were milling around on the sidewalk. Russell went to the door and spoke to the crowd. "They are injured," he said, "but the doctors say they are gonna be all right. We *cannot* retaliate. *I mean it.* If we stoop to the level of the people who did this, we'll destroy everything we're trying to accomplish. Now please, go home, and don't forget to come back on Monday morning." A few of the students outside grumbled, but slowly the crowd started to disperse. In the midst of the commotion, a dark-haired, older white fellow in a jacket and tie worked his way through the crowd, followed by a baldheaded white man with a Speed Graphic camera. Everyone was staring at them. As they came through the revolving door, the dark-haired fellow took a pad and pencil out of his jacket pocket and made his way over to Joseph, who by now was sitting on a stool at the lunch counter with a big white bandage wrapped around his head. The side of his face was all swollen and dusted with flour, and he looked like a character in a horror movie. The photographer was going around popping his flashbulbs and taking pictures with the Speed Graphic, and the dark-haired fellow introduced himself as Phil Robbins and said he was a reporter for the *New York Times*. He asked Joseph if he wanted to make a statement. Joseph looked at the reporter for a long time, squinting at him as though he was trying to figure out who the man was. Finally he said, "Tell 'em we'll be back on Monday morning. Nine o'clock sharp."

chapter twenty-eight

Dad waited around until we had arranged for Joseph and the others to get rides to the hospital. Five, including Joseph, needed x-rays or stitches. W.K. put them in the back of the limousine, which seemed to please them all greatly, but there were two fellows who weren't able to walk, and they had to lie inside the hearse on their backs. From the looks on their faces, they weren't happy about that at all, although someone said at least W.K. wasn't taking them to the cemetery. By that time most of the students had left. Russell, Sylvia, and I organized a few of those remaining to pick up the trash on the side street. Some of the professionals who were still there helped out and then offered to take the rest of the students home. We found a ride for Sylvia. Russell and I rode home with Dad in the Roadmaster. When Dad dropped Russell off at his house, I felt a knot in my throat as I said goodbye. "Keep up the good work, Russell," I said. "I wish I could stay."

"You do the same, Rob," said Russell. "I'll see you this summer." Dad pulled the car away from the curb, and a few minutes later we were home. Mom had a meat loaf with gravy and mashed potatoes waiting for us. We sat around the dinner table devouring every bit of the food and washing it down with iced tea as I told my mother everything about the day.

"And don't you know, Clarissa," said Dad, "we didn't see a single police officer the whole time this was going on."

"Did anybody think to call them?" she asked.

"Mom, yesterday they had a patrol car outside the store all day," I said. "Today there was nobody. That was more than a coincidence."

After dinner I stood at the sink helping Mom with the dishes. "Too bad you're going back tomorrow," she said. She was washing and I was drying, and again I felt as though I had never left.

"I'll be home before you know it, Mom," I said, and then the doorbell rang.

"Who could that be?" said my mother. It was almost eight o'clock.

I said I would get it and opened the door to find Paulette and her parents standing on our front porch. Paulette looked a little embarrassed, but she gave me a big smile.

"We thought we'd come over to say goodbye before you go back to school," said Dr. Gentry. "Are your parents at home?" I was so surprised to see them that I was speechless. "Mind if we come inside?" added Dr. Gentry, so I opened the screen door to let them in. My mother appeared, drying her hands on her apron, and Dad was right behind her with a toothpick in his hand. Everyone stood in the living room for a moment as though they were getting used to each other, and it was fine in the silence.

"Won't you have a seat?" said my mother at last, and we all sat down. I wanted to sit next to Paulette, but she was stuck between her parents on the sofa, so I sat across from her on the hassock that Dad often stretched his legs on, while he sat next to me. "I just made a lemon meringue pie," said Mom. "Would you care to have a slice?"

The Gentrys looked from one to the other and nodded. "Why, certainly," said Dr. Gentry. "Thank you." Mom started into the kitchen and Mrs. Gentry stood up.

"Clarissa, let me give you a hand with that," she said, and followed Mom out of the living room.

"Garrett," said Dr. Gentry, as if he were going to make a speech, "I want to thank you for asking me to participate in that endeavor today. I was proud to be a part of it." I looked at Paulette and she looked at me, rolling her eyes at her father's choice of words. "And I want to thank *you*, Rob, for your work in helping to organize the protest. I'm sure it wasn't easy to interrupt your studies to come down here. Paulette tells us that you're quite a student." Out of the corner of my eye, I could see Paulette's eyes rolling again as she looked, all the while, out the window. "Have you considered a career in medicine?" said Dr. Gentry. "We could certainly use a fellow like you." Paulette's mother appeared carrying two silver pitchers, which she set down on the coffee table.

I shook my head no to make it clear I didn't want to be a doctor.

"Tell me, Rob," said Dr. Gentry, "have you started to think about college?"

"Not really," I said. "A lot of the fellows at Draper go on to Yale, but I don't know if that's the best place for me."

"Yale's a fine school," he said, with a smile that seemed a little forced.

"Where did you go to college, sir?" I asked.

"Dartmouth," he said. "Then medical school at Howard. I applied to the Ivy League medical schools, but, even with an undergraduate degree from Dartmouth, I couldn't get one to accept me. And when I finished medical school, I couldn't get a residency either, but the United States Army saved me. Six years of my life I gave them, but I got the training I needed to become a surgeon." He was having iced tea with his pie, and he took a swallow. "It's given me a good life too, a comfortable life for my family, but I've often wondered what would have happened if I'd chosen a different path."

"What do you mean?" asked Dad. His eyebrows were raised at the comment.

"When I was at Dartmouth, I wanted to become an English teacher. In my senior year, I won the English literature prize for a paper I wrote on Milton. The faculty made a big fuss about it and told me I could have a brilliant future as a professor, but when I came home—my people are from South Carolina— everybody in my family was out of work and hungry, and my mother told me she couldn't wait until I finished "that school," as she called it, so I could get a job and help out. I worked my way through medical school and I've been able to help the family and take care of my mother, but I've often wondered what would have happened if I'd listened to my heart instead of my head. I still read Milton, when I get a chance."

"'How soon hath Time,'" said my father, "'the subtle thief of youth, stol'n on his wing my three and twentieth year.'" Everyone except Mom looked wide-eyed at Dad. With a little smile, Mom was looking at her hands in her lap. "Milton," said Dad, with a smile of his own. "I was an English major, too." He leaned over and put his hand on my shoulder. "You have to listen to both your heart *and* your head, son."

"Rob, why don't you and Paulette clear the dishes and take them into the kitchen," said Mom, after everyone had finished their pie. We put the plates and silverware on the tray and collected the napkins, and Paulette started to pick up the crystal glasses.

"Handle those carefully, honey," said her mother. "They're very delicate." We carried everything into the kitchen, and we took our time cleaning up. I was washing and Paulette was drying, and we were laughing and sneaking kisses every so often. I told her about the sit-in, and how the men had arrived with lunch and how her father had served lemonade. She laughed, but when I told her what Russell and I saw when we ran inside to the lunch counter, her eyes filled with tears.

"Daddy said Joseph was knocked out," said Paulette. "I hope he's going to be all right."

I told her what Joseph said to the reporter.

"Well, then, he can't be hurt too bad," she said, and we both laughed.

"Joseph will be there on Monday morning," I said, "even if W.K. has to bring him in the hearse!" When Mrs. Gentry appeared at the kitchen doorway, we were leaning against each other giggling.

"Paulette, we're getting ready to go," she said.

"I'll be right there, Mama. We're almost done." Her mother smiled and went back to the living room. Paulette put her arms around my neck and we kissed, and I could hear our parents chuckling in the front of the house.

"I'll be home in six weeks," I said, "and we'll have the whole summer together."

"Does that mean you've definitely decided to go back to Draper next September?"

"I think so. I'll see how I feel about the place when I get back."

chapter twenty-nine

It was raining the next morning when I climbed aboard the train to return to Draper. As the train pulled out, my parents stood on the platform under a big black umbrella that my Dad was holding. I gave them one last wave from my seat inside the coach before they vanished. The rain came down in sheets. When we passed through little towns, streets were flooding and people were standing in the windows of row houses looking up at the sky.

In New York, it was still raining when I switched trains and boarded the coach that would carry me the rest of the way. It was empty and there were scattered pieces of the Sunday paper discarded on the seats and on the floor. I picked up a front section and took it with me to my seat. As the train pulled away from the station, I leaned back and opened the paper. It was the *New York Times*. Under the headline "Student Sit-Ins Spread, Violence in Virginia," there was a photograph, printed in crisp tones of black and white, of the Woolworth's lunch counter at home, the row of vacant stools, the CLOSED signs, the empty pastry case—

objects I had seen just the day before with my very own eyes. It was thrilling to see them on the front page of the Sunday paper, but when I studied the photograph more closely, I could see the bloodstains on the floor, the spattered drops on the counter, and the flour that had been spilled on the vinyl seats of the stools, and my eyes filled with tears.

The cab driver was waiting for me when the train arrived at the stop for Draper. He was wearing a yellow slicker and holding an umbrella as I stepped down from the coach with my suitcase, and he ushered me to his station wagon.

"Helluva mess out there today," he said when we were both inside the cab. He started it up and headed for Draper. We rode together for a while without speaking. "How much longer you got at the school?" he said, breaking the silence.

"Two years," I said, "if I decide to stay." It was still light out, and a small herd of dairy cows was standing in a pasture.

"Them cows have been gettin' wet all day, happy as can be," said the driver with a laugh, and he drove on. "Whatsamatter?" he said lightheartedly. "Don't ya like it up there?" I took a long time to reply because I had been thinking that I would never like Draper, even if I decided to stay, but that maybe I could manage to put up with it and graduate, if it meant I could do whatever I wanted with my life when I left. And at that moment, it dawned on me that I was free, as free, it seemed, as it was possible to be.

"It'll do," I said, as the cab pulled into the school driveway. It was dark, but all the campus lights were on. He stopped in front of my dormitory, and I got my suitcase and paid him, including a small tip for his company. He offered to escort me to the door with his umbrella, but I turned him down and walked up the footpath alone.

It was quiet inside the dormitory, and I was exhausted from the trip. I decided to prepare for bed, even though I hadn't studied at all for my classes the next morning. I climbed into my pajamas and was about to turn off the lights when I heard a knock at the door. "Come in," I said, having no idea who it could be at that hour. It was Gordie.

"How'd it go?" he said. He was wide awake and curious. "I heard something about it on the radio. WQXR. And there was a front-page article in the *Times* today. Did you see it? I guess some people got hurt, huh?" He wanted a blow-by-blow account, but I was bushed and in no position to give him one.

"It was amazing," I said, sitting down on my bed. "Incredible. But I'm too tired to talk about it right now. Let's get together at breakfast and I'll tell you everything."

"Okay," he said. "Get some rest." He turned to leave and then stopped and turned around to face me. "Oh, yeah," he said, "I guess Mazzerelli is gonna pack it in. There's a rumor going around that he's withdrawing. He's supposed to leave tomorrow morning. I thought you'd want to know."

I was stunned. The school year was almost over. Since January, I had been so preoccupied with organizing protests and keeping my grades up and attending to my relationship with

Paulette that I had almost forgotten about Vinnie. Occasionally I would see him by himself in the hall and we would exchange greetings and talk a bit, but since he had moved out of the dormitory, we never really got together like we used to. He was in the infirmary and I was in the dorm. I guess he decided that he'd had enough, though.

"I'll go over and see him tomorrow morning," I said, getting into bed and pulling the covers up. "Switch the light off when you leave, will you, Gordie?" I said, and he did.

Garlands of mist wreathed the gray-green hills in the distance when I awakened the following morning. The sky was overcast, as though it had not quite recovered from the rain the day before. I dressed quickly and bolted down the dormitory steps, peeling off from the other students, who were going to breakfast in the dining hall, and heading across the campus to the infirmary. I walked inside and the nurse was at a desk by the door. "You're here to see Vincent, aren't you?" she said with a maternal smile. I nodded, and she pointed to a door down the hall. I walked down and found his room. Vinnie was seated on the side of his bed. His back was curved over the edge of the bed and his head was hanging down, as though he was looking for something on the floor. The room lights were off, but the sun had broken through the clouds for the moment and the room was filled with sunlight. There was a large window that looked out onto the campus, and in the distance students could be seen rushing across the lawn to get breakfast. For a moment, I thought about my plans to meet Gordie, but I knew it was more important for me to be with Vinnie.

"Vinnie?" I said, and he looked up at me slowly. He looked completely defeated. His eyes were filled with tears.

"You were right, Rob. You were right," he said. "I never should have let Spencer put me in here. It *is* like segregation. I was here all alone. I have no friends. No one came to see me. Not even you, and you're the only friend I have." I felt awful. I thought of all the times I had told myself to stop by the infirmary to see him, and then put it off to write a letter to Paulette or to my folks or to dream about the protest, or to do my schoolwork to try to stay on the honor roll. Vinnie was right. In my struggle to keep my own head above water in the sea in which we were all immersed, I had gradually let him go.

"But why are you leaving now?" I said. "School is almost over."

Still seated on the side of the bed, he clasped his hands before him, squeezing his eyes shut so the tears fell to the floor in a tiny pool. "Because I can't stand it anymore!" he screamed. "It's worse than hell!" I flinched. The nurse appeared at the door looking worried. She was holding a glass of water in one hand and a small paper cup with a pill in the other.

"Vincent," she said in a soothing voice, "your father should be here any minute. Would you like a pill? It'll make you feel better." Vinnie nodded and she walked over to him and gave him the pill, which he took, and then he took a swallow of the water and handed the glass back to her. He was already packed. His suitcase was next to the door, along with boxes of the stuff I had helped him carry over from the dormitory when he moved in. It was a standard hospital room with a bed, a metal night table, an easy chair, and not much else except the view from the window of the campus lawn, which was beginning to turn green with the arrival of spring; the trees, which had begun to bud; and the well-worn footpaths that everyone used to get about, everyone except Vinnie, of course. I realized that he must have died a slow and painful death in this room, and I shuddered to think I had had a hand in it.

The nurse disappeared for a moment and then returned. "Vincent, I think your father has arrived." Footsteps approached, sharp against the green linoleum tiles in the hallway, and suddenly a tall, slender man in a black suit, a black Borsalino hat, and a long black cape appeared, filling the doorway. He took one look at Vinnie and said, "Vincenzo, get up. We must leave this place at once." Vinnie gave him a long look, but at first he didn't move. He just smiled a drowsy smile and resumed looking at the floor. Then his father walked over to Vinnie and took him gently by the arm, helped him to his feet, and embraced him, speaking quietly to him in Italian. When his father had finished, he turned to the nurse. "Are these his things?" he said, nodding at Vinnie's belongings at the door.

"Yes," said the nurse. "This is everything."

"I'd be happy to help you with them, sir," I said. "I can take them out to the car if you like," and I bent over and picked up two of the boxes. Vinnie's father looked suspicious.

"Who are you?" he said sharply.

"That's Rob Garrett," said Vinnie. "He's the only friend I have in the whole school." Vinnie's father seemed to relax.

"Thank you," he said. "That would be very helpful. Just give them to the chauffeur and tell him to come in and get the rest." I took the boxes to the front door of the infirmary and stepped outside to find a huge black limousine with chrome appointments that were gleaming in the sunlight. The driver was wearing a chauffeur's hat, jodhpurs, knee-length brown leather boots, and a short jacket with buttons on both sides of the chest. He gave me a patronizing smile, took the boxes from me, and put them in the trunk.

"Is the doctor still inside?" he said.

"Yes," I said, "he should be out in a minute. He'd like you to go in and get the rest of Vinnie's things." The chauffeur left the trunk door open and went inside the infirmary. I was standing next to the limousine, admiring it, when I realized there was someone inside. Although the interior was shadowy, the door had been left open a bit, enough to see a pair of tan trousers with a razor-sharp crease and, protruding from the cuffs, a pair of yellow silk socks and brown alligator-skin oxfords. I had seen alligator-skin shoes advertised in *Ebony,* but I'd never seen a pair in real life. I knew, however, that they cost a fortune. Dr. Mazzerelli walked out of the infirmary and Vinnie walked out behind him.

"I want to thank you for the friendship you have given to my son," said Dr. Mazzerelli, turning to me. His face was very grave, and his eyes, which were small and dark like Vinnie's, never left mine. "You are the only friend Vincenzo has had in this place. You are a fine young man." It was a compliment I did not feel I deserved, but I felt powerless to turn it down. "Before we leave, there is someone I want you to meet. He rode up with me from New York this morning." He opened the limousine door wide and called to the passenger inside, "Joe, come out for a second. There are some people here I want to introduce you to." And from the dark interior of the limousine emerged the massive head of Joe Louis. It was the color of butterscotch, with large, misshapen ears and a few small clumps of scar tissue around the eyes that gave him a vaguely oriental appearance, thick, plum-colored lips that held the mouth in a characteristic pout, a thinning patch of dark wiry hair, neatly trimmed and flecked with gray, and tired brown eyes, utterly without guile. Over shoulders still broad as a roof beam and a barrel chest, he was wearing a turtleneck sweater of smooth, dark gray wool and a long tweed overcoat. When he stepped from the limousine and raised himself to his full height, it was clear why his opponents had been terrified by the sight of him.

How strange, I thought, that he should appear now, at the moment of Vinnie's departure, this hero of my boyhood dreams, and I wondered, had he been brought along to console Vinnie or to distract him? Did he even know about Vinnie's plight? God, he's huge, I thought. Even now, when his career in the ring was over, when the roar of the crowd, once as big as a hundred thousand or more, had turned to silence and he had retired to a windowless room in the company of lawyers and accountants, his presence quickened the blood. But I couldn't see even a trace of a smile on his lips. Those lips, Jesus, they told the whole story. Two pressed roses of suffering under the fringe of a light mustache. Mashed, pounded, split by flying fists. Shaped by the pain of life's disappointments but revealing only resignation. Never agony. And never defeat. I wanted to ask him how, in the wake of all he had experienced, all that he had suffered, the grim childhood in a sharecropper's cabin, the stinking, run-down colored gyms, the roadwork, the brutal regimen of training, the moments of greatness, celebrated by millions, followed gradually by the awful recognition of betrayal, the evaporation of friendships, money, love, and, worst of all, the ability to take a punch, and finally, the humiliation of wasted opportunities inside the ring and out—how, in the face of all this, he managed to endure. And I thought I knew the answer without asking him the question, or at least I told myself I did. It was, I was certain, with the strength that has kept us all alive in the midst of the wilderness.

"Joe, this is my son, Vincenzo, and his friend, Rob Garrett," said Dr. Mazzerelli. "Boys, I'd like you to meet Joe Louis." Vinnie put out his hand and Joe shook it. Then I put out mine, and as I shook the hand of Joe Louis, I felt the same sense of love and gratitude and yearning I had felt toward my parents when I said goodbye on the day I arrived at Draper. Then I looked into his eyes, and I knew all there was to know about him. He was completely defenseless. He could no longer see the blows before they arrived. His eyes were haunted, like Vinnie's when I first entered his room in the infirmary. They were the eyes of one who has lost his way and been swallowed up by the world around him.

Finally, after what seemed like an eternity, Joe Louis said in a thick Alabama drawl, "How you doing, fellas?" He took a quick look around the campus. "Nice place they got here," he said. "Make a helluva training camp." For Dr. Mazzerelli, Joe's remark seemed to be a signal to prepare to leave. He told the chauffeur to start the limousine and announced that he had to get back to New York, since he had canceled his morning appointments to pick up Vinnie.

"Joe agreed to come along to keep me company, but Joe's a busy man," said the doctor. "He's got appointments, too. Isn't that right, Joe?"

"That's right, Doc. But you callin' the shots," said Joe, with a deadpan expression. I shook hands again with Joe Louis and with Dr. Mazzerelli, and then I turned to Vinnie, fighting back tears. He seemed to be on the verge of tears as well, and we shook hands for a long time, and then I put an arm around his shoulder and he did the same to me, and with our free hands, we wiped the tears from our eyes.

"It's time to go, fellows," said Dr. Mazzerelli, who was standing at the open door of the limousine with the edge of his cape gathered in his hand. Joe Louis climbed back inside first, followed by Vinnie, and then, in one smooth move, the doctor took off his hat, wrapped the cape around his body, and disappeared into the limousine, shutting the door behind him. The chauffeur started the engine and steered the car slowly down the driveway and off the campus, like an ocean liner leaving a harbor, and then they were gone.

The sun had found another opening in the sky and the campus was covered with brilliant light. I looked around and began to notice things for the first time in months. Spring bulbs had burst through the earth, filling the flowerbeds around the dormitories and the borders of the footpaths with dabs of yellow and cream and red. The last of the dead leaves left over from the winter had been raked away, and new grass had begun to fill in the brown patches on the lawn. Other than a few birds high in the trees that were plaintively calling to one another, the campus was perfectly still, immaculate, and I shuddered at the sight and ran to class as fast as I could.